HEAVENWORTH

THE UNHOLY SUMMONS

JEFFREY JAMES RICKMAN

HEAVENWORTH

The Unholy Summons

COPYRIGHT © 2024 by Jeffrey James Rickman

All rights reserved. Published in the United States by JEFFREY JAMES RICKMAN and distributed by IngramSpark/ Lightningsource Internationally.

Book Cover Design JEFFREY JAMES RICKMAN
Jacket Design by: JEFFREY JAMES RICKMAN
Photographs by: JEFFREY JAMES RICKMAN

The Cataloging in Publication Data is available at the Library of Congress.

ISBN: 979-8-9906-444-0-3

1

BLESSINGS TO:

YAHWEH,

YESHUA

AND THE

THE HOLY SPIRIT

Writing is said, to be a "continuous stream of consciousness" until, you have writer's block and then it becomes, a "brain wreck". You know, where an unstoppable force meets an immovable object?

What I'm really trying to say is, it's nearly impossible to write, edit, produce, create artwork and publish all by yourself. Self-publishing is a most difficult task and why I'd like to acknowledge my daughter, Brittney for her loving support and my editors, who helped me with their technical support, the incorrigible, Christina Hill and Collette Versoza, whose input was so appreciated editing the storyline. Also, a very special thank you, to Pastor Keith K and Journey Church, Bend, Oregon and the many "angels" who helped me on my journey.

Finally, I would be remiss if, I did not thank THE HOLY SPIRIT, for HIS insightful grace and keeping me on track. Let me say that having a "spiritual guide" is awesome, whether you believe, or not. I, especially thank, YAHWEH for giving us ALL, HIS SON, YESHUA!

AMEN

HEAVENWORTH

The Unholy Summons

JEFFREY JAMES RICKMAN

CONTENTS

Chapter 1

"Inbound"

The full moon crept slowly through the dark storm clouds, separating them with ease. The day's earlier rains filled potholes with shimmering reflections of orange pools, scattered along the roadway. Turning off the main highway was an old prison bus defying a lower gear. The blue behemoth lunged forward, ambling its way up a long, winding hill to the origin of its destination.

Two overweight guards rode shotgun in the caged cab and one in the rear of the bus. They were hungry, tired, and very annoyed with their mission but were relieved when they saw the towers of the ominous silhouette that rested on the horizon. It was the oldest federal prison in the United States and was to be decommissioned in three years, as the new super complex was under construction. It was surrounded by vast, dark plains of space with the occasional glimmers of razor-wire fencing, which outlined the entire 150-acre site.

The guard towers were stenciled against the moonlit valley, just east of the ancient grey stone fortress that was once the only Territorial Fort in the Midwest, more than two hundred years ago. The guards grunted as they passed the sign that read, "Heavenworth Federal Penitentiary."

"There's your new home, Spook," chortled Peters, the bus driver. He looked in the rearview mirror and saw the Jamaican's nefarious outline of dreadlocks sitting chained to the inside of the bus. The other correctional officers snickered as Johnson lit up a cigarette and disrespectfully flipped the match back into the iron cage. He noticed the angry, bloodshot eyes that were glaring at him from behind a worn, brown leather mask, as he gripped his 12-guage shotgun tighter and turned his head in another direction. He kept thinking he heard a voice calling out his name but dismissed the notion by taking a deep drag off the cigarette to calm his nerves.

"I'm glad this package is almost delivered. This guy gives me the willies. I read in his file that he's some kind of voodoo dude," coughed Johnson, puffing his cigarette.

"You can say that again. The son of a dog just sits there mumbling some dam chant, over and over again. He's driving me crazy. We've been with this nut job way too long for my liking. He's a freaking witch doctor from New Orleans," Peters informed Johnson, as he tried not to look back at the circus act and keep his eyes on the road.

"Hey, Harry, you awake back there?" hollered Johnson. They could hear him snoring in the back of the bus.

"What's that? Oh, yeah, it looks like we'll get more rain tonight for sure. Look at those storm clouds to the East. Yep, it's gonna rain again fer sure," Harry garbled.

The other guards laughed at the old guard sitting in the back of the bus, knowing he was just waiting for retirement in a few weeks and didn't care about much these days, especially transporting another "no gooder" as he liked to call them. Harry rubbed the sleep from his eyes and was suddenly startled to see the large hairy heads of the grazing buffalo alongside the road. The government took great pride in raising the great herd nearby the prison, symbolizing the reemergence of the vanishing mammals that once covered the prairies in droves of thousands and were nearly hunted to extinction in the eighteen hundreds by the wasteful slaughter of the passing railroads. Harry loved the critters, and it was his job for years to help raise the herd and feed them in the lush green pastures surrounding the prison. The administration liked them psychologically because the buffalo gave the visitors a calming effect and something to talk about when visiting incarcerated family members. Harry knew most of the heard by their appearance, naming most of them at birth as he waved at some, while the headlights flashed past the fence line proceeding up the road.

"Hey, Harry, how come some of those buffalo look, like you?" Johnson chuckled.

The other guards made fun of the old-timer, cracking one joke after another, but Harry ignored them as usual and was in his own little world—just him and his buffalo—when all of a sudden, the bus hit a pothole, jarring loose Harry's loaded shotgun. It bounced off the seat and misfired toward the front of the bus, hitting Johnson's left shoulder. The rest of the double-ought buck-shot hit the rearview mirror, blowing it off the windshield and shattering it into pieces. The bus stopped like it had hit a brick wall, and everyone was thrown to the floor. Peters banged his face, breaking his nose on the steering wheel. Steam hissed off the hot undercarriage, and the bus was dead in the road with a broken left-front axle. The herd thundered away in the darkness, as moans of pain and anguish came from inside the bus.

"You guys all right?" asked Lieutenant Spalding. His name tag was bloody. Spalding shook the cobwebs off, regaining his vision. He couldn't believe his eyes—the driver was semi-conscious, and Johnson was out cold. His white shirt was a bloody mess from the shotgun wound. Spalding's mouth hurt, and he tasted his own blood. He spits on the floor to clear his throat, and some teeth dribbled out along with the blood. His ears were ringing, but he could hear muffled laughter coming from behind him. He quickly withdrew his service revolver and aimed it at the captive inmate, making sure he was secure. Relieved that the chains held, and the inmate was intact, he noticed Harry lying on the floor beside the crazed inmate, and he wasn't moving. He felt Harry's neck and thanked God that the old-timer had a pulse.

4

He helped him up onto a bus seat as the Jamaican tried to kick Spalding, rattling his chains like a wild animal. Peters groaned in agony as Spalding leaped for the bus radio and reported the accident.

"HQ, come in! This is Lieutenant Terrell Spalding on the inbound bus. Over," he shouted into the microphone.

"This is Central. What's your 10.40? Over," squawked the radio speaker.

"Yeah, central, we are approximately a half mile from the main gate by the pasture. We are broken down in the middle of the road and have wounded onboard. We need a medical evac with security to off load personal over," he requested in pain, spitting out more blood onto the floorboard.

Spalding draped his jacket over Johnson, who had passed out. And Spalding was getting nauseated from the sight of all the blood and spatter inside the cab. The bus driver moaned, cursing, and holding his nose in anguish. Then Spalding couldn't believe his eyes. The inmate was taking deep inhales through his nose, and Spalding realized that it was the scent of blood intoxicating his derelict passenger.

"What a sick mother," Spalding thought to himself. Then the stark realization came that made him shake with a bone-chilling numbness. "What if this psychopath caused the accident?" he shuddered. Spalding was injured and stumbled backward onto the steps of the bus from the revelation he just encountered. The dreadlocked mask was staring right at him, chanting something again.

He swallowed hard and was full of fear, oblivious to the voice on the radio. Spalding was mesmerized by the inmate's hypnotic gaze that was focused squarely on him. Spalding's vision blurred, as he suddenly visualized horrible images of terror, blood, and death raging in his consciousness, as the inmate intensified his gaze on Spalding. "Come in, Spalding! Damn you! Answer me! This is Warden Stevens. What in the blue blazes is going on, down there?" the Warden demanded.

There was no answer.

Chapter 2

"Captain Ron"

The prison floodlights illuminated two rows of silver maples into bright bouquets of crimson, outlining the long driveway approaching the domed rotunda of the Administration Building in front of the prison. Three white-paneled vans sped through the main gate as it rolled open and then closed behind them. The first two vans emptied their passengers to the waiting battalion of guards in front of the penitentiary. The heavily armed officers escorted three gurneys and a wheelchair along the maze of fencing near the side entrance of the Admin Building, with the bus driver still cursing up a streak. Then the main tower opened another gate, where the third van pulled into a different entrance and was met by a SWAT Unit of 10 guards, who opened the side door and unloaded the chained miscreant into a wheelchair and carted him off into the bowels of the main prison complex.

"I don't know what happened out there, Captain Tatum, but I expect you to secure the situation and have a full report on my desk first thing in the morning. Am I perfectly clear on that?" scolded Chief Warden Walter P. Stevens, as he checked the time on his gold wristwatch.

"Yes, Sir, Warden," said Captain Ronald "Ron" Tatum, with a standing salute. "You can count on me, Sir, to get to the bottom of things and contain the situation in strict confidence. Sir, do you want this report to be official or off the record?"

"Hmmm! You are probably right, Captain. We don't need this type of thing getting out of control and embarrassing us in front of the Regional Office. Let's keep it down low. Get a wrecker and get that bus off the main road before visiting hours tomorrow. We don't need civilians asking questions and raising concerns about the safety of this institution, now do we?" he quipped.

"No, Warden. We wouldn't want to ruin our service record. It's been nearly 660 days since our last conflict. I believe we are the only correctional facility up for an award this year, Sir," stated the captain proudly.

"Yes, and let's keep it that way. I didn't get to be the country's best warden without that sort of nuisance now, did I?" he asked, waving at his wall of fame. Twenty gold plastic accommodations outlined the wall behind his desk, making him smile.

He helped to design the low, medium, and maximum-security complexes, and he was hoping that the Bureau would name it after him at his upcoming retirement.

"Captain, you are on your own. I'm late for my fundraising dinner. I'll have the inmate road crew repair that awful pothole first thing in the morning. The damn thing broke the front axle, disabled the bus, injured those poor bastards tonight, and almost accidentally blew that officer's head off," Stevens grumbled, slipping on his Armani raincoat. "If that happened, we'd be totally screwed and wouldn't get our award this year that I've worked so hard to achieve. This place is a catastrophe waiting to happen, and I'll thank my lucky stars if we leave this place intact to the rats, who are the permanent tenants of this property."

"Yes, sir," chuckled the round Captain, knowing the warden was truthful on many counts.

Captain Tatum saw a rat near the cooking vats in the kitchen early one morning, nearly scaring the crap right out of him. "It was definitely the biggest freaking rat I have ever seen in my life," he told his lieutenants earlier that day.

"When we saw each other, both of us froze, waiting for the other to make the first move. I drew my piece out at it, aimed, and hollered (BLAMMO!). It didn't even flinch. They are getting so big and brazen, that I heard one of the black inmates tell me he saw "little dogs running around the garbage dock.""

"I hate those things, and if one ever bit you, well, I want those exterminator-inmates to get on it, and trap those rats, and burn them in the incinerator."

Captain Tatum envied the Warden, watching him from his office window as he pulled his new, black Land Rover from its private parking space and raced away down the tree-lined corridor.

"Spoiled ass," snarled Tatum. "I run this show around here, not you." He pulled his baton out, slapping his cupped hand harder and harder. He was angry that he always took the fall and covered up "Mr. Goody-Two-Shoes'" mistakes in management, like all the other pencil necks that worked in this shithole prison.

Tatum sat down in the Warden's leather chair and threw his boots up on his desk. He liked the feeling of power and absolute authority.

He took the orders from his superiors but always, changed the procedure to accommodate his well-being, and people in the prison knew that for a fact, from top to bottom—from the administrative secretaries to the inmates—Captain Ron was no one to cross and have mad at you. He ruled the prison with an iron fist, and the army of two hundred officers followed his every order—they had to, or else. Tatum's command had more cover-ups than the CIA. He was a murderous coward and beat inmates to death if he had to, just to get his point across. Heavenworth Federal Pen, was one of the most notorious prisons in the entire correctional system and a total sham when, it came to upholding justice.

The inmate designators in the entire U.S. Government sent the worst inmates in the country to it. There was more union corruption and more bribes taken than anywhere else in the nation. The corruption was rampant, and the captain ran the prison gangs as well. He called the shots and put the contracts out on would-be kingpins. He funneled narcotics into the prison and coerced visiting families into prostitution and drug trafficking.

Captain Ron was straight-up pure white trash, but he was trained by special-forces in the U.S. Army to be the killer that he was. Correctional employment is where they hire people like, Staff Sergeant Ron Tatum after they "Go Rambo," taking out the innocents when you can't identify the friends from the enemy.   They all melt into one big pot, and your trust instinct is totally blown, so you just get whoever is in your way, out. They send guys like Captain Ron back to the secret detox rooms in Langley and reprogram them into a better way of life, as noncom-personnel. They then hire these para-military thugs in the privatized correctional systems in America because they are just what the system ordered. Who else could police the "human zoos" that are positioned as global warehouses of criminal misfits?

Yes, Captain Ron had an agenda, as he leaped up from behind the desk, drinking the rest of the cold, leftover coffee from the warden's U.S. Department of Justice's gold-emblazoned mug.

He marched down the marble corridor, swinging his stick and wondering what happened to his men, and just who is this "spook" they brought into his house. He crossed the inlayed War Eagle on the marble-tiled floor and nodded to the main control block.

The guards checked the surveillance cameras to recognize him and let him into the main security corridor that led into the domed complex. They saluted their superior officer, but he ignored them as two tons of iron barred door rolled right and then closed left behind him with a booming (CA-CHUNK), as the steel lock slammed home. His heavy boot steps echoed his arrival at the Central Command, as three more officers stood and saluted him. The Captain was in the house!

Chapter 3

"Welcome to Heavenworth"

"There, Spalding! You look a lot better than Peters and Johnson," said Dr. Loomis. He was the Chief of the Medical Staff and was used to patching up inmates and prison personnel after riots and apparent suicides. He was a horrible surgeon and lost more patients on the operating table from incompetence and alcoholism than most major hospitals. He usually cited the inadequate working conditions he had to deal with inside the ancient facility.

"How's Harry?" Spalding asked the Doc, checking out the eight stitches over his upper lip.

"He's OK. He's a tough old bird—took a couple of aspirin and went home. However, Peters and Johnson were a mess, and we sent them to Heavenworth General by ambulance where they can convalesce. Johnson's probably disabled for the rest of his life. A few inches to the right, and the blast would have taken off his head. Very, very lucky!" he said, sarcastically.

"Lucky? My ass! In twenty years of service, I ain't never seen a bigger freak show than what happened on that bus tonight. I need a stiff drink, Doc!

Where's your bottle?" Spalding asked.

"First drawer, second file cabinet on the left," said Dr. Loomis.

"Pour one for me, too, if you'd be so kind?" Dr. Loomis grinned.

The lieutenant poured two tall glasses of Scotch whiskey and handed one to the Doc. They clinked their glasses together and sat down at Loomis's desk. Dr. Albert Loomis looked pale from fatigue, working his usual fourteen-hour day, and stressed to the max from the inmates' daily death threats to him and his family. He gulped the Scotch, opened his top desk drawer, and removed a pack of cigarettes. He offered one to Spalding, but he said he didn't smoke.

"No thanks! Those things will kill yah," joked Spalding.

The two men looked at each other and laughed, knowing how ridiculous it was that they might die from nicotine instead of being murdered in the prison.

"These are the least of my worries," said Loomis lighting up, taking a big inhale, and blowing it up into the dim fluorescent lights. Spalding took a long painful drink, washing the metallic taste of blood down his throat—followed by another, and finishing the glass. He lost himself for a few seconds just staring into the glass.

"Got any more of this stuff?" Spalding asked, "And any painkillers samples I could have too?"

The Doctor gave him a smile, opened another drawer, and opened another bottle of Scotch.

He leaned over and poured them both another glass, leaving it open on the desktop. He reached in his coat pocket, shook a bottle of pills in front of Spalding, and tossed it to him.

"Help yourself, Lieutenant. I have plenty of those, too!" smiled the Doctor.

"Just what the hell went on out there tonight, anyway?" he asked.

Spalding chased down two tablets with his drink and gave the Doc a nasty glance.

"I don't want to talk about it!" barked Spalding, feeling his lip tenderly.

"Your kisser is probably, going to change a little, but it won't leave too big of a scar," said the doctor.

Spalding got up and looked into the mirror at the repair. He studied it closely and said,

"Looks like you did a pretty good job, Doc!"

"Thanks. I've had enough practice. The only thing I'm good at is sewing people together," Loomis chuckled, taking another drink.

"There's going to be one hell of an investigation into what happened out there tonight. I am sure the warden is all over the captain, and then he'll be all over me! What a fucked-up day!" Spalding cried, rubbing his temples.

"Yeah, shit rolls downhill, my boy. Sure you don't want to tell me anything—off the record?" asked the Doc, winking at Spalding. "Well, I guess the whiskey is working. How about one of those smokes?" he asked, smiling.

"Surely," said the Doc, and he reached over and lit the cigarette for Spalding and another for himself. As he did, the lights in the prison went out, temporarily. It was pitch black in the office, and Loomis flicked his lighter on. He held it up, and Spalding took a puff and coughed.

"You look like Boris Karloff, in these dark shadows, did you know that?" joked Spalding.

"Gooooood evening!" the Doctor said cynically.

"That's par for the course. There's probably another storm blowing through the valley."

"Yes," said the Doc. "We've had outages all day long. It rained like hell, and we even had a flash flood, or so I heard."

"Well, that would explain the potholes we hit. It knocked the shit right out of us and broke the front axle in two pieces," waved Spalding, taking another drink.

"So, who was the inbound?" Dr. Loomis asked.

"Oh, that guy is the spookiest mother I have ever seen. His name is Mutumbo Watini, a Jamaican from New Yorker. He got twenty years for second-degree manslaughter. He apparently led some cult into a ritualistic killing of four college co-eds from Columbia University. We picked him up at the Oklahoma City transfer station. Everyone said this guy is really bad news and, so far, I agree with them.

"They say he's a witch doctor and does voodoo curses and all kinds of weird shit. Hey, Doc, maybe you two got something in common," Spalding slurred a little laughter.

"Very funny!" said the Doc, lighting a candle and putting it on his desk.

The candle flickered atop the Doctor's desk, as Spalding told him about what happened on the bus. Spalding was fearful, and Dr. Loomis knew, that Captain Ron's first lieutenant didn't scare easily. He was very nervous and described the event in vivid detail. They both leaned in and lit cigarettes off the candle, discussing the ordeal, when the lights came back on.

"That's quite a story, Lieutenant! I'd be careful on what you report to the captain, though. You don't want this to get out of hand," cautioned Dr. Loomis.

"Yeah, you're probably right. It was a good thing Harry woke up and saw what I did. He clobbered that "spook" and knocked his ass unconscious—or we might all be dead. I'll tell you one thing, Doc, that bastard is not human. I know people—and I have seen the worst—but this character is definitely a badass. The boys put him in Level Three Detention underneath the solitary confinement block. He ain't going to see sunlight for a while, after tonight's little episode. We'll make him wish he wasn't born, by the time we get done with him," said Spalding.

There was a knock on the door, and the nurse informed them that Captain Ron, was waiting to speak with them both in his office—immediately, before the count. Loomis blew out the candle, and they both finished their drinks. Then Spalding said, "Wonderful. The greater of two evils, and I get to see them both tonight."

Chapter 4

"Count Time"

It was 10 p.m. and time for "count." The Nation's prisons simultaneously, do a physical headcount of every man and woman incarcerated in the United States of America. All inmates, must either stand up, or be in their cells, or dormitories by their assigned bunk beds and be counted by the correctional officers on duty at the time. There are four counts per day in each and every prison. The times are as follows: 1 a.m., 4 a.m., 4 p.m., and 10 p.m. The most important of all of them is the mandatory 4 p.m. count. Each inmate must stand up and be counted, whereas the others are a mere formality, and most of the general population is sleeping in their cells, reading a book, or shooting some dope. The 4 p.m. count is when each facility reports the national consensus of the general population to their respective regional office. The region then reports to the National Center of Crime and Statistics for the Department of Justice in Washington D.C. The reason for the accounting of each inmate, is to verify the accounting records, which are not as easy as it may sound. The general population is constantly in a state of flux due to the judicial sentencing of newly inducted inmates and the release of expired sentences of inmates.

Then there are those inmates on furlough (which, is visitation rights for good behavior or funerals), and then you have the sick or injured who go to local hospitals and clinics and, of course, the inmates who die while incarcerated.

The count is the pulse of the Department of Corrections, which operates fiscally under the Department of Justice. The DOJ puts you in jail, and then turns the control over to the DOC from the point of sentencing and during your probation, parole, or what's commonly known as "supervised release."

Most inmates learn really fast that you do not want to screw up the headcount at any time, or you will suffer the consequences—which is revocation of most of what little privileges you have. If it really upsets the officers, they will take away other inmates' privileges, too, which in retrospect, the other inmates will beat you to a pulp for your screw-up. It's relatively a pretty simple system but, on occasion, it happens most often from the imbecile guards who lose track or count one head twice, and then they still punish you because it is never their fault.

The correctional officers at Heavenworth Federal Penitentiary were mostly local, gorillas with shaved heads. You could hear their blasphemies a block away, as they chastised the local inmates.

It was the 10 o'clock count, as two unshaven guards, made their way around the cell blocks.

"One, two, three, four, five, etc., etc.," they counted until the lights went out, again. This was a very scary moment for a guard, because if, the cells were not on lockdown, someone could get hurt really bad, usually the guard on duty. Momentarily, the darkness froze the thoughts of each man's actions of what he would contemplate doing and then what would be the consequences. The guards' prayers were answered, and the lights flickered and came back to life.

"Son of a bitch! I hate that," remarked Lieutenant Lonnie Parson. He was an old-timer, black and mean as hell. He put more inmates in the hospital than any other guard in the system and was proud of it. His eyes were always wild, like he had too much coffee to drink. The inmates knew better than to mess with "LP" as in liquid petroleum gas—highly combustible.

"You don't mess with LP or BOOM! You all could get hurt real bad," he'd shout. Well, it was a warning, but LP, for the record, should have been dead four times after inmate assaults. LP had been stabbed once, shanked twice, and clubbed, then hung with his own shoelaces, but he lived through it all. "You gotta love a guy like that," quipped Captain Ron.

Their jailhouse keys rattled and clanged as they strolled through the prison blocks and finished up their counts. In C-Block, cell number 313, there were two African Americans playing dominos until it was lights out, which was usually at 10:20 p.m.

They were prisoner #030719-038, Bartholomew L. Jefferson (aka "Bubba") and his bunkmate (or bunky), inmate #021476-042, LaVernious Tyrell Coleman (aka "LT").

"Hurry up, LT! Shuffle dose damn things, or we won't be able to finish up da game," whined Bubba, pushing up his thick prison-issued glasses. They were duct-taped on the nose bridge and on both ear stems. They were broken and repaired more times than the men he clobbered, fighting within the general population. His biceps were 24 inches around, and his massive chest was 56 inches in circumference. He tipped the scales at 375 pounds. He was an NFL washout, three years pro, who played right tackle for the Saints. He was doing 15 years for second-degree manslaughter. He accidentally killed his agent who was cheating with his now ex-wife. They extorted his bankroll and partied all over the cities where Bartholomew was playing football. One day, one of his teammates told him to leave after a game and go straight to his hotel suite where he'd find out what a tramp he'd married. He did. Bubba lost it when he caught them both "doin' da nasty" and threw his naked-ass agent from the 35th floor to his death. Bubba admitted it in court to the Judge, saying, "It was nothing but blood, sweat, and tears," but he also admitted that he really thought there was a swimming pool below. The gavel hit, and the Judge gave him two consecutive terms of 15 years. That was six years ago, and he was the strongest man in Heavenworth.

On the other hand, LT was the smarter of the two—well, if you can call two guys behind bars smart, that is.

LaVernious was from Detroit and had a rap sheet in his case file that was five inches thick. He was a habitual offender with more than twenty-eight convictions. He started out in "juvey" (juvenile detention) at age 14 and had eight arrests for stolen vehicles. He started selling drugs in high school and was a junkie on heroine by age 17. He finally made the "big time" by committing armed robbery—starting out small, hitting convenience markets and, eventually, popping banks. He was incarcerated at age 20 and was now 38 years young, with ten more years to serve. LT was one of the unfortunate kids raised in the projects on the south side of Chicago. Fatherless like most black kids and his Momma was a junkie and a prostitute herself. He had an older sister who raised him for the most part, but she was killed in a shootout when he was 12. He loved her more than anything. Her name was Latticia Ray, and he still had a photo of her hanging next to his top bunk bed. He talked to her every night before going to sleep, pretending that there would be a day that they would see each other again—in heaven. The only thing LT believed in was that there had to be a better life than the one he and Latticia Rae had—or didn't have. "C'mon, Bubba! You are slower than the second comin', I swear," lamented LT.

Bubba rubbed his chin, plotting his next move, and gave a big grin, knowing he had the move when he picked up his domino to slam it down. That's when the lights went black.

"Oh, no!" cried the big man. "Shoot! I had da game, man. I had you stone cold, bunky!"

It was dark in the cell with very little light coming through the bars. LT put the dominos back in a thick wool sock..

"C'mon, man. Who you talkin' to, fool? You never had a chance at winning! The only thing close was my sentence ending—your big old dumbass is so slow," he jived.

"Don't chu talk to Bubba like dat, unless'n yo want a whup ass!"

"All right, all right! I's sorry, but you got's to learn how ta play faster, dat's all I'm sayin'," said LT, holding his hand up and putting the sock in his locker. Bubba pulled down his pants and sat on the cold, stainless steel toilet.

"Damn! Dat's chilly!" he said as he farted.

"Man don't stink it all up, now! I's goin' to bed," moaned LT.

"Hey, man, did you eat dat sorry ass spaghetti?" asked Bubba, grunting.

"Hell yes, I did! It was plain nasty! All sauce and no meat! What up wit dose noodles?"

"It's called pasta, ya dumb ass!" came a voice in the dark from the next cell.

"Who's talkin' to your dumb ass, niggah?" grunted Bubba again.

"Yeah! You betta get cho ass ta sleep, so I don't havta com through dis wall and bust your dumb ass up," chimed in LT.

The night banter was common between the "brotherhoods" on C-Block. It was the inmates' way of bonding with each other in a crass kind of way. Many nights the guys would trade barbs with each other and get a pretty good laugh, taking their minds of their troubled souls. Suddenly, something upset Bubba's constitution, and he leaped up off the toilet seat, screaming, "EEEEEYYYYYYAAAAAAHHHHH! What da hell's dat?"

LT sat up quickly, saying "What on earth is wrong now?"

Bubba danced around the cell like he was on fire, shaking his hands in the air.

"There's sumthin' in the toilet, LT! It grabbed my equipment! Look see here! Der's somethin' movin' around in there!" he said in a panic. LT busted out laughing, watching the 375-pound man dance half naked in their cell. His hands were flapping like a little bird, and then he threw a roll of toilet paper at the toilet. LT was in hysterics, and so was Bubba, but for different reasons.

Then a flashlight beamed in on the two troublemakers. It was none other than Lieutenant Parsons (aka "LP").

"What da hell's going on in here?" he growled.

"Somthin' grabbed me when I was sittin' on the toilet, LP!" said Bubba.

The beam was aimed at the toilet seat. "I don't see nuttin'," LT mumbled.

The other inmates were all making wisecracks and jeering Bubba on.

"That's enough out of you guys, or I'll lock dis bitch down!" screamed the lieutenant.

LP no sooner said that when he flashed the light back in the cell, and the toilet paper jumped out of the toilet and onto the floor. It scared LP, and he screamed a shout and dropped the flashlight on the concrete.

"What da hell is dat?" LT cried. "It's a freaking rat, I'll bet," he shouted, nervously. "I hate dose tings!"

Bubba was freaking out holding, his pants up around his waist, and standing on a chair. LT was quiet, his eyes big as saucers.

The toilet paper jumped again, and the three men screamed—again.

"You guys better not be playin' sum kinda joke with me, or I'll send you both to the hole! Do you hear me?" shouted the angry lieutenant. He scrambled with his keys and opened the bar door. Holding his flashlight and pulling out his baton, he swung at the moving toilet paper and hit the menace. The toilet paper jumped again, and he swung harder hitting it again.

"Kill it, LP! Kill it!" shouted Bubba, dancing on the chair.

Soon the whole Block was chanting, "Kill it! Kill it! Kill it!"

The toilet paper quit moving, and the scene settled down. LP slowly lifted it up with his baton and uncovered a dead frog.

"Well, son of a bitch! It's a frog! Must have come up the sewer drain from all the rain we got today," surmised the lieutenant.

He shined the light at it and gave it another rap with his baton, popping its head open and blood ran out on the cell floor.

"There! Clean this shit up and get to bed, hear me?" he commanded the two inmates.

"Yes, sir, LP," they both replied.

"What was it? The boogeyman?" hollered another voice in the dark.

"OK, boys. The show's over! It was a frog," reported LP.

"A FROG? Did ya kill it, LP?" asked another voice enthusiastically.

LP locked the cell door again. He took his baton and rapped the knuckles of the inquisitor next to #313.

"OUCH!" he cried, jerking his hands back behind the bars. Sometimes the bars protected the inmates from the guards—or even other inmates. "I killed it and popped its head wide open! I'll do the same to the next sum' bitch that opens his mouth," LT promised.

What was uncontrolled laughter and mayhem was instantly changed into dead silence, except for the toilet flushing in cell #313.

Chapter 5

"Who dat?"

The SWAT Team was watching the new arrival, as scientists would study a new species, or form thereof, on the surveillance monitor. The inmate was now identified by the open file record sitting on the desk of Sergeant Fred Rogers, Night Commander of the SHU—otherwise known as the Special Housing Unit. The inmates affectionately called the SHU, "the hole." It was really a prison within a prison but simplified with less accommodations of luxury like a bed, toilet, or any type of windows or barred doors. The SHU is as close to solitary confinement as reform goes but has virtually no contact with anyone other than the Correctional Officer on duty. The environment was all pre-formed concrete. The bed and floor were one, with no furniture or locker of any type. Bare and void of any comfort, the design of the SHU was to break down an inmate for "bad behavior," and deny him any means of attention or lack thereof. The COs usually dressed the inmate down, to wearing an orange jumpsuit with large black letters, "SHU," stenciled on the back, a pair of boxer briefs and a pair of navy blue, slip-on tennis shoes.

The basic issue for day-to-day prison-issued clothing consisted of a khaki shirt, a pair of second-hand battle fatigue pants, a white cotton T-shirt, a pair of cotton boxers (used or maybe not), two pairs of tube socks, and a thick pair of black work boots—all made in China.

However, none bothered to dress the inmate down because of the special chains and shackles that the dread-locked Mutombo Watini was wearing. He was wearing a leather half-face mask with steel inserts in the mouth opening like the ones they issued to "Hannibal the Cannibal." Watini was a biter, and that meant real problems for everybody because of the infection that was usually delivered to the wound. It was well known, that the human bite was among the worst documented injuries in the correctional system. Medical treatment for such a wound, was usually large doses of steroidal ointments, externally and internally. If, the infection got out of hand, it usually led to amputation as a last resort, since most bite wounds were on the arm or leg. Bites usually resulted in a Staph infection of one strain or another, but the dominant virus among crowded living conditions, such as in hospitals and prisons, was the dreaded MRSA (Methicillin Resistant Staphylococcus Aurous). Most inmates called it the "mutant maker" because of the painful disfigurement caused by the disease. The virus habitat was everywhere but mostly, it was in shower stalls, toilets, sinks, water fountains, gymnasium floors, and weight-room equipment— and, of course, the telephones.

MRSA is one of the most puzzling of viruses because you could have it in your bloodstream and not even know it until you had an outbreak from an open wound or sore. The infection is rampant and very damaging to the human cell and can result in death, if not treated immediately. The C.O.s' studied every move, as the inmate investigated his new cage, shuffling around the cell, mumbling chants, and occasionally, sipping water from the water fountain. Watini's file was thick with psychological evaluations and incident reports that labeled him as a Level Five Security Risk and to use extreme caution when around him.

"Why on earth did Region send this nutcase to us?" asked the obese Sergeant. "This guy belongs in a 'Super Max' with those freaking terrorists and other weirdo lifers in Colorado. Put 'em all deep in the ground with the other cockroaches on the planet," he grumbled, chewing a huge wad of chewing tobacco while reading the file. The more he read, the less he chewed, as he drooled some black juice on his stained white uniform shirt.

Most of the inmates dubbed him, "Inbred Fred," because of his grotesque chewing habit and his body structure of an English Bulldog. His cowboy belt buckle had his nickname engraved on it, Fredneck. "Would you look at this 'profile' report from the FBI? It says here, that when they got word about this Watini guy from the Sheriff's Department and sent a unit out to arrest this guy, they all disappeared and have not been located.

It comes about that this dude was practicing 'black magic' in a swamp in the North Parrish of Piedmont, just outside of Slidell, Louisiana. When the second team of seven FBI agents from Quantico came to arrest him, it says they encountered a, ah, ahem, . . . no, no this can't be right! It must be a typo or something!" he muttered, looking dumbfounded. His office chair squeaked, as he rested backward in it.

"What is it, Sergeant? What did they encounter?" asked Officer Peacock, pulling off his helmet.

"It was a, uh, a 23-foot alligator. It bit one of the troopers in half and kicked the hell out of the rest of them. It broke two agents' legs from whipping its tail and clawed another's right foot clean off."

"What? You can't be for real! Let me see that," ordered Captain Ron. He walked in the room just as the Sergeant was reading the report.

"Ten hut," the SWAT Unit saluted him, startled from his surprise entrance.

"Yeah, OK. At ease, guys. What is this all about, Fred?" he jumped the desk jockey.

"We're reading that wild animal's profile that the DOJ sent here, Captain. The guy is a bonafide nut job, Sir. Take a look at him on the monitors," moaned Inbred Fred.

"I've been watching him since you buffoons brought him in here, at my office," the Captain growled.

He read the report and scratched his head. Then he flipped the pages back and forth, not believing the reports he was reading. He leaned over the desk and stared at the monitor.

"Boys! We got us a real prize here, with us tonight. He's bad news and a real troublemaker. I just spoke with Lieutenant Spalding, and he swears that this inmate used some kind of voodoo on him and the rest of our guys. Tyrell says he chanted some kind of spell on them all. But for all we know, it was an accident from the bus hitting a pothole created by the storms earlier. I don't want you jumping to any conclusions about this Mutombo character other than, he's a psychotic, paranoid hostile, and we treat him like we treat all of those types, that come to visit us here at Heavenworth."

The Captain opened a metal door and went inside, turning on the light. He reappeared holding two fully charged 15,000-watt, taser guns. He sparked the firing mechanisms, as they sizzled, burning the ion in the air, and gave a big smile.

"Boys! Let's give Mr. Watini a big 'Rock, Chock, Jayhawk' welcome," he said as he handed one of the stun guns to Bulldog, who responded with a big grin, and spat his chaw into a full coffee cup.

Chapter 6

"Big Red"

T he wind was cool that Saturday morning, but it felt great to the men working out in the three-acre yard located in the center of the prison. It was the beginning of a new day, as the sun cast long shadows over the steeply pitched rooftops and east towers of the complex.

The COs walked along the massive, old brick wall, which surrounded the entire prison. It was five feet thick and forty-two feet in height. The west wall was over a thousand yards in length, with two-gun towers on the north and south ends. The yard was dwarfed by its ominous size, built psychologically just for that fact. It gave prisoners that "shut-in feeling" like they were being suffocated by the mere oppression of the facility and what it represented. Rarely, did an inmate see anything outside of the yard. It was the only green grass that they ever saw. Some of the inmates worked in the south terrace garden growing vegetables.

They grew some carrots, peas, and tomatoes in the sparse sunlight that came over the east rooftops, and they could all see the silver dome at the front of the complex. It looked like a giant UFO resting on the red brick, rectangular structure of the administration building.

The dome had a giant seventy five foot flagpole jutting up into the sky that flew "Old Glory" and, of course, the Kansas State flag just below it. It was a symbol of freedom for the surrounding countryside of local Kansans, but it was a stark reminder to all the incarcerated inmates of their misgivings in life and what they had lost.

"Loud and Proud," was what most of the natives called the largest employer in the area. The U.S Government's oldest prison was like a huge "fiscal black hole." The facility was so outdated and wasted so many resources that it was hard for the BOP (Bureau of Prisons) to justify its massive drain of funding on the entire system. Still, it was a place that could warehouse 2,243 lost souls: Murderers, mobsters, rapists, pedophiles, drug lords and addicts, bank robbers, gang members, extortionists, cyber hackers, pimps, and thieves.

Then you could classify the above miscreants according to their status in life, those who were doctors, lawyers, judges, law enforcement officers, politicians, congressmen, mayors, council members, nurses, teachers, scientists, professors, diplomats, businesspeople, developers, contractors, engineers, etcetera, etcetera, there's no prejudice when it comes to crime.

Time served is the common bond shared, between people in prison. The really sad scenario of the incarcerated is a person who is more likely to die or commit another crime while serving their time. The lifers, or people serving longer than twenty years, usually were serving another predator, while in the system. It was a universe within a universe, of painful conflict from the day-to-day hustle of corruption, collusion, sex, injury, and death. While incarcerated, you never know who the enemy is and that included the people who were paid by the U.S Government, to watch over and protect you from the general population.

The recreation yard was the marketplace to do business if you were an inmate. The shots, bribes, payoffs, and pledges all went down inside the walls. The integration was cruel, to say the least, as the kingpins would call shots or put contracts out on the weaker, non-affiliated inmates. Much of the insidious business was conducted by the legions of obedient soldiers who played by the rule of the land—which was to kill or be killed. Once an order was given, it had to be executed or else. If an inmate feared for his life and reported the incident to the authorities, that person was marked as a "RAT" and would be exterminated sooner or later. If the BOP felt that the rat was in real danger, they would transfer him to another prison, seemingly giving false hope that the inmate would be out of harm.

The system was designed for bribes and snitches, which made it virtually impossible to hide under custody protection.

It was just a matter of time before the rat person was found and dealt with. You can run, but you can't hide! The overlords extorted money in many different ways—usually on the outside from a target's family member.

The sweat poured out of Derek Jackson, inmate #237350-041, as he ran lap number 26 around the quarter-mile track. His grey sweats were two-tone from all the perspiration he had generated from his intense workout regimen. He was six feet tall, weighed about 194 pounds, and was solid muscle. He could bench-press 450 pounds and deadlift 650. He performed a hundred sit-ups daily, along with two hundred push-ups. Derek was 38 years old and divorced. He was doing an eleven-year sentence for trafficking methamphetamines to support his tennis habit. He played on the professional circuit bu,t couldn't get sponsored. "It was fast, easy money," he said, selling to addicts, but he never touched the stuff himself. He was an athlete and hard up for money to cover his expenses traveling around the country playing tennis.

His supplier was his younger brother, Kyle Jackson, inmate #323357-041. He was the cook and "go-to" guy when Derek needed some cash. The false promise of tennis fame and glory would lead them down a road frequently traveled by aspiring athletes of many sports.

The sponsorship funding came from laundered drug monies and was easily tracked by the FBI, resulting in equal opportunity for the two brothers—behind bars. Kyle was the total opposite of his brother, but he tried hard to get in condition after damaging so many brain cells while ingesting the powerful chemicals used in meth manufacturing. He was six feet, two inches, weighed 223 pounds, and could run about two miles—usually meeting his brother on the track near the end of his workout. In prison, everyone usually, called the other individual's first letter, instead of their full name.

"Hey, D. Slow down a little, man, before you rupture something," whined Kyle. "It's about time you got off your butt and started working out," D chastised.

"Man, didn't you see me over there doing my leg stretches with Raul?" he boasted.

"Yeah, I saw you stretching your jawbone and flapping your gums," he grinned.

"Well, for your information, Raul knows more about what's going on in this place than the warden." He hocked up some phlegm and spit. "There goes some more lung," he joked.

"You know that isn't funny! It's probably the truth, for all you know." Kyle punched him in the left arm kiddingly, hurting his right wrist, "Ouch, that hurt!" He shook his hand lamely, running next to his brother.

"You are so darn hard, you could probably run through the wall and knock it down. Why don't you do that so we can get out of this dump?" Kyle advised. Derek wiped his brow and looked up at the armed guard above them walking the wall.

"That's why! We wouldn't make it twenty yards, before we'd be both shot dead, even if, I could knock a hole in that thing. Besides, a tank couldn't drive through that thing. There's more rebar and brick in that wall than a skyscraper," said D.

The CO looked down at the two of them, and Kyle gave him a friendly wave.

"What are you doing, man? Don't let other guys see you waving at a guard, for Pete's sake!"

"Oh, I was just sharing the love of Jesus with him," said Kyle.

"Well, just don't do that if you know what's good for the both of us. This place is straight-up evil and that's all you have to do to get beat up real good, is a wave to an armed guard. Besides that guard is "Dead Eye Dick." He's only got one eye, and that's why he's an expert sharpshooter. Nothing distracts his aim when he shoots. He killed those two idiots that tried to climb up the smokestack from the powerhouse last year and nailed them both from six hundred yards, with a night scope. The inmates shot, were real time brothers. They were both saved, two years ago, when they first came to Heavenworth at the weekly prayer service conducted by the local Chaplain, Reggie Burns. The Chapel was located in the southeast wing by the cafeteria.

"You're probably right. Look at all the pockmarks and chunks blown out of the wall from bullets hitting it," Kyle gulped, feeling intimidated.

"Well, most of those rounds were shot, long before we got here not since the last riot in 2003. The Cos' killed thirteen inmates, and the inmates killed five guards and one civilian," said D, hesitantly. "OK, this is the last lap, Bro."

"Praise the Lord" puffed Kyle. "I'm starved! I hope they have a good meal for us today.

You know, some fresh hard-boiled eggs and French toast with maple syrup," he said.

"Kyle, you've been here long enough to know that's what they serve every Saturday since we've been here," D reminded him.

"Well, I'm still hungry, and that's why I'm running my tail off to burn calories, right?" he asked. "Yes! So, what gossip did Raul have this morning?"

"Oh, the usual," he answered. "I guess there was a beat down, in the SHU on some 'witchdoctor dude,' who came in late last night. Raul cleans the SHU, you know?"

"Wait a minute!" Derek stopped running and grabbed his brother's hoodie, stopping him in the middle of the track. "Did, I hear you right? Did you say they brought in a warlock?"

"No! I said they brought in a witchdoctor from Louisiana," Kyle said poignantly. "Wow! Now that's something else. I ain't never heard of a witchdoctor in prison, before.

What did they bust him for—selling batwings illegally or something stupid like that?" Derek joked.

"Don't know! Don't care! Raul said there was a lot of blood in the holding tank, and he had to hose down the entire room into the drain. He said the Sergeant told him that Captain Ron and he and four other SWATEES, tazed the dude silly, and then beat him up real bad."

"I guess," Kyle continued, "he made the transfer bus crash near the pasture late last night. One of the COs was wounded by a shotgun blast to his shoulder and almost blew his head off!" Kyle said as he told him the gruesome news.

"Say what?"

"Yep, that's what Raul said. He also sai,d they're sending some Cos' to the main confluence of the storm drains. Seems there's an outbreak of frogs invading the prison. The COs were chasing the critters all over the place and rounding them up. I guess C-Block had a lot of them come up through the toilets. A lot of the inmates killed them and threw them off the tiers at the passing night watchmen. I guess it was a real mess. Raul said, the guards were sliding on froggy innards, all over the place."

"That's just crazy!" Derek laughed at the visual thought, of the mess they had to clean up.

"Yeah! They blamed it on Bubba and LT," informed Kyle. "They are both in the hole. Raul said they started the whole thing and ole Lieutenant LP went crazy, wondering how they got all those frogs up there in their cell in the first place. I guess he slipped on a frog and skated halfway across the mezzanine on one foot and finally crashed."

They were both laughing and hanging on to one another.

"Raul said LP went bonkers and started to chase them frogs around with a mop. He was hitting them like hockey pucks at the inmates, in the lower cells. Ole LP, almost started a riot because he made those guys so mad., I guess everyone got into it down there. They were throwing the freaking frogs, all over the place. C-Block is locked down. That's why the yard looks so vacant, this morning," opined Kyle.

They both looked around and noticed that it wasn't crowded at the weight pile. C-Block was the toughest block in the prison where they housed a lot of the long-timers together. They dominated the weight pile, lifting weights at recreation time.

"You know, now that you mentioned it, Kyle, I was wondering where, Brother Bubba was? He's always at the weights hollering and motivating the others to lift more," said Derek, as he wiped his face off with a white towel from around his neck.

"Yup! Our big Christian Brother, Bubba's in the hole and probably won't be singing with the chapel choir at Sunday service, either" lamented Kyle, who sang in the choir, too.

"Yes, we'll have to pray for him and LT that they both get out of there as soon as possible. The SHU sucks!" said Derek.

"Did you just curse?" asked Kyle.

"No! Sucks is not a curse word, it's an adjective."

"I don't know about that, Brother D. I think it's a curse word." Derek was getting mad at his brother and swatted him in the back of the head.

"Hey, don't do that! Now you better seek forgiveness for cursing and hitting your brother, too!" laughed Kyle, who shoved his brother backward and dashed over to Raul, who was doing wind sprints in the grassy field. "Oh, Raul!" called Kyle.

"You had better run! If, I get my hands on you, you'll 'croak' like one of those frogs did last night," chuckled the older brother.

Raul Ibanez, #112875-031, hailed out of Tijuana, Mexico, via Brownsville, Texas, where he was busted ten years ago for smuggling twenty pounds of horse (aka brown heroin) over the border.

He was thirty one years old and serving a one hundred eighty-month sentence.

He was a millionaire by age nineteen and moved a ton of heroin annually, over the border. His code name, was "El Cohonnes" because, it took some real balls, to pull off the size of deals he made with the DEA undercover. He started early in life at age eleven, like most of the young street rats in Mexico. Ibanez's first five years were served in Pelican Bay F.C.I., in California, and was immediately pimped, because he was young and very handsome, not good while serving at the toughest prison in the U.S.A. He was a Sorreno Gang member, and his "jeffé" was known as "Mantobahn the Mercilous." He was one of the cartel kingpins, alive in the Bureau of Prisons. No one messed with the kid, but he was involved in a lot of bloodshed in the "Can-Can Wars" in 2004. That was what the FBI called the turf war between the Mexicans and the African Americans. More than five hundred inmates died in a two-year period, not counting another thousand who were maimed or injured until, a truce was agreed upon in 2007. The gangs will one day rule the world, because the fatherless and greedy young men and women have nothing to live for, except to follow the orders handed down to them by their superiors. "Kill, or we will kill your entire family, before we kill you," was their motto.

Raul was number three in the system before they finally turned on him. He was stabbed nine times before the sharpshooters killed his two assailants one sunny afternoon while walking around the track with his boss. Montobahn was shanked thirty times and bled out on the track next to his three-man crew. Raul was the only survivor of the attack and was hospitalized in a coma for fourteen days.

Raul woke up and told the prison doctor that he had met Jesus, that Jesus was his new boss, and that He had a lot of work for him to do. Raul's punctured left lung and severed right femoral artery were miraculously healed. The doctors couldn't believe they were the same X-rays taken just two weeks earlier. The Bureau transferred him out of Pelican Bay to Heavenworth Penitentiary, where he joined "God's Gang," preaching the "Good News" to inmates. The rule was that when you enter prison, you became affiliated with a tribe or gang immediately, if you wanted to live longer than thirty days.

The "protection" was the only way to survive the ruthless miscreants and their powerful alliances. Being a "Christian" was a sign of weakness but, nevertheless, respected if you were a believer, or not. Even the hypocrites, respected the wrath of God Almighty. Just look at what He did to the Jewish Nation all those centuries before. The unbeliever just never got the message about Jesus Christ, but that was prophesied by the ancients long before they were born.

That's what the Christian Brotherhood was all about, but now the Islamic faith was crowding in on their turf, which was starting to pose real problems between the gang bangers because the Muslims continued their gang relationships The yard was busy with lots of inmate activities such as die-hard softball games, bocce ball, soccer, weightlifting, boxing, martial arts training, and some men playing handball. Also, the prisoners' favorite pastime was "smoking cigarettes," whether contraband roll-your-own or the usual corporate brands purchased through the commissary. About eighty five-percent of the prison inmates smoked, not worried they would die, from lung cancer, as opposed to receiving a mortal shank wound, someday.

The brick wall was affectionately named, "Big Red." Inmates watching the softball games offered to fetch the balls that were jacked over the short right-field wall, next to the field. Of course, the guards would smile and tell them to go ahead, knowing the inmates were just kidding around, but they weren't. Heavenworth Federal Penitentiary was built in 1887 and located in the State of Kansas. The enormous facility sat alone in a valley, just east of the Missouri River. Rolling green hills with spotty forests lined the valley, and Fort Heavenworth, was two miles north of the prison. Inside the yard to the south was the domed rotunda that was designed to look similar to the U.S Capitol Dome in Washington, D.C. It was octagonal in shape and painted silver, with eight round windows for sunlight to pass into the dark interior of the massive building underneath it.

The four-story administration building, had four, sixty-foot columns in front of it, which housed the business offices of the penitentiary and the visiting center for the inmates. It had two flights of thirty steps that lead up to the entrance of the fortress, of pale grey concrete, from the parking area inside the grounds. The smell of ancient mold, permeated the atmosphere from the underground labyrinth, beneath the complex that went as deep as three stories. Most of the heating, was still a steam-generated system with pipes running through twenty miles of tunnels. The powerhouse was an old coal-burning unit that was converted to a natural gas boiler system in 1952, and it still had an eighty-foot-tall smokestack jutting up inside the north wall. The medical infirmary/hospital was adjacent to it. The rusted steam vents belched vapor plumes every seventy yards along the paved roadways that wound through the maze of buildings.

"So, Bro, how are the lungs feeling after that workout of yours?" asked Raul.

"Man, I'm beat! I'm looking forward to some chowtime," Derek responded, clasping hands with his Christian friend, while still wiping the sweat off his head.

"Brother D! I wished I'd have half the muscles you got and could run as fast as you can. I would still be in the pro soccer league in Mexico City if I was in your condition."

"You played professional soccer, Amigo?" asked Kyle.

"Yeah, Hessé! I played three years in the minors for Guadalajara, before I moved up to the big time, like your brother here."

"I didn't know that! What happened, Raul?" asked Derek, perplexed.

"You know, the usual sex, drugs, and rock 'n roll, man. They took me down faster, than you running the forty-yard dash. I got addicted and went to pieces in one and a half years. I owed a bunch of money to my friend, who was a cartel hit man. I ended up selling drugs for him to other athletes, kind of like these pimps do in America. I think they call them agents. Anyway, I started moving a lot of drugs through Tijuana, when the DEA caught up with me. They wanted my superiors, but I didn't snitch them out and found a really good lawyer. I still got one hundred eighty months, but it could have been much worse."

Both Jacksons looked at each other, thinking their 120-month sentences were paltry in comparison, to Raul's time.

"Anyway, that's all behind me now. I just want to serve God, become an Evangelista, and preach the scriptures, saving souls for the real Boss of it all," he grinned.

"Amen!" responded the brothers.

They walked back slowly, toward the entrance of Cell Block-B, where they were housed, discussing the events of last night.

As, they passed the smoke filled, Native American, sweat lodge, Running Bull appeared coughing from the tent of wet blankets. His three hundred forty-pound frame, was glowing red from the hot steam, he had just finished. He gave a mean stare to the three Christians and gave a big grunt and started doing a Cheyenne war dance, hopping around outside of the tent with the tom-tom drums beating inside. His braided hair swung around the tattooed eagle stenciled on his back shoulders. His real name was Jeremy Curtis, #15633-036, B-Block.

He was an intimidating inmate, acting out what he wanted to be while inside working for the "white man." He went by his real name, Jeremy except, when doing his lodge thing. Then he was 'Running Bull' and his new gig until, he grew impatient with it, like he had all the other religions. He was in search of a higher power and was like a lot of lost souls wandering throughout the network of prisons, trying to establish some sort of identity. He was dubbed semi-schizophrenic with a real bad attitude. He was intelligent but always acted superior to others after he learned more about who they were. Some people act out who they want to be instead of who they really are. Prison, is that kind of place, where you could be anybody you wanted to be, because there was no way of really checking up on you, unless you had good informants on the outside.

Most of the incarcerated masses, were habitual liars, and Jeremy Curtis was one of the best. You couldn't tell if he was lying, or telling you the truth, he had such a convincing tone about him.

Derek tried not to laugh at the dancing bull, as they kept walking by the lodge.

"Man, what a waste of humanity," stated Kyle.

"Now, Kyle! You know not to judge your brothers in, er,.ah? Well, you know what I mean," exclaimed Raul.

"Ugga, bugga,, ugga, bugga! Yes, me, understand, Brother," mocked Kyle, folding his arms together, like a chief from a movie scene. Suddenly, two other tribal members jumped out of the sweat lodge, dancing around in their cutoff khakis. The steam rolled off their backs, like they were fresh out of a kettle, as they tried to cool off by drinking water but crying from the painful sting of the burn.

"Man, I don't know about you, but smoking a peace pipe and almost passing out from heat exhaustion is not my idea of getting closer to God. Know what I'm saying?" he boasted, shaking his head in disbelief at the ceremony being performed.

"Yeah, it makes me think of what hell, will be like for people who end up going there," remarked Derek. "Only, it would be so much worse."

Meanwhile, over at the weight pit, Lance Smith, a new inmate, #030467-045, was enjoying the cool morning air and about to bench press three hundred pounds, when he was rudely interrupted by another monster lurking in the pit.

"Skuse me, but I was working out here," replied the ogre staring down at Lance.

"My bad! I didn't see anybody here, so I was going to do a few reps."

The ogre's name was Malcom "the Monk" Samansky, inmate #11832-029. Lance was wise to cower before the giant looming over him. Samansky was no one to cross, as Lance slid off the bench and started to walk away. The scarred, six-foot-six gladiator glared, making him feel queasy to his stomach. Samansky was a school bus, with legs. His legs were wrapped tightly, so he could lift the free weights without blowing out his knees. Smith didn't know it yet, but he was about to meet some of the regulars who were targeting him. Smith was recently incarcerated for selling anabolic steroids to a network of professional trainers in college football. He primarily sold HGH (human growth hormone) before, it was even known to the sports world. The media focused on him since he had played college ball as a linebacker for Florida State. He graduated with a B.S in "sports science" and was working for a large pharmaceutical company, marketing their performance-enhancing drugs right out of college.

He was earning well over six figures, when the Feds pulled the plug on his little retail clinic, sending him and his doctor girlfriend to prison. She received 10 years in Oxford FCI in Wisconsin, and Smith the same.

"Hey, Holmes, you the new schoolboy we been hearing about?" asked the stocky, tattooed Mexican who appeared from behind Samansky.

His name was Chino Morales, leader of the dreaded Sorrenos Gang in Heavenworth. Lance stopped, as he was circled by Chino's crew. Wisely, Lance kept his mouth shu, as he remembered an ancient proverb, "mouth open, battle lost." One of the Sorrenos, shoved Lance from the back, knocking him to his knees in front of Morales.

"Oh, Hessé! You tripped on your bootlace. Let me help you up, Holmes," smiled Chino. The number "13" was tattooed on his neck, which was their gang sign. He reached down and lifted Lance up and then dusted him off, giving a little smirk and said," You see, Holmes, we take care of our people, and we want you to know that we would like to take care of you. But we cannot do that, unless you join our little community." Chino put his left arm over Lances shoulder and pulled him close to him. Chino had to reach up, being five inches shorter than Lance. He gave him a light slap on the cheek.

"You see? We are all brothers in here, Hessé, and you cannot live amongst us, alone as some Hombré and disrespect our cause.

We are 'the south of the border gang' and the largest community in this piece of crap prison. The guards are on our payroll, and many of the administration, too!"We love the 'gringos' here in the U.S.A., but unfortunately, they don't like us. That's why we are infiltrating the population, Holmes, so we can integrate, and all be one big happy family. Do you know what I'm saying, Holmes?" smiled Morales. The others laughed, at the mockery the boss was lavishing on the terrified "newbie." Lance was ready to throw up, he was so scared. Chino fed off the fear coming from his victim and held him a little tighter.

"Holmes, you scared man? You shaking like a little Chihuahua, Hessé."

The gang all broke into laughter at their leader's exploitation of power and joviality. But Lance was numb with paranoia, as it washed over him from head to toe. He closed his eyes, praying for help, when he heard a bold, loud voice come into the circle. He then felt another hand grab his right arm, it felt like ,a vice grip.

"There you are man! We've been looking all over for you, Brother," said Derek Jackson. Lance opened his eyes, and his prayers were answered, as the Jackson brothers and Ibanez rescued him from his assailants.

"Thanks, Chino! We've been trying to find this ding-dong all morning. He's helping us put the Christian choir together," said the confident Jackson, who knew he was on the verge of having a contract put out on him for interrupting the initiation process.

"Hey Jackson, you got some cohonnes, coming in here and not minding your own business, Holmes," Chino said angrily, not letting go of Lance's left arm. The turf war was on, as the Sorrenos circled the rescue team. Kyle looked around at them and smiled saying, "Good morning," although gulping nervously. Ibanez clenched his fists around his towel draped neck and stared at one of the Hispanic soldiers.

Chino then saw the wall guard, Dead Eye Dick, take aim at him with his rifle. He knew he would shoot him because of his stature in the general population, and Dick wasn't on the take.

The gang leader released Lance's arm, gave a big grin and said, "Hey, Holmes, you a singer? You might have to come and sing for us someday," he laughed mockingly. "Hey, Jackson, you lucky you got some angels with guns up there watching down on you Puttas, or you would all, be bled out on the ground by now," threatened Chino, looking up at the guards gathering on the wall. They knew something was going down. Chino winked at his men and washed his hands, which was a sign meaning, "not now."

"C'mon, Chino, the guy's a Christian. Leave him be," Derek pleaded. Chino looked back at them and aimed his finger at them, pretending he was shooting, and sauntered away into the busy weight pile.

"Thanks, you guys! That was a close one," said Lance introducing himself.

"Any time! Do you realize how close you were to death, right there?" admonished Ibanez.

"Yeah, dude! You could have got us all killed right there! This thing ain't over yet," warned Kyle.

"Why? What are you talking about?" asked the new kid.

"What we are saying is that you need to learn more about the yard and what's happening around you, man.

You don't just wander into the weight pile, like you do some gym on the outside, for crying out loud. That is strictly a no-no, and you are very lucky, or blessed that we were here to save you," informed, the muscular Christian.

"Hey look, man, I didn't know, OK?" Lance said, defensively.

"And for your information, I'm an atheist. I don't believe in that, JESUS, mumbo jumbo, Son of GOD stuff, and I definitely, didn't join your little choir, either!" he shouted at the threesome who were walking back to the chow hall.

"I'm not joining any gang, do you hear me?" he shouted to them, wiping the dirt off his pants and following behind them.

"You are too late, for that!" chimed Kyle, as the three of them laughed.

"What do you mean?" Lance asked.

"What we mean, Brother, is you were just indoctrinated, as a Christian, and if you don't like it, you can go back and see Chino. He'd love to have you be his bitch," said Raul.

Lance stopped and looked back, thinking of the harsh reality of prison life and that he dreaded being some thug's girlfriend, as he saw Chino blow him a kiss and the gang members, burst into laughter again. Samansky grabbed his crotch and shook it at him, scaring him further.

"Hey, you guys! Brothers! Wait for me," shouted the convert, loudly.

Chapter 7

"Chow"

The 10 o'clock Saturday morning count was finished 20 minutes ago, when the order was given to let the men out of their cages for breakfast.

"A-Block, chow!" shouted a raspy voice on the loudspeaker. The annoying buzzer sounded, and a loud clank of the door locks opened and rolled to the left slowly, letting the hungry masses out. Men would squeeze out of the heavy bars before they opened just to get in line as fast as possible. Saturday chow call was the most anticipated meal of the week. If operations ran relatively smooth during the chaotic week, the men were treated with a little better than average quality of food. The men behaved themselves marching in single file down their respective walkways. Each block had two wings divided into three-story tiers. As the buzzers bellowed, you could hear the inmates' shoes shuffle a steady rhythm as they paraded into the massive mess hall.

Once again, the armed guards walked on the security tier above them, all monitoring their every move.

The chow hall was more than a football field in length and likewise in width. Red brick and mortar towered with an outline of iron braces supporting the monstrous octagonal roof. The staff called it the "rusty web" as it appeared that some freakish arachnid had spun a web of iron across the ceiling. Eighty ceiling fans spun vigorously, trying to keep the humidity down that emanated from the kitchen's ten, hundred-gallon, gas-fed vats that roared in the rear of the cafeteria. The widows were caked with a combination of ancient dust and moisture that formed a mossy sun shield across the twenty enormous, twenty by forty-foot barred windows facing the west side of the cafeteria. The clamor was near deafening as the men hollered obscenities at one another and were served their morning meal of biscuits and gravy, four strips of bacon, scrambled green eggs and a wormy, apple.

The executive committee formed a line just behind the counter, as the inmates entered the great hall. It was comprised of Chief Warden, Walter P. Stevens, and his administrative secretary and concubine, Shirley Hunt; Administrative Warden, Pete Dodd; Chief Warden of Operations, Theodore (Ted) Brewer; Captain of the Guard, Ron Tatum, and Chief of Psychology, Dr. Henry Arnold. It was a show of authority, as well as the bureau's feeble attempt at public relations for the inmates, like it or not.

They talked among themselves, never exchanging eye contact with the inmates. They were arrogant and haughty in their demeanor, looking down on the general population as basically their product.

Not much respect was given other than a nod if, someone said "hello," which was usually followed by a smirk or a wisecrack from one of the other staffers. They stood just far enough away from the counter so as not to be overheard by the line of humanity passing before their eyes.

Captain Ron was the only one, to "jawbone" boisterously, and he would occasionally challenge an inmate to a stare-down. The inmates would usually yield, knowing that if they wanted to survive their sentence, they had better not cross the murderous officer. Torture was not uncommon to the hard-core gang's shot-callers. Most of them earned respect from surviving the masochistic treatment of the Captain and were admired by their peers for enduring countless months in the hole. Besides, most of the executive staff had their own little games of extortion and evil that were perpetrated among the inmates.

The evil was so prevalent that it fed off the fears harbored by everyone in the complex. It was as if you could feel the spirit of darkness hover over the institution as would smog on a warm day.

The staff pretended to entertain each other, knowing full well that most of them should be walking in the line with the rest of the incarcerated souls before them.

"How much food do we go through in a day?" asked Ms. Hunt.

"Oh, I'd say about a ton a day. Isn't that right, Pete?" asked the Warden.

"Well, that's pretty close, Sir, but more like a ton and a half," said Dodd.

The Warden knew exactly, how much food went through the complex, or in and out of the gates. He knew the take on sales from the thieving correctional officers, who raided the inmates' best food that was received off the freight trucks and stored in the warehouses located on the complex. It was the biggest black market in town, and everyone knew it.

The good U.S. citizens, who paid their taxes had the funds appropriated through the Department of Justice in their annual budget to Congress. The tax dollars purchased mass quantities of food and would be accounted for by Receiving in the Department of Corrections and then distributed to the seven hundred institutions in America. Once received by those institutions, the fox was in the henhouse, as the crooked Food Service Managers would distribute the groceries out to the Correctional Officers who would pay twenty-five cents on the dollar and sell the groceries to their families and friends for fifty cents on the dollar. The bevy was enormous as millions of dollars were pirated out of the taxpayer's pocket and created a "free enterprise" zone within the Bureau of Prisons.

This was highway robbery right under the accounting nose in Washington, D.C., and made many politicians, executive administrators, and institutional personnel rich beyond expectation. The paperwork was lost in the sea of bureaucratic expense, which no one accounted for except the malnourished inmates who received less than adequate nutrition while incarcerated.

The crooked administrators would purchase other wholesale trucks of expired foods from the national supermarkets or animal suppliers in the world and ship it into the empty warehouses that were looted.

A lot of old military surplus that was warehoused was emptied, and they performed the same food scam on U.S military bases around the world. The intergovernmental black-market operation was just the tip of corruption that was known in the offices of administration, but no one would admit to the thievery that was happening. If someone filed a report, it would disappear somewhere into the "big government."

The food hustle didn't stop there, either. The inmates had a game going on inside the institution, too. The culprit behind the scenes was none other than the main supervisor himself, Owen Haslip. The overweight, unkempt "cretin of the kitchen" sold more food illegally than was ever accounted for. Of course, the executive administration knew full well what he was doing—selling high-protein foods and fruits to the inmates who could afford them.

The kitchen help would cook chicken, barbequed ribs, and steaks. But the number-one commodity was hard-boiled eggs. Once cooked, the orders were delivered to the cells in exchange for the only currency at hand, which was U.S Postage Stamps. Books of stamps were the underground currency used to pay for the "black market goods." The inside hustle produced more than $1,000 per day and on weekends nearly twice that amount.

The "Fat Man" was Haslip's nickname because, he personified a dumpster, with shoes. His white shirts were never washed clean, and he was a three-time loser, when it came to marriage. He was the admin's perfect patsy to run the food service end of things, and he was cunning enough to handle any extortion problems without a hitch. He was responsible for more beat-downs than Captain Ron. If, an inmate cheated the food hack, it was a known principle that there would be bloodshed.

"Well, how's everyone doing this fine Saturday morning?" jeered the Fat Man, as he marched down the counter to greet the executive line.

He wiped his hands off on a filthy towel wrapped around his waist and offered a handshake to Warden Stevens, who snidely was repulsed by the thought of even touching Haslip and put his hands in his pant pockets.

"Hello, Mr. Haslip. How are you today?" replied the warden's bubbly concubine.

"Oh, I've been better. The stench in the back kitchen is awful. I think the rains are backing up the sewers. Is anyone looking at that, Pete?"

"Well, of course, Owen. I'll have someone check it out right after chow. Captain Ron has a team to inspect the sewers and the main cistern of the well. Those bloody frogs are coming up all over the place, and we have to investigate where they are coming from and poison the little buggers."

"Well, they created one hell of a mess last night in B-Block," said Warden Stevens.

"They nearly started a riot, for God's sake. The inmates threw them off the upper terraces at the nightshift guards. There were hundreds of those slimy buggers dead all over the institution this morning. We had to bring in a tractor and shovel them in a front-end loader and drive out the east gate to bury them. The inmates complained about the horrid stench coming from their rotting soft tissues," reported Dr. Henry.

"Yuck! That is so gross. Have we ever had an outbreak like this before?" asked Ms. Hunt.

"Nope, never since I've worked at this dung heap for over twenty-seven years," said Dodd.

"Too bad we can't cook' em up for the inmates. They would probably enjoy some fine fresh, food," joked Haslip, his belly jiggling with laughter.

The Warden smiled at the thought, but he knew that if, it ever got outside to the Bureau, he would be the laughingstock of the Region. He checked his gold watch and said, "Today is payday, isn't it, Mr. Haslip?" giving him a wry smile. The other's eyes grew wide with greed.

"Ah yes, Warden, it is. Why else, would you be here on a Saturday morning? Isn't this your day at the country club?" sneered the Fat Man.

"I suggest you watch your mouth, Owen, if you know what's good for you. It's none of your business, what I do on my days off, let alone question my presence at this institution. You can give Ms. Hunt my envelope, and she'll bring it, to me. Now if you all don't mind, I have to square away the paperwork on yesterday's little disturbance, get the transfer orders to region, and move the little problem we got locked up downstairs," said Warden Elliott, giving Captain Ron a stern look as he passed him by and said, "I'm going home in an hour, and I don't want any disturbance, for the rest of the weekend. Do you understand, Captain? Deputy Dodd is on call this weekend, so if we have any problems, you may buzz him," he nodded at Dodd.

"No worries, Sir," saluted Captain Tatum. "Things should be back to normal again."

As soon as, he said that, a big toad lunged out from the counter, landing on the serving bar, scaring Ms. Hunt, who responded with a blood-curdling scream: "EEEEECCCKKK"

The Warden leaped in the air, startled, as a dead silence fell upon the entire chow hall. No one stirred, as the terrified secretary scampered into Haslip's office, as if, she were being chased by the amphibious monster. It seemed to be stalking her, leaping after her, and landing on her thick right calf. She shrieked again, crying as Captain Tatum swatted at her hopping assailant. The Warden shook his head and pointed his finger at Ted Brewer, Chief of Operations.

"Ted, those slimy things better be gone, when I get back Monday morning, or it's your ass I'll be kicking out the door—not some frog's. Do I make myself clear?" he said angrily.

"Yes, Warden, I have my best man looking into it right now—as we speak," he informed him nervously.

Warden Elliott angrily, stormed away from the roaring, laughter of two thousand inmates, who were in hysterics as they watched the Captain try to apprehend the toad. It hopped and dodged the baton of the wicked Captain, like the artful dodger it was, as it ducked underneath the salad bar. The inmates made catcalls at the Captain, who was now on his knees, infuriated at the green escapee. Soon another guard joined him and they had it surrounded.

Haslip rolled the salad cart away, as the frog sat there and gave them a frightened look, "RRRIIDDUUUPP!", it croaked. The two officers swung their batons, at the same time, and the frog leaped vertically into the air, as Captain Tatum's baton hit the other officer in the head, nearly knocking him out, he rolled in pain on the floor.

"You dumb ass," growled the embarrassed, Captain, who lunged up and caught the frog in midair with his left hand. The inmates were in tears laughing as the guard continued to roll in pain, rubbing his head. Captain Ron rose to his feet, his face beet-red with anger and hatred. He snarled like a beast— holding the frog in one hand and his baton in the other—and daring anyone to make another wisecrack. Again, it was silent in the mess hall. Warden Dodd pushed a garbage can over to the Captain, who shook with anger. His hatred toward the inmates emulated in his fierce stare-downs, over the incarcerated men.

"You think this is funny? I'll show you what's funny!" He then lifted the helpless frog higher and squeezed it until its eyes popped out, and its blood ran over the Captain's knuckles. He made an example out of the frog to the inmates, communicating his evil desire, of what he'd do to the next inmate who made a mockery of him. The staff all walked away disgusted with his violence, all except Haslip, who enjoyed all the mayhem.

The inmates went back to eating their meals and just shook their heads in disgust. They knew it could be them and not some frog that the murderous Captain would annihilate.

"Come on, Ron, let's go get you some money and have a drink in my office," said Haslip nervously, handing the maniac a towel to wipe off his hand.

"Damn those things stink, don't they?" asked Haslip.

Captain Tatum wiped off the entrails and dropped the frog and the towel in the garbage can.

"Yeah, they do, and so do those damn frogs," replied the Captain, referring to the inmates, then chuckled, entering the Fatman's office and closed the door.

Chapter 8

"Mutumbo Watini"

D r. Henry Arnold, PhD., Chief Psychologist for Heavenworth Federal Penitentiary graduated Magna Cum Laud from the University of Kansas, in Lawrence, Kansas, only hours from Heavenworth. He was 47 years old, married for twelve years to Dr. Mary Ellen Arnold, M.D., a local gynecologist in Kansas City, Missouri. He had a budding young family comprised of a son, Josh, aged 16, and a beautiful and talented daughter, Erin, aged 13. They had it all going for them, materially speaking: A new home, two new cars, all were in good health, money in the bank, and both were very active with their young children's education and extracurricular activities. Keeping their busy schedules was insanity, at best. Henry constantly fretted over the family calendar and spent hours each evening scheduling everyone's agenda for the next day, week, and month. He even scheduled their vacations each year in advance, booking their flights and hotels well in advance, and he obtained any discounts that he could. The good doctors discussed their travel plans as they planned their kid's future for going to med school.

Chief Warden Walter P. Stevens had 40 years of exemplary service to his country, proudly protecting America from its harbored enemies. He was dressed for success, wearing expensive suits and handmade leather shoes. Stevens was a handsome, fit 60-year-old and was happily married with a family of three. He had two sons, Jacob, aged 28, and Lowell, aged 25, and a daughter, Margaret, who was 19. They all attended his alma mater at the University of Kansas, and he lived on the nearby military base at Fort Heavenworth Military Academy.

He was a retired Lieutenant Colonel in the U.S. Army, and he served three tours in the Middle East. Stevens was three years from retirement from the U.S. Department of Corrections and proud to be a director on many Government committees. He couldn't wait for his retirement, and he regularly daydreamed of fishing and traveling about. He was late for a fundraiser at the base and was perturbed over the incident that had taken place. He wanted to retire with the decommissioning of the prison as its last Director Emeritus and lock the doors behind him when he leaves and the new super complex opens, which was his pride and joy.

Dr. Arnold was well liked, by the inmates and staff at the institution, but he was secretly planning on opening a private practice next year in Kansas City so that the family could be closer together. As it was, he had to drive a hundred and twenty miles daily to report to his easy government job. He knew everybody's problems and exactly what prescriptions they were on. His mind was well organized, and his recall was impressive. He was a guest lecturer at many high-level meetings with the Department of Justice, speaking about the "criminal intellect and its effect on society." He was writing his fifth breakthrough paper that was being published by the <u>Ph.D. Today Magazine</u>.

Yes, you might say he had it all, brains, money, and Freud. However, he was mystified by the subject, Mutumbo Watini, whom he was monitoring through the two-way mirror in Level #3.

He scribbled notes furiously as he sat on the edge of a wooden table with his feet perched on the seat of the chair and studied the celled creature who was just yards from him. The motley, dread-locked wild man was nearly primordial in his jaw and skull structure, which utterly fascinated the young Dr. Arnold as he pushed his designer glasses up to his nose bridge with his mouth open in awe. He marveled at the thought that this throwback of evolution could be his ticket to "Paradise" among the elite of psychiatry.

The masked man paraded the cell confines, like a fly trapped in a jar. He crawled on the floor around the perimeter and then studied the corners, seeking a way out of the concrete bunker that housed him. Over and over, he would "study," crawl forward, and then, much to the Doctor's amazement, he'd crawl backward like an insect.

The actions excited the Doctor so much that he didn't even hear Sergeant Rodgers enter the darkened room. The SHU Commander touched the Doctor, who leapt off the table and into the window with a bang, dropping his clipboard and notes.

> "Yaaaaaaaahhhh! What the hell are you doing sneaking up on me like that, Sergeant?"
>
> "I'm sorry, Doctor. I knocked on the door, but you didn't answer it," he apologized.
>
> "You damn near made me wet my pants," he bemoaned further.
>
> "I brought Watini's file in, Sir. You said you wanted it immediately. We had to locate it and finally found it on Captain Tatum's desk. Apparently, this guy is generating a lot of attention."

Then the big Sergeant froze, watching the inmate stare into the mirror, like he understood, what they were talking about.

Dr. Arnold picked up his scattered notes off the floor and moved toward the glass.

He raised his hand, touching Watini's hand in the same place he was. Watini jerked his head at the connection and stared intently through the glass.

"I wouldn't do that if I were you, Doctor. That thing in there is not human."

Dr. Arnold said nothing as he slowly moved his hand down the glass partition, and Watini's hand followed it perfectly—as if they were connected. The doctor gave a stymied laugh at the exactness of movement between them.

"Well, will you look at that? How does he know you are moving your hand?" asked Rodgers inquisitively.

"I have no idea," said the perplexed psychiatrist, giggling at the continued movement on the glass. "He can't see through the glass, can he?"

"There's no way he can. That's a four-inch-thick safety glass two-way mirror. He can't see or hear anything we say in this room. So, how's he doing that trick?"

The doctor pulled his hand away. Watini then punched the window in anger and went ballistic. The Sergeant walked up to the window and laughed, "Look at that freak! He's insane, I tell you. We went in last night and stunned him with 20,000 watts. He dropped like a brick and made like bacon sizzling in a frying pan, jiggling on the ground. We taught him a lesson, by God, and he'd better straighten up after pulling that stunt on our boys on the bus," smiled the jailer.

"What happened on the bus?" asked Dr. Arnold.

Sergeant Rodgers told him the entire story while Dr. Arnold read the inmate's classified documents in his file. His eyes grew wide in further disbelief as the jailer bragged about their heroics. He wasn't even listening to Rodgers as he went to the glass again, rubbing his shaven face and observing the unique "witchdoctor" from New Orleans—via the Virgin Islands.

"Sergeant, I'm going in to interview him, and I want that mask removed before I do," ordered Dr. Arnold.

"But, Doctor, that freak is a biter! It's in his profile along with all the other weird shit he's done. He's got some kind of voodoo powers of sorts. I don't trust him, nor do I think you should go in there alone," warned Sergeant Rodgers.

"I'm not going in alone! You are going to accompany me with another guard," he said.

"Well, OK, if you say so, but I don't feel good about this, Doc. The guy's a real spook," he worried.

"Look, he is a 'paranoid-schizophrenic,' I agree with you, but he did just exhibit a strange talent that needs to be investigated, and I'm going to want a camera filming the interview. Whatever he is, he has something unique to provide to the field of science. Let's begin in one hour. I'll get a sedative for him if that makes you feel better," he smiled assuredly.

They both watched the inmate lay down on the concrete bed and clasp his hands in a relaxed position over his waist, as if he knew something was happening.

"That's the first time, I've seen him relax since he got here," said Sergeant Rodgers.

"You see, there's nothing to worry about," said Dr. Arnold confidently.

Chapter 9

"Warden Stevens"

The fluorescent lights flickered in the warden's office as he rose slowly from behind his desk, fastening his belt buckle after, having sex with Ms. Hunt. She laid on the posh green carpet half naked, wearing only her thigh stockings and high heels. She lit up a cigarette, like some cheap hooker in downtown Kansas City. Of course, that was where they first met one rainy night when the Warden was on a drinking binge. The low-class hooker discovered whom, he was and had taken a video in her apartment bedroom and blackmailed him for the current position, as the Warden's secretary, even though she could only type twenty words per minute and could not spell, worth a hoot.

"Get dressed, will you before someone sees you lying there, for Pete's sake." He sat down at his desk, opened the drawer, and removed a bottle of Scotch.

He poured a stiff one, into his precious Department of Justice coffee mug. He grunted, watching Ms. Hunt slip her short skirt on and helped her to fasten her Victoria's Secret bra. She was a full-figured woman, with large round breasts. She just turned thirty six years old last week, and so, the Warden took her to Atlanta, Georgia, as a birthday present. He lied to his wife, telling her that he was attending another boring Bureau of Prisons' Conference.

He knew that she was sick and tired of attending them, after being married all these years, and she hated the bureaucratic phonies and their wives. He hardly attended any of the meetings anyway. Instead, he golfed at the best courses in the area and, usually, he had an expensive suite in a lavish hotel, all, of course, paid in full by Uncle Sam. He was very discreet with his secretary, ordering room service only while they were at the hotel and taking separate cabs to dinners when out on the town where they were cheating. He was near retirement, and he planned to divorce his wife and dump Ms. Hunt at the same time within the next two years. He opened the envelope lying on his desk that Ms. Hunt retrieved from Food Service.

He counted the money that was in hundred-dollar denominations, and it totaled, thirty seven hundred doolars. He smiled, as he sipped his whiskey and handed three hundred dollars to Ms. Hunt, who was standing next to him and brushing, her auburn hair.

"Gee, thanks, Walt. I'll buy another nice secret outfit for you," she said tucking the money into her tight-laced bra. She took another long drag off her cigarette and blew it into the air. She grabbed his mug and almost finished his drink, like a sailor at a bar.

"Here, you better brush your hair. It's a mess," she said, handing him her brush. He walked to his private bathroom, washed his face, and brushed his hair back to perfection. He checked his bleached teeth for stains, running his tongue across them. He gave himself a wry smile, feeling superior in his conquest of being a womanizing gentleman. He saw Ms. Hunt count the money he had put back in the envelope and quickly walked back to his desk.

"Does that envelope interest you, my dear?" he asked snidely and backhanded her across her face, before she had a chance to answer. He knocked her to the floor and grabbed a handful of her thick mane. He jerked her head back and said,

"You need to mind your own business and not be so nosy. I'd hate to mess up that pretty face of yours, if you know what I mean?" he snarled viciously.

Ms. Hunt shook with fear, never witnessing this side of her lover before, but it was bound to happen sooner, or later. He was a coward and a wife-beater for years, ever since his life was threatened, as a deputy Warden in Mississippi, twenty years ago.

Dr. Henry Arnold, tried to help him with his issues of insecurity, but the Warden never grew comfortable, with trusting anybody again after that night of terror. He was held hostage by three gangbangers, who were trying to escape prison. The three desperate criminals tortured him, for more than thirty hours. They beat the tar out of him and killed two guards, before authorities detained the convicts and killed all three in a hail of gunfire. Warden Stevens, was wounded by a stray bullet in the stomach and had a nasty scar, where they had removed it from him that night. He almost bled to death.

However, he miraculously held on and lived through the ordeal, which changed him for life. He was surprised at how hard he had hit Ms. Hunt and the shock of rage that left him feeling empty inside. He warned her again and told her to get out of his office. He told her that he was leaving because he had a golf match in Independence later that afternoon. Ms. Hunt grabbed her purse, straightened her skirt out, and stormed out of the office. She could not believe what had just transpired. How could anyone be so ruthless after making love to a person she wondered. She slammed his office door, and the plate glass window exploded into a thousand pieces. She left the main office, went down the administration corridor, and out of the main doors.

He watched her from his office window, while sipping another glass of Scotch. She bolted across the parking lot, as the tower guards whistled at her, like they usually did, when she left the building. She flipped them off and went over to the Warden's car and kicked the passenger door panel, putting a dent in it with her spiked heel. As, she walked away, her heel broke, and she fell down on the asphalt, tearing her expensive hosiery. The guard called her "Grace" as she again flipped them off, threw her shoe into her BMW roadster, and "smoked the tires" out of the lot.

"She's really going to get it the next time I see her," he growled, gripping the glass tighter. He entertained the thought of murdering her right after his golf match, killing her with a nine iron—no, maybe a sand-wedge instead." He got on his intercom and buzzed the captain's office, "Yes, Warden, what can we do for you?" a voice asked.

"Have Maintenance repair my office window. The damn thing broke all over the place."

"Yes, Sir, I'll do that right after Jakes gets done in the storm drains," informed the young lieutenant.

"Why is he down there?" asked the warden, finishing his Scotch.

"Captain Ron said that you wanted to poison those frogs before they ruined the plumbing."

"Oh, yes, I did say that. Well, carry on but do have it cleaned up before I get back tomorrow morning. I have meetings all morning and don't want this glass lying around on the floor," he said sternly.

"Yes Sir. What exactly happened, Sir?" asked the lieutenant.

"Oh, I er, ahh, chipped a golf ball through it while practicing my swing. I didn't mean to hit it that hard, but it nonetheless, broke. Don't put that on the incident report though. Just put that housecleaning broke it with a vacuum cleaner or something like that," he lied. There was a long pause.

"No problem, Warden. I'll take care of it for you."

"Thank you, Son. What is your name?"

"Reynolds, Sir. Second Lieutenant John Reynolds."

"Very good. As you were!" slurred the Warden. He clipped a fresh cigar from his desktop humidor and took a deep inhale, dragging the stogie across his upper lip. He thought, "life is good," as he stuffed the envelope of cash in his inside jacket pocket and proceeded out the front door, saluting the guards in the tower in the front parking lot. He marched, like a proud man and inspected the damage to his Land Rover. He looked sheepishly back up at the guards who had it all on video tape. He shook his head and then lit up the thick cigar outside his door. He looked up at the dark clouds rolling in, wondering if it was ever going to quit raining.

He started the engine and noticed the black tire tracks leaving the administration parking area. He acted, like it was no big deal. He turned on his windshield wipers and drove down the hill, premeditating Ms. Hunt's demise, but first a short stop at his favorite strip club. He looked up at the rain clouds thinking, "Maybe, it will quit raining."

Chapter 10

"The Fallen Angels"

Raul Ibanez played the upright piano, and Kyle Jackson strummed his six-string guitar, while his brother, Derek, rehearsed the songs with the music director, David Kairabedian. The twelve-man choir, were affectionately known, as "The Fallen Angels," who were all, born-again Christians. The Chapel was a blessed sanctuary, from all the chaos that went on outside of its doors. It was always busy with inmates thumbing through the religious books in the library and seeking some kind of solitude inside the walls of the "red monster" that held them captive.

The congregation was a tattooed parlor, of the not-so-rich and infamous. Most of the inmates were adult children locked inside their huge muscular physiques, wondering what happened to them and how did they end up in a place like this. Their newfound belief was no hoax, as they were looking for a reality that was elusive to them while living on the "outside." Here was the one place where they didn't feel like a square peg trying to fit into a round hole.

Here they could release their fears and explore something they never experienced before, which was an unselfish love of a GOD, whom they had never met, until now.

David led the choir, moving his hand in cadence with the rhythm of the guitar. The men sang quite well, except for a couple of them. That didn't matter, to Kairabedian, who wanted everyone, to have the chance to express their love to GOD. Bubba was off-key, as usual, upsetting the others, but who was going to argue, with the strongest man in Heavenworth? Derek, liked Bubba a lot and was proud of the fact that he tried, so hard at everything that he did, even if music was not his forte. Bubba towered over most and was a leader to most of the men, who were threatened by the other gang members, who criticized their community.

"JESUS, oh JESUS, how I love you so . . . oooh . . . ooh. Come into my heart," they chortled.

"OK! That was good but, Brother Mongo, you got to pick it up a little more," admonished the Music Director.

"You have got to learn to form your words, by using your lips better, and sound out the high notes," David pleaded, pursing his lips into a pucker.

Mongo's eyes grew wide, watching him and tried to mimic the director's gestures.

"Man! That's just too gay for me," whined, the convicted bank robber.

The men broke out laughing, as they heard the big man's comments. It embarrassed Mongo, aka Lamar Archibald Robiuellet, inmate #43522-021, the most notorious armed bank robber in U.S. history, next to his dead hero, John Dillinger. He was a three-time loser, serving twenty years for robbing, twenty-six banks and stealing more than three million dollars. His crime spree went unchecked for five years in the southern states of Georgia, Alabama, Mississippi, Florida, North and South Carolina, and his home state of Louisiana. Next to Bubba, he was the toughest inmate there. Mongo, was an ex-Marine and mixed martial arts fighter, who could beat the snot out of just about anybody he wanted to.

His claim to fame was the absolute punishment of five correctional officers, who tried to take a picture of his mother away from him one day, as punishment for hospitalizing three fellow inmates, one of whom, was Monk Samansky. He was serving his twelfth year, in his fourth different prison and had become a Christian a year ago. Derek met him, while on a shared work detail stripping and waxing floors in the main auditorium. Derek really knew what he was doing, and the floors looked like new, when they were finished. The staff was so impressed during a regional inspection of the facility that they gave them and Kyle Jackson special privileges in the institution. Derek witnessed to the powerful man as he accepted Jesus Christ as his Lord and Savior while playing ping pong one evening. They became best friends, and Mongo had changed so much, that no one could believe he was the same man.

The tattooed giant, was six feet four inches and weighed in at two hundred ninety pounds. After the whup-ass, he did on Samansky and the guards, everyone called him "the Ragin Cajun," but he preferred Mongo, instead.

"You look like you're trying to give Bubba a kiss or sumthin'," cracked LT jokingly, getting a few more laughs, until Bubba's big hand grabbed his neck. Mongo turned red, made a fist at LT, and threatened him to shut up, but Derek gave him a look that was not the acceptable behavior, of a loving Christian. Mongo yielded to a calmer demeanor and apologized to LT. Bubba let go of his neck, giving him a shove.

"OK! Let's do another song here," said David, when the Chapel door opened and their recent acquisition, Lance Smith, walked in.

"Good morning," he nodded nervously to the unshaven choir.

"Men, this is Lance Smith. He became a member of our little society this morning after speaking with Chino and Monk, earlier," smiled Derek. Once again, the choir burst into laughter, embarrassing Lance. He opened a book and flipped its pages, trying to ignore the rude barbs from his new gang.

"Can you sing?" asked LT.

"Who me? Ah yeah, a little bit, but I play the drums better," said the financier.

He pointed to the dusty drum set stacked in the corner behind the piano by Ibanez.

"Well, praise the Lord! Do you see, gentleman, how GOD works? Our drummer was transferred two weeks ago, to another FCI, and it just so, happens that we need a drummer," smiled Derek.

"Yeah, but can he play the drums? If you know what I'm saying," winked Ibanez.

"Yeah, man, we don't need any pretenders," Kyle said sternly.

"Oh, I'm not pretending at all! Let me show you," said Lance, lifting out the dusty snare drum and set it up in front of the choir. They all sat down on the metal steps and watched the fledgling fumble with the drum set and set up the top hat cymbals.

"Is there a stool, to sit on?" he asked. Raul was using it, instead of the wood bench and reluctantly gave it to him. Derek winked at Raul and sat on the wood bench with him, curious to hear Smith play. He could tell Lance definitely, had a stage presence and was in control of the captive audience. Many of the men joked about how cute he looked, kiddingly of course, trying to intimidate the young musician.

"OK, anyone have a request?" Lance asked, looking into the dumbfounded audience. "Well, let me see," he said, adjusting the seat cushion.

He rattled the set, banging the foot peddle into the bass drum, and tightened the snare adjustment, like a professional. Kyle gave a big toothy grin at his brother, knowing they were in for a show. Derek winked an acknowledgment, back at Kyle, as Lance took off his grey sweatshirt, leaving his thin T-shirt on with its ID number emblazoned on it, reminding them all, of the same demeaning psychology, that they were just a number, in a big system. Lance pushed his long bangs back and clicked the drumsticks, above his head. He proceeded to pound the drum set fiercely, like he was going to break the sticks in half. The percussion thundered off the bass drums, as the snare reverberated its roll of taps. The new kid played, like he was playing in a concert. Lance had learned how to play from his older brother, who played professionally with a real rock and roll band, named "Shockwave." He also, played in his high school band and did some independent gigs while, attending college to earn a few extra bucks and especially to meet the girls. His brother told him that it was the best part of playing, meeting the babes.

"First you pound the drums and then you pound the babes," was his brother's favorite mantra. Lance followed closely, in his brother's shoe steps, but he found that playing professionall, as a real "rock star" took its early toll on your health. His brother had died from alcohol poisoning after a concert in Miami, Florida, at the age of thirty two.

Lance loved his brother, so much that when he played the drums, he was tremendously emotional, because his brother was his best friend, and he never accepted his death, when their father notified him in person, while attending college. He banged the drums and rang the cymbals, like a man possessed to the adoration and whistles, coming from the choir. He made them forget the old drummer fast, because they could recognize good talent. Raul's and Derek's eyes were wide in disbelief, as were most of the men of drumming when they heard it. The little Chapel had a seating capacity of two hundred, but well exceeded it, becoming packed to the walls while Lance Smith performed "live" for the inmates. Pretty soon Raul kicked in playing an old Bob Seger tune, "Rambling Gambling Man." Raul stood up on the piano, as Lance synced perfectly with both of them, singing vocals. The crowd clapped their hands, loving every minute of the drum exposé performed, especially for them. When the song ended, Lance flipped the drumsticks over his head, exciting the men further, who whistled their approval. He stood up after the ten-minute demonstration and took a bow. Derek stood up and clapped, walked over to their new member, and gave him a welcoming, bear-hug.

"I don't know! What do you guys think? Is he in, or what?" asked Derek. They all broke out in laughter, as they cheered their approval of a real talented musician. Bubba slapped Lance on the back, almost knocking him off his stool.

Lance looked up at him and said, "Take it easy, Big Fella," rubbing his left shoulder realizing, just how powerful Bubba, actually was. Bubba and Mongo laughed, all the louder, jubilant at their new friend. Then Lance realized something profound. It was the first time that he really heard laughter and had seen sincere fellowship, for more than two long years. His heart pounded with the warmth and safety, he felt inside the Chapel. The men showed their appreciation as Lance, realized what he had taken for granted by his new fans. They walked out of the Chapel feeling jubilant, when Derek excused them, so they could get some fresh air and yard time in, before the afternoon count.

"Man, you have a real gift from GOD, Lance. Where did you learn how to play the drums, like that?" Derek asked.
Lance wiped his face off with his sweatshirt and told Derek about his brother. They sat down, and Derek soon realized, Lance's loss. Derek was a good listener and understood a lot more about Lance. Derek knew that GOD, brought Lance to Heavenworth, for this exact time.

Derek explained, how important it was for men like Lance, to acknowledge his fellow inmates and pay the respect given they all had to earn. Derek was well-educated and explained the dynamics behind the harsh ways of living life, behind bars. Most all of those, who were drug addicts or alcoholics, at an early age having dropped out of school. The National Crime Lab statistics revealed that over sixty eight percent of the males and females, who are incarcerated had never graduated from high school.

The general population was 42 percent African American, 37 percent Hispanic, 16 percent Caucasian, and the rest were a composition of Asian or Native American descent.

Another revealing statistic, was that over thirty one percent, never knew who, their father or mother was. The prisons were, in fact, massive "orphanages" operated, by State or Federal governments. The Bureau of National Crime and Statistics, also illustrated how poverty levels of family income that were supported by welfare programs contributed to a whopping, 68 percent of all convicted felons and 82 percent of all misdemeanors, that were committed in the United States of America. Furthermore, the "recidivism rate" of returned criminals is over sixty seven percent.

"That's incredible," Lance remarked, astounded at Derek's information.

The problem has escalated, to a bureaucratic nightmare, as politicians promise more programs of the same caliber, which only exacerbates the problem further. There are ways to deter crime, and it starts with the family. It is not a guarantee, but it's what the communities must focus on doing and try to establish better parenting skills to help our younger children, who are cannibalized by older children, and who then are cannibalized, by adults. The food chain of humanity must establish, a better parental system in order to stop itself from imploding, into a society of total moral decay.

The evident reality of it all was that the "man-child" needed attention and love but never got it on the home front, or on the streets.

Who else, but God could fill a need so great? Who else would caudle the losers in society and help them to regain their lost identity through Jesus Christ, the Son of God? It was Jesus, who was recorded throughout history.

HE healed the sick, fed the poor, gave sight to the blind, delivered people from their demons and gave hope for a better way of life by establishing a belief system that was backed by action and not just words. Jesus, the man from Galilee, established the only logical covenant to an insane world. He established it in only three years' time, and it has lasted for well over 2,000 years. Jesus Christ developed a "perfect epoch."

"Jesus is the solution to the problem. As a child, He shared Holy Scripture that was written by ancient prophets with the rich and poor, alike. He baffled the brilliant and convinced the high priests that He was the Messiah. His own people betrayed Him to a foreign government because they were threatened by His truthful righteousness. They witnessed a Son who loved His Father, who was God of them all, and the Jews became jealous that God would bestow the power of Heaven in a common man. It was selfish guilt fueled by greed, and the Jewish priests tried to eliminate this new regime of grace and mercy preached by Jesus Christ, the Messiah. So, they killed him by torturing Him and crucifying Him on a cross, fulfilling the prophecy in the Scriptures. Jesus died for our sins. Yours and mine, Lance," pointed out Derek. Lance's eyes were filled with tears, as he felt the compassion of Derek's strong witness of Jesus' story.

"Listen, Derek. You are a nice guy and all, but I came from a religious upbringing in a large church. They were well organized, and they were all a bunch of hypocrites, as far as I'm concerned. My mom and Dad were the worst, but they tried their best to shove all this Jesus stuff down our throats, and I couldn't wait until I was old enough to run away from it all. I think it had a lot to do with my brother's death, too," he stated.

"Well, I doubt that. You can't put your brother's overdose on JESUS. As, a matter of fact, it had nothing to do with HIM at all, but I'll tell you who was behind your brother's death. It was Satan! You know, Lucifer, the god of evil in this world," said Derek as he stood up, looking Lance in the eyes.

"That's nonsense. Satan, the boogeyman, and JESUS, are all a myth. Brother. Do you really believe all that stuff?" Lance asked.

"Oh, yeah! There's no doubt in my mind. Look, Lance, I dropped out of college for two reasons. One was to further my chances to play professional tennis, and the other was that I didn't care for the university's teaching of evoluation or Darwin's "theory of origins." If you want to believe, that you are nothing, but pond scum and a descendent of a tree-swinging monkey, then be my guest," Derek huffed.

Lance stood up, stretched his arms, and put his sweatshirt back on.

"Listen, Derek. I'm trying not to get emotional about this, OK? I learned the same things you did in college, but the creation and GOD, are a lot for me to swallow. I enjoy people who are friendly, and that's why I'm here with you now. So, don't push this on me right now. I'm still trying to deal with this whole prison mentality. I do believe there is such a thing as evil, but I don't necessarily agree, that it all comes from some devil guy that pissed off GOD one day and was banished to Earth. There's no proof or evidence that this stuff ever happened, and science is proving more each day that we are not alone in the universe."

"Well, Lance, you are entitled to your opinion, and if you ever want to talk about anything with me, then I want you to know it's alright," Derek said, as he handed him a Bible.

"What's this for?" asked Lance.

"I just want you to read the New Testament for me. It will give you something to read besides, all that other junk in the library, and it will give us something to talk about, when we see each other. In the meantime, I'm not going to say anything to the rest of the congregation about you being an atheist. That's all we need is a drum-playing atheist in the chapel playing Christian songs just because you want to play the drums. Besides, a Bible will protect you from Chino and the rest of the predators inside this place," Derek winked opening the door.

"Oh, man, you're right. What was I thinking—or not," said Lance as he held the Bible tightly.

"Lance, this is a big place, and you need to have some allies on your side, like Bubba and Mongo. Don't take that for granted. They established a "no-touch zone" for us Christian believers, so don't be running your mouth off that you don't believe in GOD. The last thing you want is for them to find out that you don't. They both were almost killed in an ambush, one day, three years ago, by eight different gang members in the laundry room. They were hurt really bad, but they nearly killed those other fools, who tried to mess with them. The Warden got rid of the gang members, by transferring them out, but he decided to keep Bubba and Mongo, here for the time being. Believe me, as you hear other men's testimonies about salvation and God, you might become, a believer yet," smiled Derek. "Come on. Let's go play some basketball in the yard. It's a nice fall day out there.

"What are you talking about? It's raining outside," Lance whined.

"What? You scared of a little rain drop or two?"

Chapter 11

"No one down here, but us frogs"

The Maintenance Officer, Gerald Jakes, fumbled with his large key ring as he held his flashlight tightly underneath his left armpit. The keys jangled against the rusted metal gate that led into the boiler room and eventually down the long, damp corridors to the main cistern located deep below the prison. It's a trek the maintenance man has made hundreds of times, taking inmate crews down to replace broken steam pipes that heated the ancient behemoth or to repair a tunnel from a cave-in after a heavy rain like the past two days.

"Frogs, indeed, the miserable little sons of bitches," grumbled Jakes, as he spits a wad of tobacco juice at a scampering field mouse along the brick ledge that was next to him. "You, too, you lil' bastard," he said as he tried to hit the scampering rodent with a sewer snake that he was carrying in his right hand. But he narrowly missed. "I hate this freaking place," he cursed, opening another metal door.

"God almighty, they put more doors in this place than a whorehouse in Topeka," he spit again. His teeth were stained yellow, and he was missing a top front tooth from running into a pipe valve one day. He was affectionately known, by his new nickname, "Fang," because of his missing tooth and nasty disposition. Jakes, like most of the guards, was an alcoholic and had worked in the prison, for more than thirty years. Most of them couldn't wait for their day, to finally retire from the "red beast" that held them captive, too, just like the inmates.

Although free, they reported for duty every day, making sure they clocked in and nursed their union paycheck each month, paying their union dues and then paying all of their bills at home. Most of the guards married their girlfriends' right out of high school and started a family, then bought a small house and got into debt, like every other blue-blooded American who chased that elusive dream. The biggest lie ever perpetrated on the American public was not a dream, but the reality of a nightmare that wouldn't go away.

The mortgage made to the local banks made everybody a slave, or bondservant, hating their lives and what it stood for as they went to work each day, trapped by the yoke of responsibility of raising a family and trying to have something for retirement in 30 years. The only dream was to have their mortgage paid off.

Jakes was one of those people who just wanted it to be over— sooner, rather than later. His wife never worked a day in her life, grew overweight, and had diabetes like so many others, literally ending their sex life. Besides, after having three children, feeding everyone, paying the mortgage, and having to pay his wife's medical bills, Jakes barely had enough money to go to the bar every night with the rest of the good old boys after work.

"Just who is in prison, here," he'd said to himself every other minute, day in and day out, for twenty years. It was no wonder his attitude was lousy. He hated life and he hated himself.

"I hate that smell," Jakes cursed again as the sewer stench rose from the mildewed brick labyrinth. "Christ, you'd think I'd be used to that smell by now. Damn this place to hell anyway."

He went through five different gates and traveled well over a thousand yards as he descended lower into the bowels of Heavenworth. Jakes didn't mind working by himself, he could drink alcohol, and no one would bother him. His favorite was the cheap vodka that he would sneak in his coffee thermos, each day. He stooped over and put down his tool bag and removed his thermos. He twisted the top and took a hearty chug from the dented metal canister and then twisted the top back on again. He wiped his mouth, reached into his overalls, pulled out a pack of cigarettes, and lit one.

The match glowed eerily, as he peered down the tunnel, thinking he saw something move. The match burned his fingers, causing another stream of curse words, as he opened the thermos once more and took another swig.

There was little pleasure in Fang's life, except for his bad habits of alcohol, tobacco, and hunting whitetail deer, along the Missouri River. It was his ultimate fantasy, twenty four seven, just thinking about shooting a big buck each year. He loved eating the tender venison from his hunting trips. It was the one thing everyone talked about, getting ready for the campout, for two weeks each year. Jakes was a great shot, too. Something he prided himself in, earning his expert marksmanship trophy each year, at the institution's gun range.

The prison, had a shooting range that was located just a half mile west of the prison camp, where the requirement was two hours of target practice each quarter. Jakes served as a sniper on the prison SWAT team because he was so accomplished as a marksman.

He finished his cigarette, flipped the butt into the drain channel and moseyed down the tunnel, checking his wristwatch. It read 1:35 p.m. He was making good time and was almost to the cistern when he cursed and batted away the huge cobwebs with his flashlight. The tunnel opened into a huge brick cylinder, pouring tons of water fed by the underground wastewater system.

The noise was deafening, as the water thundered into a huge pool at the center of eight, twenty foot corridors, that all dumped into the main cistern. Jakes couldn't believe his eyes. What he kept seeing in the distance was movement beside the wastewater, and now he understood what it was, as the lights glowed near the opening of the tunnels.

"What the hell is this? Mother-freaking frogs! There must be thousands of the sons of bitches," marveled the operations engineer.

Jakes watched waves of green amphibians as they, jumped into the main cistern, flopping about in the frothing, wastewater. He started laughing at how insane the place was and how, many frogs there were. He couldn't believe his eyes, as he rubbed them with disbelief. Some of the frogs, literally flew through the air, elevated by the cascading downpour of the tunnels.

"They're freaking flying," he laughed out loud. He could feel the misting vapors that emanated from the downspouts as he sat back on some pipe railing that outlined two gang walks crossing over the giant cistern. He could see a rainbow in the haze of dew over his head as he opened his thermos for another drink. It reminded him of a fish ladder his father took him to when he was six years old.

He and his dad watched the trout runs fly through the air during their spawning season, reminding him of nature's impressive feat of survival. It was silly, but comical, as the frogs flipped and performed somersaults in mid-air, making him laugh hysterically. The gang-walk seemed to glow, as a lime-green moss, covered the metal grating below the railing. Jakes noticed large veils of moss dangling from the fifty-foot-high vaulted ceiling, which had grown in twenty-foot lengths over the past hundred years in the foul-smelling cistern.

"Yaggghhhhhhhhh!" Jakes shrieked. Something cold, wet, and slimy landed on the back of his thick neck. "Damn it all to hell," he cried, dropping his thermos of booze into the water. The frog hopped off and landed just in front of the angry oaf. He tried to kick the frog into the murky water, but he slipped on some slime and landed with a thud, hitting the back of his head on the railing, and knocking him out cold. He was out for only a couple of minutes,when he groaned in pain, as he felt a large bump on the back of his head. His vision was blurred as he sat upright on the gang-walk, shaking the green slime off his hands and cursing up a storm.

"Ridduppp," went a frog hopping past him.

"OK, I'm gonna fix you little, sons a bitches up real good," he cursed again, reaching into his tool bag and pulling out a bright yellow canister with a label that read, "Danger-Poison" on it. He slowly bent down to his knees, leaned over the railing, and twisted the top off the lethal canister.

"Yep, this will fix you boys' right up, quick like," Jakes gave a sinister chuckle, as he shook the white powder into the water. Suddenly, from out from nowhere, a brisk wind blew the poison back into his face. He cursed, stumbling to his feet while, holding onto the rail. The toxins burned his eyes, and his throat felt, like he drank fire. Jakes stood upright, knowing he ingested the poison, and the situation had turned into, a perilous plea, for help. He tried to wipe the substance out of his reddened eyes, as they started to hemorrhage. He looked like a ghost, with a white face, as he tried to stumble back up the walkway. He tried to navigate the slippery surface, as the toxins worked rapidly, blinding him, further. He could hear the thundering waters and a faint croaking sound coming, from the pool. Jakes was dying, and he knew it. He turned around and balanced himself, against a brick buttress, when he saw a frog sitting in a drain opening. It croaked in defiance, heaving its throat out, in a puffed billow and then leaped onto Jakes' face. Jakes grabbed the cold frog, but lost his footing and fell backward over the railing, into the churning waters.

"HEELLLPP!" he gurgled, flailing his thick arms around the churning currents, as he quickly sank out of sight. Strange as it seemed, Jakes' last vision were hundreds of frogs sitting on the walkway's edge, watching him, struggle for his life. It reminded him of a grandstand full of fans at a football game, he had attended the night before.

Chapter 12

"An interview with Evil"

"Is everything ready?" asked Dr. Arnold, standing behind Lieutenant Rodgers and the SHU dayshift officer, Lewis Peck. They briefed each other as to the protocol of the upcoming interview and procedures of security that Lieutenant Rodgers wanted to have outlined before they went inside the room. "Yes, Doctor. The cameras are set up and recording, and the microphone is live," said Officer Peck, smiling like he did his job right. He was a young recruit and never had much training other than at the military academy at Fort Heavenworth. He was recently married a few months ago and was up for promotion to Sergeant. He helped Lieutenant Rodgers open the heavy metal door with a Taser shield ready, and they entered the SHU interview room. Peck then led Rodgers with the doctor trailing behind. They saw inmate Watini still lying on the concrete ledge, casually waiting for them to get on with it. Lieutenant Rodgers locked the door behind them and hooked his keys back on his large key ring.

"Get on your feet and turn around, Watini. We are going to remove that mask from your face, but before we do, we will secure your arms behind your back and shackle your feet," barked Rodgers forcibly.

Watini stood up and put his hands behind his back as ordered. Dr. Albert was nervous and studied the inmate closely. He noticed how thin Watini was, maybe he weighed one hundred forty pounds, wet. The doctor took great comfort knowing that Rodgers and Peck towered over him, and there would not be any problems to worry about if there was a physical altercation. Rodgers clicked the handcuffs tightly around Watini's wrists and then dropped to the floor to attach the iron shackles to the prisoner's scarred ankles.

"Now please remove the face mask, Lieutenant," ordered Dr. Arnold.

Rodgers stood up straightening out his stiff back and pulled out the special screwdriver, which unscrewed the lock clasps on the back of the leather mask. Peck stood firm, flexing his arm holding the stun-shield's trigger ready for any sudden moves from the foreign inmate. The stun-shield would put 20 thousand watts into him instantly, if he tried to harm any of them. Plus, it was a security measure for a known "biter" in the Bureau.

"You could use a good shower and haircut, Watini," growled Rodgers, flipping some of his ratty, long dreadlocks out of the way while, removing the mask. Watini didn't say a word or make any irrational gestures, knowing he was going to be free of the awful restraint wrapped tightly around his face for over a week. His body ached from hunger after eating non-solids for months because of the mask. Dr. Arnold noticed the strange tattoos all over the prisoner's neck and arms. They were all zodiac references, with other drawings of witchcraft insignias and writings. Dr. Arnold pulled out a chair and threw a pack of cigarettes on the table because he had read that Watini liked to smoke. It seemed to calm him down enough to speak with the other Bureau psychologists. It was against the rules to smoke inside the institution but, after all, everyone smoked inside the walls. The nicotine calmed nerves and who needed, more aggravation by following the rules that look good in writing, but are not effective when it came to real time situations like, running a dangerous facility like Heavenworth Federal Penitentiary?

The mask dropped to the floor, and Rodgers bent over to pick it up when he noticed in the rear corner of the room there was a dead rat. Not an unusual site in a prison, but the rat was skinned like a deer and hanging by its tail, which was nailed to the wall.

He picked the mask up and went over to investigate what had happened, while Watini stretched his jaw and rubbed the creases out of his sore face. He turned and faced Dr. Arnold, giving him a diabolical stare that made the doctor's hair raise up, on the back of his neck. Watini's face was looking like a skeletal frame, with high cheek bones, sunken red eyes and had dark circles, under them. His nose was broken like a boxers, and he had a wicked scar that ran diagonally from the top of his right eyebrow across his face to his left jaw. Dr. Arnold also observed, the scar of a pentagram in the middle of his forehead. Watini glared at him and sat down at the table across from the nervous doctor. He wasted no time shaking out a cigarette and putting it in his mouth. He looked at Officer Peck as, if he was nothing and back at Dr. Arnold, raising an eyebrow, suggesting that he needed a light.

Dr. Arnold was completely entranced with Mutumbo Watini, thinking this inmate was unlike anything that he'd ever met or read about after 16 years in practice. The term "spook" was not nearly the paraphrase he would use for this inmate. Dr. Arnold leaned over the table with a lighter and lit Watini's smoke. He inhaled the cigarette slowly and then let the smoke out slowly, drawing it up his nostrils and inhaling it again. Then he blew it out into the air above him while still working the kinks out of his neck.

"What the hell is this about?" Lieutenant Rodger's asked, pointing at the skinned rodent. Dr. Arnold stood up and walked over to the horrid site and asked Watini, if he did this. Watini. He never even bothered, to turn around, enjoying his cigarette ignoring, his inquisitors. Dr. Arnold bent over and couldn't believe his eyes, when he saw the rodent's skinned carcass and a chalk drawing below it. The drawing was a pentagram, like the one on Watini's forehead, with an inscription written next to it. It was covered in the rat's blood, and he couldn't decipher what it said. He looked at Rodgers who made a face like a monkey and gestured to the doctor that this guy is a whacko, by circling his head with an index finger. Lieutenant Rodgers lifted his boot and kicked the rat from the wall and then walked back to Watini saying, "You're gonna clean that up before we leave, Watini, or I'll make you eat the damn thing," he threatened. Watini merely nodded his head in compliance, as he crushed out the cigarette butt, on the steel table. He shook out another cigarette and put it in his mouth, turned and looked at the rat lying on the floor, and then startled the three staff members by saying his first words.

"Don't worry about that rat, but worry more for yourselves," he said grimly in an Oxford style of English, which surprised all of them with the eloquence of the threat. Dr. Arnold couldn't believe his ears and sat down at the table with his eyes as wide, as saucers. He pushed his glasses up on his nose and asked, "What did you just say?"

"Whom am I speaking with," asked Watini.

"The name is Dr. Henry Arnold. I am the head of psychology here at Heavenworth."

"Hmmnn, interesting. You sound like an educated fellow. Would I be correct, in that assumption?" Watini asked candidly, blowing everyone's mind with his Colonial English accent.

"I don't like you, Watini! You are one spooky S.O.B. If you make any false moves, even just one, Peck here will nail you with 20,000 watts from that shield he's holding. Do you understand me?" barked Lieutenant Rodgers into his face, trying to intimidate the inmate. Watini never even looked at Rodgers but, nodded his head in compliance once again. The response from Watini completely surprised Dr. Arnold, who was still trying to grasp the reality at hand and who he was dealing with presently.

"Remarkable! Patient, confident, almost borderline arrogant—hardly the symptoms of a paranoid schizophrenic, as per his profile," he thought to himself.

"Excuse me, but could I possibly get something to drink? I'm terribly dehydrated," Watini asked politely.

Lieutenant Rodgers put his baton under Watini's chin and said, "You think you're a smart one, do you? Well, how would you like to swallow this stick, smart boy?" he pressed the baton firmly. Watini gave him a stare that imparted, such fear in Rodgers that he stumbled into Officer Peck backward. Somehow, Watini telepathically sent a shockwave into Rodgers' uneducated mind by merely fixing his gaze on him and uttering some kind of gibberish that no one understood. Peck accidentally blocked him with the stun-shield, knocking the two of them to the concrete floor. Watini casually got up from the table, took the shield from the young officer and stunned them both with the high-voltage weapon. He then just dropped it on the two unconscious officers. Dr. Arnold tried to move, but he was frozen in his chair and couldn't move. Watini reached into the doctor's coat pocket and took out the lighter and lit his cigarette, while patting Dr. Arnold's shoulder. Watini sat back down in his chair, "Now, where were we before that rude interruption?

Ah, yes, I remember. You were wondering how you became temporarily paralyzed. Is that correct, Dr. Henry Arnold?" smiled Watini. He laughed again, and smoke billowed from his nostrils like an enraged beast. His eyes focused squarely into the doctor's eyes, and he was speaking to him now without moving his lips.

"It's elementary, my dear Doctor, hypnotic suggestion by means of telepathic signals. Oh my! Does that surprise you that a native man like myself could render such a powerful subliminal brainwave? Well, the answer is yes, I can, and I have much more to show you but so little precious time. You see, Dr. Albert, I have been sent here on a mission from my Master. So, yes, Doctor, I can read your mind. You merely think what it is, and I know what you are saying before your mouth does. Isn't that fascinating?" asked Watini.

"You see, I studied at Cambridge University and then transferred to Oxford, where I met some very interesting people who called themselves Druids. These people came from all over the world, and we met while I was attending Oxford and studying Telepathic Hypno- Transcendency. I do believe you studied it some, being the well-educated doctor that I know you are.

"Oh, what did you ask? Yes, I had a fix on you the minute you entered the mirrored room a bit ago. I actually put the interview together and imparted the thoughts to you by reaching and touching the glass partition," Watini explained. "Anyway, they introduced me to their powerful cult in Old Britain and taught me how to practice the 'dark arts' or, as you educated folks call it witchcraft. Druid worship of Baal and the earth brought me to a whole new understanding of control that science hasn't even discovered yet. Oh, scientifically speaking, higher education is trying to impress the general public with its form of knowledge and dissection of wisdom into a form of higher learning. But as you can see clearly, it has no meaning to what we can do by serving the one true alchemist of this world, and that is Satan," said Watini as he blew on the hot ember of his cigarette and reached over to Dr. Albert's left hand and extinguished it, burning his flesh. He didn't feel a thing, even though his mind knew that it should have been very painful.

"You see, Doctor? No pain. That's because you are paralyzed by hypnotic suggestion, and you will be very comfortable when I sacrifice you and your associates very soon," Watini said, smiling.

"Oh, my dear Doctor," Watini added, "don't you worry about a thing. I'll make this, as bad a nightmare, as you could ever realize in your wildest imagination.

"You see, its 'smart people' like you, who we control and prey upon the most because you are so easy to manipulate. Higher education detours the fabric of 'creation' by means of biological evolution. This science devours the closed mind, and opens it to a new dimension, or what you call 'enlightenment.' "What is it you are asking, Doctor? Oh my! You are so open-minded that your brains would fall out if it were not for your skull. This is our stronghold in the institutions of the world that teach the concept of 'self-realization.' Darwinism was the perfect delivery system for higher learning to deceive the young minds of the world, who pay outrageous sums of money as tuition to be deceived, and yet it is through this deception that 'our Master' prevails. I know, I know what you are saying, Doctor, that GOD does not exist, but that is simply not true. This must come as quite a shock to you, at this time in your life, which is about to end very soon, to discover how wrong you have been all these years and to know that there is a GOD out there and that you, my friend, will be going to Hell. But, it is, what it is! "The root of it all, is simply 'un-belief.' Our plan was to get rid of that meddlesome Jew, known as the Son of God, whose name I am forbidden to say out loud because of its powerful effect on me and others like me. You see, Dr. Albert, higher education is a plan to eliminate the fact of creationism and replace it with self-centeredness.

"   Why do we need a God when we can be gods unto ourselves? Thus, I learned after eight years of intense education, discovering there are indeed powerful principalities and strongholds working in the universe that our mere mortal arrogance cannot possibly understand. Oh, I know what you are saying, Doctor, but the true reality exists in a hidden dimension where the battle between good and evil rages on—an invisible war that is so fierce and being fought in other dimensions known by your colleagues as 'the third dimension,' or the 'interverse.'

"This is why I have been sent here, believe it or not, to stop someone from exposing a truth and to help usher mankind to its ultimate fate, which is not death but the lake of eternal fire. Oh, yes, Doctor, there really is such a frightening place, and you should be proud that you will be seeing it firsthand very soon. Who am I? A much better question is, what am I, don't you think? Well, I am a demon, who has possessed this poor soul known to you as Mutumbo Watini. My name is 'Hedeku.' You see, Dr. Albert, our Dr. Watini was a smart, well-educated man like yourself, and when he graduated from Oxford and began tampering with Druid worship, he met me and invited me into his being.

"You see, Dr. Arnold, science investigates the supernatural workings of the psyche in this world. There are so many phenomena happening around you that cannot be explained, even though you waste so much money on research trying to uncover the things that aren't supposed to be discovered. Oh, true, Doctor, mankind has evolved greatly through its achievements by developing a lifestyle that is comfortable yet perplexing. Higher education is a good thing to develop the human potential through the sciences, but you must ask yourself, Doctor, is it really?"Because of man's unbelief, we the forces of evil can manipulate all the processes of achievement through our plan of deception. Your accomplishments are merely a deluded psychology that you think you are better than GOD, so there is no other god than yourself. "Mankind's greatest paradox is believing more in themselves, rather than a spiritual creator, who punishes everything he makes. That's why our Master convinced the others of his kind to revolt and try to overthrow God and take over His Kingdom of Heaven. The revolt was crushed, and we were banished to the Interverse, to live in exile, until the fulfillment of scripture in the Book of Revelation for the second coming of the Jew, who is the Son of God. Then we will have our final war, here on the battlefield of Eden, or what you call the Earth. That is why we are infiltrating the ranks of humanity through your own visions of grandeur in your thinking that it's all about you.

"Yes, Dr. Arnold, the Interverse is the dimension of spiritual reality where man can open channels to good or evil by the power of belief," Watini/Hedeku declared.

"You must know by now that knowledge is the lamp to understanding," he went on. "The more you are trained in a belief, then the more wisdom you can benefit by that field of belief. "Engineering, Architecture, Medicine, Agriculture, Psychology, Liberal Arts, Physics, Mathematics, Language, Geology and Religion are all derivative forms of Knowledge. Nothing has really changed when it comes to the basic needs of mankind's quest for knowledge. This is the root of personal loneliness in the Universe, seeking inside their inferior minds for more knowledge and truth, rather than accepting the fact of creation.

"In summation, Dr. Arnold, we are all spiritual beings. This is the truth that evades all 'higher learning' and its purpose in understanding that man did not evolve but was, in fact, 'created.' It is man's unbelief that separates him from the great 'I Am.' How else, could man possibly explain its accomplishments through the power of creativity? If a man can create, then why is it so hard to believe that a God couldn't? The most intelligent seek out other means of self-expression than what was taught by the ancients, since the beginning of time, and that is how we have come to power.

"The crack in the fear of the unknown is doubt. This is how the man Adam lost the key of creation. It was when our Master deceived him and the woman Eve, by making them believe that they, too, could be like God. Nothing has changed over time, only man's inhumanity toward himself—of course, with a little help from us.

"How old am I? Why I have no idea Doctor, because in the Interverse, there is no measurement of time. It merely exists as a world of spiritual relativity. It is nothing you could imagine because you are from this world—not mine. Now, with that said, it is time for you to help me to bring another spirit into this world from the Interverse, which is the real purpose of our meeting." Hedeku explained.

He then searched the unconscious bodies of Rodgers and Peck and found what he was looking for—a buck knife. He opened the folding blade and tested it by cutting off Rodger's right ear. The demon smiled and flipped it on the table in front of the frightened doctor, who screamed for help, but only figuratively, since he was under Hedeku's spell and could not move a muscle. Hedeku started dancing around the room, chanting words that Dr. Arnold couldn't understand but had the feeling that something bad was about to happen. He glanced up at the surveillance cameras, praying that someone was at the watch desk monitoring the insanity that was taking place in the SHU interview room. Only the red light blinked underneath the camera lens, recording the horrifying events that were happening in the room.

After twenty minutes of incantations and carving up the two unconscious officers, Hedeku painted their blood on the concrete floor, making three signs of the Pentagram. Then he cut off Dr. Arnold's jacket, tie, and shirt and painted signs on his upper torso with blood. He swirled the human finger paint over the doctor's face, who was helpless and unable to move. Dr. Arnold suddenly realized in a moment of clarity what the demon was going to do, as he looked in the corner of the room and saw the skinned rat. Horrified, he pleaded with the demon, but to no avail.

Hedeku miraculously levitated the two officers into the air and placed them upside down from the overhead sprinkler pipe. He removed their belts, tied their feet to the pipe, stripped them naked, and dressed them like a deer. When the demon was finished, he spun around, swinging his dreadlocks, and hissed violently at Dr. Arnold, revealing a serpent's tongue. His blue eyes were completely covered by his black dilated pupils, further revealing something more hideous than anything the good doctor had ever seen in his lifetime. The demon flipped the knife in the air, reversing his grip, and plunged the blade into Dr. Arnold's sternum. He rocked back and forth, sawing his chest open and removed his pulsing heart. The creature then licked it with its forked tongue and held it in front of the fading psychiatrist. "Goodbye, Doctor! I'll see you in Hell."

Chapter 13

"Riot"

The afternoon wind grew brisk, blowing the colored leaves of autumn throughout the compound. The yard was at its peak during the day, with most of the inmates exercising in the yard. Gray sweats and white tennis shoes dotted the landscape as the men worked out their frustrations from another week in the "red beast." The tall smokestack bellowed a thick rolling gray plume of smoke, filling the air with the essence of refuse that was being incinerated. The tower guards studied the monitors closely, looking for any criminal activity going on in the yard. This was the time when the gangs pedaled drugs or called their shots out, against each other. Nothing went down for the past couple of weeks, and the pressure was building between the gangs for something to happen—at least that's what some of the snitches reported. The correctional officers wore their blue wool coats, hiding their body armor and fearing the worst that could happen. The snipers polished their weapons, getting ready, if this was going to be the day everyone was dreading.

Dead Eye Pete, walked an average of three miles per day back and forth across the massive wall to the west. He knew exactly how many bricks it took to build "Big Red" and that it went 10 feet beneath the ground surface, deterring any large moles in the prison from tunneling underneath it. Dead Eye glanced up at the orange windsocks that were mounted on the rooftops of the guard towers, checking out the crosswinds, as the flags revealed a southerly breeze. A good sniper knows about such things because when it came time to act swiftly, there was no margin for error. The winds swirled inside the giant yard, creating downdrafts that affected their marksmanship.

The gangs were wise to the eyes in the sky, so they usually created diversions if there was a hit put out on someone. It would happen fast, and it usually resulted in a death because the contracted assassins would shank a victim with five to ten thrusts in the neck or chest, bleeding the victim out before help could arrive.

Derek Jackson was a stout, handsome Christian man at 38 years young, and he was one of the fastest runners in Heavenworth. Flag football was the game of choice with most of the inmates because it was as tough a game inside as a pro game outside. The teams would draw big crowds, and some of the best fights would break out during the free for all.

Lance Smith was asked, to quarterback for the injured Christian regular quarterback, Lamar Johnson, who was knocked unconscious, early in the third quarter after a late hit by Hector Gonzales—a huge Norreno gangbanger from Guadalajara, Mexico. Gonzales played for the North Mexican team, "El Diablo." This was the semi-championship game, and the winner would advance to play the African American team known as "Whup Ass" for all the tuna packs bet during the season. The inmates pledged more than 200 packages of tuna from the commissary for the winning team and, of course, bragging rights for the year. This was a big prize paid out because it was the best source of protein in the prison, besides the pilfered eggs from food service.

The score was tied 21-all, with two minutes left in the fourth quarter. It was the "God Squad" team's ball on their own thirty five yard line. Jackson was the team's fearless running back, and his brother, Kyle, played left guard next to Mongo and Bubba. LT played special teams and wide receiver, leading the league with twelve touchdowns in only six games. The league was comprised of four teams and played each other twice in the short three-month season.

The huddle broke and everyone took their positions on the sparse field of grass. Lance called out the numbers and took the snap.

He stumbled backward, almost losing the ball, and then he rolled left—smack into Gonzales' right outstretched arm, close-lining the rookie on his backside. It knocked the wind right out of the kid as Bubba tackled Gonzales to the ground and shoved his head into the dirt.

"One more dirty play like dat, Brother, and Christian or not, I'll shove dat ball up where da sun don't shine, Baby! You got dat?"

Derek and Mongo helped drag the giants away from each other while trying to restore some semblance of order to the game. Gonzales took a swing at Mongo, and Mongo caught his hand in mid-air. The tattooed lineman squeezed his vice-like grip as hard as he could, driving Gonzales to his knees in pain.

"No, you don't, Brother! Uh ah," he roared over the Norreno. Gonzales winced in agony, slapping the ground for mercy as Mongo jumped around on his back and then put him in a chokehold. The War-eagle tattoo, on Mongo's right bicep bulged out like a block of cement as he shoved Gonzales's face back into the dirt.

"Don't hurt him, Mongo. Let him up right now," ordered Derek trying to pry away his death grip on the big Mexican.

"It ain't worth it, man," said Bubba, helping Jackson.

There was a lot of shoving and pushing going on between all the players as LT helped Lance catch his breath and got him to his feet. A whistle sounded from the guard tower, and a guard barked over the loudspeakers for everyone to stand down. Mongo relented, controlling his rage, and giving Gonzales another shove, getting off him quickly. Gonzales got up and wiped the crumbs of dirt and saliva from his bloodied face. He said something bad in Spanish that no one understood, but it was not good, whatever it was.

Suddenly, after things seemed to have settled down a bit, Lance blew up in a fit of rage, kicked Gonzales in the cahones, and cursed him for the cheap shots delivered, not only to him but to Johnson, too. Derek tried to leap into Smith's kick, but was too late. The fight was on. Bodies were flying through the air as Bubba grabbed others and tossed them, as if they were rag dolls.

Derek dragged Lance backward, who was still trying to kick the ailing Gonzales, begging him to pull it together before he got hurt. Then they both saw Chino and another Norreno burst from the pack, hiding something in their hands. Lance knew they were coming for him after their little row earlier. Derek let Lance go so he could defend himself. He grabbed the football off the ground and hurled it point-blank in the face of the other Hispanic.

Mongo hollered to Jackson, trying to break free of three El Diablo players, when Chino pulled out the jagged metal shank and attacked Smith. Chino swung wildly and slashed Lance's left forearm, as he tried to protect himself. Derek wrestled with the other hit man, holding his wrist in the air, trying to disarm him. Lance was still winded after the big hit Gonzales put on him and tripped backward, losing his footing.

Chino came at him again holding the white-taped shank high in the air to deliver a deathblow to the rookie inmate lying on his back. Chino grimaced at near victory, revealing his gold-capped teeth, standing over Smith. Kyle Jackson screamed to his brother when shots rang out in the mayhem. Just as Chino's hand was raised to strike, Dead Eye's two hundred fifty-grain round exploded into the back of his head, killing him instantly. He fell on top of Lance, who rolled the <u>Jeffé</u> off him, not believing what he just saw. He thought he was a dead man, but instead, Chino was. The whole yard had broken out into a full-blown riot. The guards shot tear gas into the yard, and Dead Eye blazed away using lethal force.

Lance was stunned until he heard the sirens blaring in the background of the huge complex. He punched another Hispanic, who was not armed, but then got clobbered by a barbell from Monk Samansky.

It hit him in the right leg, nearly breaking his femur. Lance fell in pain, holding his leg, until he was hoisted by Bubba's massive black arms and thrown over his shoulder. "Put me down," Lance cried in agony but felt relieved that he was in good hands.

Mongo threw a cross bodycheck into the flailing Monk and knocked him to the ground. Bubba cleared a path for the God Squad, charging through the mass of humanity like a huge black bull running through the battling inmates, who were at each other's throats. Mongo tried to get off the ground before Samansky could but was tackled by three more Norrenos. They punched, gouged, and bit him all over his muscles. As he'd push one away, another would take his place.

The Monk rose up and started swinging the lethal steel barbell around his head like a Gothic barbarian in battle. The pipe crushed anyone in its path as Samansky moved closer to Mongo wanting to finish him off, once and for all. Mongo finally grabbed a fistful of dirt and swatted the pests off him and stood in front of the Monk, challenging him to the match. Bullets ricocheted off the ground near the behemoths, who were unaffected by the hail of rifle fire from the angry guards.

"C'mon, Monkey Man, I'm ready for you," chastised Mongo.

Samansky hated, the boyhood curse of that name "Monkey," fighting kids his whole lifetime defending his nickname. Enraged, he charged Mongo, swinging the pipe and barely missing him as Mongo ducked and rolled on the ground. Mongo threw the cloud of dirt in Monk's face and temporarily blinded the madman. Quickly, he went behind Samansky and slugged him as hard as he could in the Monk's liver, dropping him like a sack of potatoes to the ground. Samansky picked up the pipe and raised it above his head to strike the deathblow onto his opponent's head. His huge biceps flexed as Kyle Jackson jumped in front of him and pleaded with Mongo, not to hit him.

"Remember, Brother, Jesus loves him, too!" shouted Jackson holding up his hands. Mongo was infuriated, telling Jackson, "Get out of the way, Kyle, or I'll kill you, too! So help me, I will! You can both go meet Jesus right now or get out of the way!"

Kyle wrapped himself around the helpless Samansky, who was still blinded and trying to remove the dust from his eyes. He knew Mongo had the upper hand and was at his mercy. Then LT covered Jackson, pleading with Mongo not to do it. Mongo swung the pipe as hard as he could into the ground, purposely missing the Christian brothers.

LT and Jackson closed their eyes—fearing the worst—but when they heard the thud on the ground, they were relieved that Mongo had relented in his attack. Samansky couldn't believe his red eyes that Mongo spared him. Jackson and LT jumped to their feet, as more bullets ricocheted around them.

"Let's get out of here before we get shot!" Kyle warned them all, helping Samansky to his feet. They ran for their lives as the bloody onslaught raged within the yard. They witnessed outrageous violence escalating at a fever pitch. Kyle tripped over a dead inmate, and his brother, Derek, screamed for him to get up. A bullet hit the dead inmate's head, popping it like a ripe melon, and gore splattered on Jackson and Mongo. LT hobbled along and helped Samansky into the weight pit. It had three sides of cinder block walls that shielded the other Christians who were taking shelter. Derek counted over a hundred dead bodies lying in the football field, and there were more every second as the guards fired round after round of ammunition. He couldn't believe his eyes, thinking this was as insane a riot as he had ever witnessed. The gangs were murdering each other, along with the guards. He looked up at the wall and saw Dead Eye on his knee shooting at will into the throng of inmates.

"Look over there," shouted Bubba, pointing to the administration building. A battalion of armed correctional officers marched out of the exit doors fully clad in black body armor. They moved like a long black snake in single file, led by none other than Captain Ron. The soldiers had stun-shields and batons raised, charging into the center of hundreds of inmates who were still fighting on the field. The other inmates who sought shelter threw whatever they could at the rampaging guards as they clashed into the middle of the mayhem.

"STAND DOWN, DAMMIT! STAND DOWN!" echoed the loudspeakers.

Samansky was still jawing it out with Mongo, inside the pit as Derek, Kyle, Lance, and Bubba ran onto the field and carried the wounded back to safety. LT pointed his finger into the Monk's thick chest and told him to help them and quit arguing—that he was lucky to be alive. Samansky grabbed his throat and thought about breaking LT's scrawny neck, but finally realized the Christian was right and that he just risked his life to save him. He let go and grabbed a ten-pound flat weight from the bench press and stood outside the pit. Mongo wondered what he was up to, when he saw the Monk curl the flat weight around his back, spin a ten pounder and flung it, like a discus into the air.

The black weight hit the wall and deflected into the unsuspecting Dead Eye, hitting him in the face and knocking him off the wall into the mayhem. He landed on the ground on his back, breaking it and paralyzing the "Cyclops" on the field. He couldn't move and screamed in agony, as ten armed inmates charged him and pulverized him to death.

The other tower guards blasted away, killing most of the inmates who attacked the ruthless sniper, when a hailstorm of disks showered the shooters. Mongo, Bubba, and the Monk hurled the free weights at the other guards atop of Big Red, forcing them to seek cover inside their tower.

"OK, men. Let's run for our lives," shouted Derek Jackson, leading them all in their escape back to the main building, away from the bloodshed. There were a hundred and fifty of them who sprinted back to the building as the guards opened fire again, dropping them one by one. Miraculously, many of the Christian Brothers survived the wretched onslaught that afternoon. Derek and the others looked through the chow hall windows at the war raging outside.

He could see the armored giant, Captain Ron, shouting commands to his dwindling forces to not break rank and keep fighting until the end. He reminded Jackson of a Roman General, clubbing his way to victory. A third of the battalion was dead, but the body count was overwhelming as the inmates continued their hopeless siege.

"Man, this is really bad," Lance choked, not being able to fully swallow from the dehydration of the afternoon's events. His bloody arm was wrapped in a T-shirt.

"Look at all those men still fighting! They don't stand a chance in hell," said another.

"It's like a nightmare out der," moaned Bubba, nursing a pulled groin from running for cover.

"It's like dey all in some kind of trance or sumthin! They're like a pack of animals attacking the way they do. I ain't never seen nothin' like this before," reported LT.

"What do you make of it all, Brother Jackson?" Mongo asked, stupefied.

Jackson shook his head and wondered the same thing as he winced while watching the guards pick off others who were trying to run for safety.

"It's really a bloodbath! I'm sure the National Guard, is on its way, now. This place is going to be under a lockdown for months until they sort this out," Kyle recanted.

"The Army? Holy cow! I forgot about them! The military base probably heard the gunfire. They probably think there's a war going on over here," cried Jacob Porebski in his thick native Ukrainian tongue. He was a transfer and tight end for the God Squad.

He no sooner said that when a huge shadow traveled overhead. It was a Blackhawk gunship thundering overhead, and it spun around, holding its position about a hundred feet in the air. The men could see the wing gunner hanging out from the side door and aiming the 55mm machine gun.

"Put down your weapons," a voice bellowed from the chopper. Captain Ron ordered a retreat to the rest of his men as they made rank in a line formation that was similar to a Roman Praetorian Guard moving away from the inmates who were still fighting amongst themselves. The remaining seventy-plus miscreants were a bloody mess powered by something far greater than hatred. The grey sweat suits were blacked by the blood spatter from the altercation with each other.

Suddenly, a crack of rifle fire came from the shadows of Big Red. It wasn't the guards who fired because the shots were coming from the ground.

A Cartel bandito, was firing Dead Eye's 270mm rifle, at the Army gunship. Sparks hit the front cab, startling the pilot, who reared sideways to try to avoid any further hits. The inmate adjusted the high-powered scope and scored a direct hit, severely wounding the pilot in the chest. The chopper spun around, and the wing gunner opened fire. Thick chunks of brick blew apart from the walls as the shell casings fell from the sky. The inmates cheered and shouted obscenities, while raising their fists in defiance of the tour de force. Another stream of machine-gun fire ripped through the compound, killing cops and robbers, alike. Captain Ron cursed, and his men broke rank, running for their lives back to the administration building. Everyone knew things were terribly out of control.

The pilot struggled with the controls and veered off to his left. The gunship's landing gear bounced off the west tower rooftop, collapsing it on top of the guards inside. They hit the deck, and covered their heads, trying to protect themselves from the falling debris. The bandito fired another shot, which ruptured a piston in the main engine, causing a thick stream of black smoke to twist in the tailspin of the failing helicopter. The gunner was relentless, trying to hang onto his weapon and continuing his malaise of gunfire.

Gold flashes sparked from the heated weapon and shattered the thick plate-glass windows of the cafeteria and administration building. The pilot took his last breath of life and miss-fired a Harpoon rocket. The red-, white-, and blue-striped missile streaked across, the yard and pierced the prison infirmary. The warhead ignited a cache of nitrous cylinders in the emergency ward and blew the building with its seventy-three occupants inside into smithereens.

Jackson and the others were speechless as the infirmary turned into an inferno. Captain Ron barked orders over his radio, trying to regain sanity to his fleeing troops who were seeking shelter deeper inside the prison complex. If anything, it was a good bunker from outside attacks but never in their wildest imaginations, or emergency training, were they ready for anything like this. Captain Ron took off his riot helmet and threw it across the room hitting a picture of Warden Elliott and knocking it off the wall.

"Son of a bitch! What the hell is happening?" he raged in frustration, scaring his bewildered lieutenants. "You guys go and round up some inmates and put that fire out, now, before it burns this whole freaking place down. I can't believe this freaking mess. Shit! They are kicking our asses, yet we have the manpower and the weapons! So, will someone, please tell me how this is possible?" screamed the Captain Tatum.

A young lieutenant stood motionless with his mouth gaping wide open, as he pointed nervously out the window. Captain Ron turned, just in time to watch the smoking chopper spin wildly in front of them and then crash adjacently into the executive wing of the administration building. "Take cover!" he yelled. Captain Ron leaped behind the file cabinets, pulling the young lieutenant down to the floor with him as the explosion rocked the entire facility.

Warden Elliott was just about to sink a three-foot putt on the 13th hole when he heard the thunderous boom. It disrupted his swing midway, and the ball lipped out to the right, missing the easy putt. He cursed and turned to see what made the noise. He noticed the other three golfers in his foursome were all mesmerized by the enormous fiery plume billowing up on the western horizon. When the Warden asked what they were looking at, he turned, dropped his putter, and his cigar fell out of his mouth, "WTF."

Chapter 14

"Lockdown
"

D eputy Warden Dodd wiped the smoke from his sweaty face. His eyes were as red as beets after putting out the fire in the infirmary. It took them four hours, but they got the job done. The prison was now on lockdown, and the remaining 1,485 inmates were secured in their cells.

Warden Elliott Stephens was exhausted, and his head pounded after assessing the damage and counting all the dead bodies in the prison yard and infirmary. Captain Ron Tatum was explaining his actions to the Bureau of Prisons Regional Section Chief, Eldon Bunn, who flew in by helicopter a short while ago, along with General Rocky Oswald, the U.S Army base's Commanding General at Fort Heavenworth. The penitentiary was surrounded by two Abrams K-51 tanks and two hundred armed soldiers, who were deployed making a camp and triage center in the front courtyard of the parking area.

The tanks were situated at the south gate and front entrance of the prison, and emergency lighting flooded the damaged executive wing in the administration building.

"Good God Almighty! This place is a national disaster," puffed Chief Bunn. "I just got off the phone with Senator Ewing, and he's furious over what happened here today. The media is already having a hay-day out there, speculating about what went on in here, and it won't be long before the national networks arrive. We got security breaches all over the place, and more than four hundred people dead, with another two hundred wounded. This facility is now under quarantine until we can figure out what to do with the dead."

"Yes, I think the best idea right now is to make it look like this is an outbreak of some kind of disease. That will hold off the press and locals from coming near this place," advised General Owens.

"We have another hundred reserves, being called up who will be here in the morning, but until then, we have got to clean this up and put our best efforts into practice." Warden Stephens then pulled over a wastepaper basket and threw up in it.

He was experiencing, an early hangover and possibly faced with early retirement. The others walked out into the hallway, until he was finished hurling his lunch from the golf course.

Deputy Dodd explained their lockdown procedure and illustrated the command center's point between the three wings of each building and, of course, the gates and control center in the hub of the prison were not affected by the chopper's explosion.

"The good news is that no prisoners have escaped the facility, and our electricity and boiler rooms are all operational and supplying the necessary heat and lights for the duration of this lockdown," said Dodd.

"Good job, Dodd," said Chief Bunn. "We'll need the Army's assistance, General, until we can address the nation and inform them of our plan. Whatever that will be, I have no idea, so I'll let Washington spin something up for us. They are the best when it comes to these types of internal catastrophes. Captain Tatum, under the circumstances, I'd have you under arrest right now for dereliction of duty and letting this riot escalate to the proportions it has, but I need you to assist the Army in evacuating the dead and establishing a safety net around the perimeter of Heavenworth.

"I also, need to get the names of the officers and inmates who are dead, so that we can notify their families. We have twenty-four hours to establish a communication link for our people to assist with the details, forthcoming."

"The local authorities, including the Kansas State Patrol, the Sheriff's Department, and the Heavenworth Police Department are securing all interstate exits and local roadways within a five-mile radius from us as we speak, Chief Bunn," informed General Owens.

"Excellent! Thank you, General. Can we get some air support during the night? We must secure the entire complex. We don't want any civilians penetrating the safety net, either do we?" asked Captain Tatum.

The general nodded his approval as Warden Stephens stumbled into the doorway, moaning about how bad he felt and complained that none of this was his fault.

"I'm holding you personally responsible for this, Captain," he scolded. "You and Dodd will be held accountable for the disgrace that you have brought upon this prestigious institution.

"I can't believe, that when I left here, but a few hours ago that all hell has broken lose. Your officers went way over the line killing more than three hundred inmates!

What were you thinking, for God's sake, man? People are dead out there!"

"Listen here, Stephens," chastised Chief Bunn, "There's plenty of blame for everyone here, including you. The Captain, has been advised to help us with the lockdown and remove the bodies from the courtyard. We have the Army's complete support to get this mess cleaned up with minimal damage. We are notifying Washington that the prison has had a severe outbreak of airborne disease and we are now under quarantine, within a five-mile area. That should give us time, to figure out how to handle what really went on here today," explained Chief Bunn.

"Might I suggest that we set up our command post here in the main corridor just in front of the 'bubble' so we can monitor all the wings during the lockdown? We can control access and transport the deceased by loading them in freight containers and drive them out through the south gate," offered General Owens. "We have a tank guarding the entrance now, and it is the only road into the yard. Is that correct, Captain Tatum?"

"Yes Sir, but we will have to wait until daylight to start loading the bodies," replied Tatum.

"Why wait until morning? We need to get them loaded on semis tonight under the cover of darkness. We can't let the media see all those bodies laying out there, now.

They could fly over in a news chopper, photograph the whole thing, and blow our cover," said Chief Bunn.

"True, but the chopper hit our main power terminal and destroyed a transformer bank. We are operating under auxiliary power right now, and it isn't very dependable," said Captain Tatum. "It will barely keep the lights on, let alone move the gates internally."

"Tell me, do you have a backup generator in this dump?" asked Chief Bunn.

"No, Sir! We requested one seven months ago, but the Bureau keeps rejecting our request due to budget constraints," said Warden Stephens snidely, to the Regional Chief.

"I don't mean to interrupt you guys, but I promised the inmates, if they went to their cells we would feed them tonight," Deputy Warden Dodd butted in.

"How can we do that? The kitchen is closed due to the lockdown and, to my knowledge, still trying to get rid of those cursed toads," argued Captain Ron.

"They are frogs, not toads," corrected Dodd.

"What are you two talking about anyway?" asked Chief Bunn, who pulled up a steno chair and sat down, rubbing his temples.

Warden Stephens explained, the wild tale of the frog invasion and what a mess they had caused inside the sewer pipes and the rest of the facilities. "GOD, they were everywhere!"

General Owens shook his head in disbelief, as he listened to the Warden's saga of what had transpired. He rubbed his bristly, bearded face, and scratched his head. Then he came to a startling epiphany.

"I've got it! We'll leak a story out to the media and tell them that an amphibian epidemic, tainted the prison's food supply, and that's what caused the lethal poisoning of 361 inmates and forth-eight correctional officers. We'll call it some kind of 'salmonella outbreak,'" he beamed, removing his helmet.

"Yes! That's very good, General. I like your way of thinking," commended Chief Bunn.

"Well, that's a real good idea, except how do we explain, a downed U.S. Army Blackhawk exploding into a ball of fire and destroying an entire wing of the prison?" asked Captain Tatum.

"Are you gonna blame that on a frog, too?" he sneered.

The Chief gave Tatum a dirty look for his insubordinate remark toward them.

"Hmmm! You have a good point, Captain. I'll have to work on that one a little longer, but regarding the food supply, we can truck over some K-rations for everyone to eat.

"We'll ship them in the semis from the base and then load the bodies up and bring them back, to Fort Heavenworth. We'll use the old Fort Road along the river, and no one will see us transporting the bodies from the prison," General Owens, answered.

"Sounds like a plan, General. Call your base, and let's proceed with the evacuation. Warden, you get on the intercom to inform the prisoners that we will serve them dinner, as soon as possible. Captain, you and Deputy Dodd organize what men you have left here to keep the peace, until we can bring some more troops in, after we haul out the deceased and clean up the wreckage from that chopper. Take the wounded and sick from the infirmary through the main corridor and out the front gate to Army's triage center set up out front," ordered Chief Bunn.

"General, I understand now, why we build prisons nearby Army installations. It is times like these, that we would be lost without your help," Bunn commended General Owens, shaking his hand.

"Has anyone seen Dr. Albert?" inquired Warden Stephens.

"No, not since chow," said Captain Ron.

"The last time I saw him, he was going to interview that so-called witchdoctor, who we brought in from Oklahoma last night. He said the guy is a real piece of work, and he wanted to interview him," said Dodd. "Yeah! He's real freak show all right," said Captain Ron.

"Well, go get him. We need him up here to help with the trauma patients, not writing a study on some derelict, voodoo nut job," ordered Warden Stephens.

"OK, men. Let's get going. The night is young and from the looks of it, it's going to be a full moon. That should help with the lighting for the evacuation. Good luck" saluted Chief Bunn. Meanwhile, in a cell two floors directly beneath them, a ritual was being performed by the nefarious witchdoctor known, as Mutumbo Watini. He felt the official's anger, as he danced between his three human sacrifices, which dangled upside down, from the sprinkler pipe in the SHU. Watini/Hedeku used their blood to paint himself with ancient pagan symbols, chanting a mantra like that used, in a tribal war dance. Little did they realize that the wicked demon had cast a spell over the prison, and it was the sole reason behind the massacre, earlier. Hedeku's power intensified, feeding upon the fear, hated, and ambivalence that emanated from inside the corrupt prison walls.

The penitentiary, was the perfect breeding ground for the demon, that had infiltrated their fortress and was busy summoning a presence of evil that would defy all human logic. Dr. Albert's corpse turned and twisted, as Hedeku waved his hands over him and then stuffed the skinned rat into his mouth—the rodent's tail hanging from his lips. Hedeku grinned, as he spat his incantations of evil over the psychiatrist's corpse. In a remote corner of the ceiling blinked a little red light. It recorded a candle that flickered on top of a table in a dimly lit room and a dark shadow dancing upon its wall. The demon performed its ritualistic gyrations, according to the tradition of its ancestry, beckoning the presence of others from the realm of darkness. The hideous mutilations, were pertinent in human sacrificial ceremonies of ancient times, known by the educated Druid physician, who was empowering himself to a new level of indecency. Hedeku savored the fear and hatred from the evil prison, like a bee on flower pollen. The battlefield's issue of blood trickled, into a wide pool of crimson red, which then overflowed into a nearby drain and wound its way down a maze of pipe, emptying into the cistern deep below the surface.

The water churned into a deep crimson froth, beckoning its amphibious theatre of croaking inhabitants. One gangly, toad leaped from the railing, high into the air, twisting its two-tone figure into a mid-air pirouette and dove into the middle of the churning waters. A bright flash of light burst, from underneath the water, summoning the remaining thousands of frogs above. The vast airspace of the red brick cistern, suddenly filled with the colors of green and white, as the amphibians leaped into the murky froth, below.

Chapter 15

"Lamentations"

The Bureau of Prison's only female chaplain, Brittney Barnett, was escorted down the dim-lit corridor of C-Block, by none other than Lieutenant Lonnie Pearson. She was a tall, elegant woman with auburn-red hair and bright green eyes. She modeled a knockout figure that was transformed by a cheap, gray polyester, sport coat and black slacks. She didn't wear any make-up, but then again, she didn't have to. She was attractive and she knew it, along with every man or woman she came in contact with.

The Chaplain, pulled her thick mane back into a ponytail, coupled by a black tortoiseshell hair clip. Her sterling cross earrings shined like stars alongside of her blonde highlighted hair. They were a gift from her father, who was a Pastor in Fayetteville, Arkansas. He gave them to his only child, who was adopted at birth, as a graduation present from Mt. Zion Seminary College in Tuscaloosa, Alabama. She was thirty three years old and totally fearless. She held a third-degree black belt in Judo and could break a three-inch board with the strike of a cobra. Chaplain Barnett was determined to be the best minister in God's Kingdom.

Whereas, other pastors reviled her, because of her beauty, they yielded to her knowledge and spiritual application of Holy Scripture. She somehow had an aura of "blessing" that could not be described because, no matter where she went, people would listen to her beautiful soliloquy of praise, and the inmates certainly welcomed her angelic-like presence.

She rotated her duties with two other chaplains who happened to be at a Spiritual Conference in Worcester, Massachusetts, for the weekend. Deputy Warden Dodd had called her in to work so she could minister to the men who were injured and grieving. She was at home preparing her Sunday sermon when she got the phone call and was told about the devastating events of the day. She lived in Kansas City and didn't have a television. Chaplain Barnett was single, but she liked to date men who were interested in Christianity.

This, of course, narrowed her field of having any kind of a relationship because most men only lusted for her body and not her belief. Her best friend was a twelve-pound Persian cat named Lazarus. She found him nearly dead in the woods where she would jog daily before going to work at the prison. The old feline must have wandered its way into the woods and was attacked by some raccoons. He was severely wounded with a gash in his hind leg, his left ear was bitten off, and he was missing his left eye.

Chunks of fur, were missing from all over his body, and it was apparent to the good-hearted Samaritan that the cat, was as good as dead. The old cat was on its last breath when she found him and knelt down to comfort him. Brittney was trained to help the sick and dying, but, she was never used to it, even after working for the Bureau of Prisons all these years. She thought it was all, so hopeless at times, watching people destroy each other, over some stupid pledge to their gang's colors.

She picked the old cat up, held it in her arms, and prayed for it. Her faith was for the living, and her spirit told her to take it home with her and care for it. She laid him on a blanket and put a bowl of cream by his head, watching his shallow breaths, before she left for work. She felt guilty thinking the cat needed a veterinarian, but then again, he was probably going to die anyway. When she came home from work that evening, she went to check on the cat, thinking the worst had happened and how she would dispose of his body. Much to her amazement, though, the bowl of cream was gone. The old warrior licked his whiskers and went back to sleep.

"Well, praise the Lord! You are still alive? I'm just going to have to name you, Lazarus, since you arose from the dead, you old mangy cat." That was five years ago, to the date, when she had found him. Today was their anniversary together.

Neither she, nor the veterinarian, knew how old Lazarus was, when she found him, but she really didn't care because the cat was the nicest pet she had ever seen. He'd lie by her side, when she read the Bible and wrapped himself in bed with her when she slept. He tolerated strangers and their rude comments about his missing eye, so Brittney sewed a black leather patch for Lazarus and put it around his head. She thought it looked adorable on him, and the cat never once tried to remove it. Lazarus had a thick, dark grey coat of fur and would rule the house when she was gone. He was constantly on her mind and would make her laugh, when she was feeling down. She remembered how funny he was, when she would put a paper shopping bag on the floor, and Lazarus went crazy chasing himself in and out of the bag. Brittney even video-recorded the event and sent it on the internet. Lazarus received over a million hits from viewers, who shared in his antics, and he was a star with his pirate patch over his left eye. She played it on the Chapel's computer one Sunday morning, giving many inmates a much-needed laugh. Some even told their families about the cat and got reports back about how hilarious the chaplain's cat was.

The inmates respected Chaplain Barnett deeply, because she gave them hope, respect, and encouragement to persevere in their captivity. But this was a totally different scene than what she was used too.

The inmates were withdrawn and scared, over what happened in the yard today. Some of the Christian men shared how "totally insane" the ordeal was and said they feared for their lives. Chaplain Barnett approached Cell #229, the "home" of her favorite converts, the Jackson brothers. She looked at Lieutenant Pearson and nodded her head for him to open the cell door. He rapped the door with his baton and shouted, "Chaplain's here," and he fumbled with his keys and opened the barred door, giving Chaplain Barnett a big smile, revealing his gapped teeth. Kyle was sitting at the table drawing some charcoal sketches, while his brother Derek read a magazine in his top bunk. It was against Bureau policy for brothers to be located in the same prison together, let alone share the same cell with the other. But Chaplain Barnett managed to pull some strings for the Jacksons because, Kyle, the younger brother, suffered from "epileptic trauma" or, better known as "grand-mal seizures."

She had convinced Warden Stephens that it was a big liability for the prison to not have a "guardian" for Kyle's condition. His brother knew how to deal with the strange disease after growing up around it all his life, whereas most people would freak out and not help him when he had an episode. Many epileptics choke to death by swallowing their own tongues, when suffering a grand-mal seizure. The warden agreed because he didn't want the liability after she had brought it to his attention.

It, like so many serious cases of illness, simply fell through the proverbial bureaucratic cracks and was never mentioned in their medical files.

"Well, how are you guys doing, this dark and dreadful day?" she asked seriously.

"Thank God we are OK! More than I can say for a lot of the others," Derek said, sitting up in his bunk and tossing the unimportant magazine in the corner.

"Can you believe it, Chaplain? Hundreds of men are dead and just lying out there. We've been in four different facilities, and we've never seen anything like this! It was catastrophic," cried Kyle.

"Yes, and all over a stupid football game," she commented.

"Is that what they told you?" asked Derek, jumping down to the ground. Chaplain Barnett was surprised by his aggression, and LP pushed her aside, pointing his baton at Derek and said, "You take it easy, Jackson. Everyone's a little tense about what happened out there today."

"Oh, put your club away. I'm not going to do anything. You know me better than that, Chaplain," said Derek, as he sat back on the lower bunk bed.

It's alright, Lieutenant Pearson," she said, as she put her hand on his baton to lower it away from Derek's face.

"Why don't you wait outside for a minute, and let me pray with these men? It's OK," she assured him.

"I don't know, M'am. I'm supposed to be by your side at all times. Them's da rules," he said.

"Very well, Lieutenant. How about you stand just outside the door, and leave it open just a bit, OK?" she asked, smiling confidently, and melting him with her southern charm.

"OK, den! But no funny stuff, Jackson," warned LP.

They waited for him to leave, and Chaplain Barnett sat down on a stool that was welded to the steel table. She noticed it was cold and didn't want to touch the cold table, either. She leaned over to see the drawing Kyle had sketched. It was an inmate screaming in agony, on his knees.

"Nice drawing. Is that a self-portrait?" she asked Kyle, smiling. She wanted to touch his arm, but she knew better than to show that kind of affection, no matter how much she trusted the Jacksons or how much pain anyone was suffering. She had already seen enough, but she knew it was going to be a long night.

"Yeah, it's my spirit crying out to God asking Him, why?" Kyle answered, gritting his teeth.

"I don't know why, Kyle. Sometimes things have to get really bad before they can get really good," she said softly. Kyle looked into to her lime-green eyes and could see her deep understanding and sincere compassion behind her statement.

"That's a real zinger, boy," chuckled Derek, clapping his hands. "You are good, do you know that?" he asked, smiling.

"No, but thank you nonetheless, Derek," she smiled back. She really liked Derek but tried hard not to let it show, especially with Kyle around. He'd get jealous of his brother, and she knew it.

"So, what's your story on what happened out in the yard this afternoon?" she queried.

They both shook their heads, bewildered, and Kyle rubbed his thick dark beard.

"Don't know for sure, but I believe something really evil is happening, and I can't put my finger on it just yet. But, believe me, something's going on," Derek said, scaring Chaplain Barnett deep inside. She didn't let them see her fear, but it was all too present, and that's why she wanted the time alone with them because she trusted their spiritual insight more than anyone in the complex.

She believed she felt, more bad vibes in the air than usual—and not just from the massacre that took place earlier. She leaned forward and motioned for them to come closer.

"I completely agree with you! There's definitely something very strange going on, and I don't know what it is, either. The warden has some higher-up's downstairs, and they're trying to spin some big story to cover up what's happened here today," she whispered, looking over her shoulder at the door. "When I was called in early, I had no idea what had happened. They said a boiler exploded, and that's what the news on the radio reported, too."

The Jacksons looked at one another in disbelief. "That's just like them, trying to cover their asses, as usual," said Kyle. Chaplain Barnett gave him a stern look about his cursing, and Kyle apologized.

"It was an Army chopper," explained Derek. "An inmate shot the pilot with a bullet from a guard's scope rifle. It spun out of control, shot a missile into the infirmary, and blew it to all to hell. Then it crashed into the executive administration wing, erupting in a ball of fire.

"I'm telling you, Chaplain, that ain't the half of it.

"When the fight broke out at the football game, it was like everyone went crazy. And I do mean, crazy," Derek confessed his feelings.

"Yep! He's right on, Chaplin. The men went bizzerko! Totally gonzo people were killing each other just to be killing each other. Gang members were killing their own kind. Now, how crazy is that?" asked Kyle.

"Really? That's preposterous," cried Chaplain Barnett, wiping a tear from her right eye.

"Hey! Is everything OK in there?" shouted the lieutenant.

"Yes, Lieutenant Pearson. Everything is fine. Leave us alone, please," she snapped back. "We're trying to pray."

Lieutenant Pearson's eyes grew wide at her retort, but he obeyed her command and disappeared again behind the door. She was visibly shaking, trying to wipe her eyes with some tissue. Derek reached out and grabbed her hands. They were warm and soft. He had forgotten what a woman's hands felt like because it had been so long since had he touched any.

"There, there, Chaplain, settle down. Things will be better by tomorrow," Derek assured her. She gave a crooked smile and pulled her hands away from his, not wanting to, but had to. Kyle handed her some more tissues, and she thanked him.

"So, what do you think is going to happen to us?" asked Kyle.

"I don't know yet. I overheard that they are bringing in more troops to help move the dead out of the yard and secure the perimeter of the prison so that no media types can get close enough to see what they're up to. In the meantime, the Army is bringing in some K-rations for you all to eat." she said quietly.

"Oh! That sucks!" Kyle cursed again. "Oops! Sorry," he shrugged.

"Well, that's fine by me. I'd eat a horse right now, I'm so hungry," said Derek.

"The horse would taste better," laughed his brother, breaking up the melancholy.

Chaplain Barnett gave Kyle a soft slap, "You're so funny, even when things are this bad." She continued, "I did hear Captain Ron complain about the inmate they brought in last night on the bus. He told everyone that the guy is a real spook, and they're keeping him in the SHU under heavy guard until they know what to do with him."

"A real spook, huh? Well, did you know about the frogs?" Derek quizzed.

"No! What frogs?" she asked, dumbfounded.

"Oh, man! We had us a frog invasion late last night during the 10 p.m. count. Frogs were everywhere. They came up through the sewers into our toilet and hopped all over the place," Kyle said, waving his hands in a hopping fashion.

"Really? Frogs?" she sat up straight on her stool.

"Yes. Inmates went nuts, come to think of it. They were screaming, catching them, and throwing them out of the cells and over the railing to their deaths down below. It was a real mess to clean up, but the guys did a pretty thorough job," said Derek.

"Yeah, right. Except for the stench from the sewer drains," Kyle sneered.

"Is that what that smell is?" asked Chaplain Barnett.

"You don't know what you're talking about, Kyle. Just shut up," Derek chastised.

"You can't make me," grimaced Kyle, sticking his tongue out at his older brother. "You guys both know that things are pretty strange when unexplained coincidences just start happening around this place. Like it doesn't have enough ghosts running around this place, haunting the prisoners' sleep, as it is," confided Chaplain Barnett.

"Yeah, like in B-Block," Kyle said wide-eyed. "I know some guys that got bit in their sleep, and they swear it wasn't from their cellee."

"Well, the guards all say they've seen poltergeists walking around the upper tiers and even heard footsteps pounding up and down the stairs, but saw no one there," said Derek.

"Do you believe in ghosts, Chaplain?" asked a somber Kyle.

"Well, the Bible tells us about demons and evil spirits so, yes, I guess I believe. But I also, believe in JESUS CHRIST, and He rules over the seen and unseen world. So that's how we develop our faith in GOD and the HOLY SPIRIT, too," she beamed.

"You see, Kyle, that's why she's such a good chaplain. She just says the right thing, at the right time," smiled Derek affectionately, letting her know of his fond approval.

"Well, I guess, I agree with the Word of GOD, or I wouldn't consider myself a Christian," said Kyle proudly.

"Well, let's pray, Brothers, that the worst is over, and we can help others with their unbelief. Let's ask for GOD's protection during these difficult times and for His Grace and Mercy to deliver us from our sins, OK?"

"Well, OK! And while we're at it, how about some grilled ham and cheese sandwiches, too," Kyle requested, hungrily licking his lips.

"Kyle! I'm going to smack you, when the Chaplain leaves," scolded Derek.

"It's OK, Derek. Philippians 4:19 says that our God will meet all our needs, according to His riches and glory through CHRIST JESUS . I don't see why we can't ask, for a sandwich, too!"

Kyle stuck his tongue out, again, at his brother.

"You know something, Kyle? You're starting to look like one of those frogs when you do that!" Derek warned his brother.

Chapter 16

"What's that?"

Deputy Warden Dodd entered the Special Housing Unit and found it vacant. The monitors were on at the front desk, but there were no correctional officers anywhere, to be found. He checked the log and saw Dr. Albert's signature on it over five hours ago, but he did not sign out. "That's strange," he thought to himself, opening the top drawer, and finding another set of keys to the cell doors. He flipped a switch and checked all the cell screens. It was a full house. There were 11 different rooms, and they revealed all the inmates were secure except, in the interrogation unit. The screen was very dark with images on it, but he couldn't make out what—or who, was in the room. He picked up the phone and called the captain's office.

"Captain Tatum, this is Dodd in the SHU. Would you come down here right now, please? Oh, and bring some men with you, too!" he ordered.

"Yeah, no problem! What's up?" quizzed Tatum.

"There's no guards down here!"

"What do you mean, there's no one there? There should be four on duty!"

"I know that, Ron! But no one is here. The main desk was empty, and the prisoners are all secured in their cells. But, the monitor to the interrogation room is on the fritz. It's dark as hell in there, and I can't tell who's in there. It's very strange, but I'm not going in there without backup," Dodd said nervously.

"I'm on my way!" the Captain assured the Deputy Warden.

Dodd took a deep breath and tried to gain his composure when he noticed something move behind the bathroom door.

"Who's there?" he shouted, terrified.

He opened another drawer, removed a flashlight, and tried to turn it on. His hands were shaking, from his frazzled nerves. He looked up again, at the door as it began to close, but not all the way. Dodd's heart raced, as he gave another command, "I'm warning you, whoever you are, come out of there right now!"

Dodd had a triple by-pass less than a year ago, and he prayed that it would not fail him now. He got up from behind the desk and slowly walked toward the door. "If that's you, Bulldog, I'll kick your ass. This isn't funny," he said, thinking that the guards were playing a joke on him.

The guards did that occasionally, just to break up the monotonous routine of watching the inmates. They were known to occupy the empty cells and take naps during their shifts on occasion because, of the lack of security and supervision. Rarely did an executive visit the Special Housing Unit, because of its subterranean chambers underneath the prison. It was a cold and grim reminder of the deterioration that had ravaged it from the countless years of neglect. It was the "budgetary black hole," where millions of dollars were spent annually on fictitious repairs and remodels. The SHU was a joke, and it smelled disgusting. The executives abhorred it, but the guards grew impervious to the rusty urine odors and undisturbed sleep over the years. Dodd opened the door slowly, holding his flashlight, like a club and thinking that he might faint from fear, as he encountered "Whiskers," the guards' pet cat. "MEEEOOOWW!" He chuckled a welcomed relief, as the old prison cat scratched in his litter box, finishing up his business.

"You dumb cat! You scared the crap out of me, too!" scolded Dodd.

The cat scampered out between his legs and ran down the corridor, turned a corner, and went out of sight. Dodd closed the door and used the commode, thinking that it was a good idea, while he was there. When he finished, he washed his hands and looked into the mirror at the dark bags, under his red eyes.

He splashed the soothing warm water up into his face and pulled out a few paper towels from the dispenser. He thought about his day ending and would soon be going home to his family and his comfortable bed. He would sleep in late on Sunday morning. He wiped his face off, thinking about what a hellish day it had been, until he looked back into the mirror and saw another image standing behind him. He whirled around, stumbled into the wall, and fell back on the toilet. Dodd was speechless, numbed with terror, as the demon struck him repeatedly with the bloodied blade.

Hedeku smiled, as his black tongue slithered out from his dark lips, killing the Deputy Warden and all his dreams. Dodd shivered a violent death throw and slumped against the evil witchdoctor. Then Hedeku heard the approaching sound of footsteps and voices entering the SHU. He closed the door, leaving a small crack, and watched the three officers standing bewildered at the main desk. Then the larger one turned around and shouted, "Dodd? Where the hell are you?" Hedeku hissed, as he recognized the fat man's voice who had beat him up the night before, and he squeezed his knife firmly.

"Look inside there," the captain ordered the young lieutenant, pointing to the interrogation unit. Captain Ron removed his 9mm sidearm from its holster and flipped the safety switch off.

"What's wrong, Captain?" asked the young officer.
Captain Ron stared at the bathroom door and aimed his gun at it.

He raised his finger up to his lips, motioning for the officer to be quiet and then pointed a command to open the bathroom door. The correctional officer held his M19 rifle up to his chest and slowly walked across the room to the door.

Captain Ron moved to his left to provide cover fire and have a clear aim at the door, when it was opened. He started to sweat profusely, sensing something was seriously wrong in the SHU. The guard reached for the door handle, pointing his rifle barrel at it, a thick flow of crimson oozed out from underneath the jam. Stunned, the young officer took a step back, when the other lieutenant shrieked in horror.

"Cap . . . aaahhh . . . tain," cried the faint voice.

The officer looked back at Tatum for a split second, giving Hedeku the time he needed to lunge out from behind the bathroom door and grab the young officer from behind. Startled, Tatum jumped backward and fired his weapon into the hostage. He emptied his clip, killing the correctional officer and wounding Hedeku in the right shoulder.

"Shoot him!" screamed Captain Tatum to the other shocked lieutenant, who stumbled out of the interrogation room. Tatum fumbled, trying to reload another clip into his gun. Hedeku crawled up the wall backward, like a spider toward the horrified lieutenant, who pointed his sidearm and fired..

He was shaking so badly, after seeing the unbelievable images in the interrogation room and now, the orange-clad spider man, was making his way towards him. Captain Tatum dropped to his knees, his mouth dropped open, as he watched the inhuman specter scamper across the ceiling and drop down on the hapless lieutenant. Hedeku straddled over him, grabbed his curly hair, and jerked his head back. The demon hissed again, in defiance, looking at Captain Ron, who relieved himself, in his pants from the sight of the monster holding the bloody blade next to the lieutenant's throat and then slitting it.

"Noooooo!" cried Captain Ron, turning an about face and running for the door. His key slipped directly into the lock, opening the metal door. He quickly slammed it behind him, and it locked automatically. Hedeku's black eyes, pierced, wildly through the safety port in the window.

Hedeku tried to make contact telepathically, with Tatum, but couldn't connect. The demon shrieked a blood-curdling cry of rage, as he clawed at the locked door. Captain Tatum sprinted down the outside corridor as fast as his feet would carry him, praying that the wild animal would not get him. He had never been that scared in all his life, as he felt the cool air against his wet pants. He didn't care about that, though. His mind was reeling about what had just transpired in the SHU. He had shot and killed a fellow officer and then panicked, not being able to load his sidearm to save another.

163

He was racing down the corrido,r when he met three National Guardsmen.

"Where are you guys going?" he asked.

"We're on our way to the Special Housing Unit. What's wrong with you? You look like you just saw a ghost, or something," said one of the soldiers.

Captain Tatum knew these young weekend warriors would be shredded alive, if they went down there alone, but he didn't care. He just wanted to kill that thing and be done with it.

"Yeah, it was something all right! Listen here, men," Tatum straightened up trying to collect himself as the soldiers stared at his wet crotch. They recognized that he was an officer.

"Don't go down that corridor. I want you to set up a guard post right there, before the entrance, where I just came from. Get some sandbags and a machine gun and block that corridor, until I come back. Don't let anyone go down there! Do you understand me? Absolutely no one! If anyone, or anything comes down that hallway, I want you to blast it back to hell, where it came from. I'm the Captain of this rat hole, and I'm giving you an order, to shoot to kill! No questions asked, got it?"

The three excited bobble heads, accepted their new orders and radioed their commanding officer. Tatum left them and continued to run down the main hallway to his office. He knew they didn't stand a chance if that thing got out from the SHU, but maybe they could slow it down before, he got more help. Tatum's thoughts were confused, as he tried to piece together, what happened. He couldn't accept the reality of seeing the demon crawl up a wall and defy gravity.

"What the hell can do that?"

He marched into the command center and unlocked the arms room, followed by six other officers. "Suit up boys, we're huntin' bear," he commanded.

Meanwhile, outside the south gate of the yard, State Trooper, Sergeant. Archie Johnson was lighting a cigarette and leaned over to light one up for the tank driver, who was seated inside the Abrams A51. His head popped out of the front hatch, like a gopher in a hole. The married gunner sat in the top turret resting on a 55mm machinegun, as the two divorced braggarts discussed their sexual conquests of the local girls in Kansas City. They laughed about their mid-life escapades, as being irreverent to the dead bodies scattered in the field beyond them. The married gunner, Private First-Class Pete Waters, chuckled at the troopers' stories, gullible enough to think that they were probably true since they were coming from lawmen. He shivered and rubbed his arms, trying to warm up as a heavy fog rolled over the valley.

He pulled his collar up tightly around his neck, to block the cool draft that was ushering in from that fog, as it was creeping up from the east bank of the Missouri River. He blocked out the jokers below him, to daydream about his brothers and cousins, who were probably drunk by now, at their hunting camp, which was thirty-five miles away from Heavenworth. He licked his lips tasting the rye whiskey, his favorite alcoholic beverage, just thinking about it.

Embarrassed, he checked to see if, the others saw him do it, but realized that they probably couldn't see him in the dark. He watched the spotlight of an Army Apache gunship, in the distance patrolling the river road for any intruders. He often fantasized about what fun it would be to hang out of the gun port and blaze away with the 75mm mini gun. Its spotlight flashed back and forth, trying to penetrate the dense fog bank along the river, as a line of headlights bounced up the road.

"There's the convoy," he pointed toward the river. "They're about thirty minutes out," he reported to the dynamic duo beneath him. They could have cared less what he said, or about the incoming convoy, as the trooper embellished, an account of a fellow patrolmen's sister that was a white-trash prostitute in the trailer court, next to the Army base. Private Waters yawned and checked his cheap watch. He pushed the light feature, and it lit a blue light, telling him it was 8:37 p.m.

He figured the convoy would be there by 9:15, and he would be relieved of duty and head for home. He'd been sitting there all day, and he needed to go to the bathroom. He stood up, stretched his aching muscles, and looked up at the starry sky above him. He noticed that the full moon was climbing over the massive east wall of the prison.

Waters waved to a guard, who was smoking a cigarette in the east tower. He could see the ember flare as the guard sucked in a deep inhale and then flipped it, spiraling to the ground. Private Waters hated smokers and thought that they were all going to die from lung cancer someday. He thought of his father, who died early at age sixty five from the dreaded disease. He remembered his mother pleading with him to stop, but he just laughed it off saying, "I'm going to die from something someday!" It never made any sense to the young private why people were so reckless with their health. He climbed down from the gun turret and walked over to a bush by the gate, unzipped his pants, and relieved himself. He focused and then the intense pressure left his prostate, as the flow of urine washed the foliage around him. "Aaaaah," he gasped, taking a deep breath of air, and pushing harder. He looked up and thought he saw movement in the dark yard beyond the gate, but he couldn't quite make out what it was, or heard, after he finished.

"Hey, Josh! Turn on the floodlight and shine it out into the yard. I think, I saw something move out there," he ordered.

"There's nothing out there, but the dead scum of the earth," said the driver, followed by a burst of laughter from the State Trooper.

"You just wished, you saw something out there. Your mind is so bored, from sitting on your sore ass all day. You want some action, don't you, kid even, if it's imaginary," Josh ribbed him sarcastically. Private Waters marched over to them, zipping up his fatigues.

"I'm telling you, I saw and heard something moving in the field over there, on the right."

"What do you think it was? It might have been a raccoon," said the Trooper.

"Well, we'll never know now will we, if we don't turn on the damn light and see."

"OK, keep your pants on and close your eyes" as the tank driver reached down for the controls. He flipped the toggle switch, and the burst of light beamed through the eerie evening fog. Private Waters couldn't see anything in front of the tank, so he climbed up to the spotlight and moved it along the gate. Then he made a pass along the infirmary to reveal the charred wreckage from the missile mishap earlier.

"What a freaking mess that is," said the State Trooper, lighting up another smoke.

"You can say that again! Those flyboys, really screwed things up, big time," said Waters, passing the light up at the guard tower. The correctional officer covered his eyes and flipped them off, for temporarily blinding him.

"Hey, knock it off, asshole," cursed the angry guard.

The tank crew laughed, as the searchlight powered its way through the twisting mists of fog, along the perimeter of the enormous red wall surrounding the yard. It amazed them how big it was, when the light illuminated the massive brick fortress in the darkness. The dew drops sparkled, as the light shined along the rows and rows of glistening, razor wire, wrapped on top of the wall.

"Hey, stop there! What was that?" asked the State Trooper, pointing at the field. The layer of fog swirled, like thick smoke hovering just above the ground. "There! Do you see that?" he cried out again.

"What the hell? There's nothing out there, but dead bodies lying in the fog," said Josh.

"Shine the light lower on the ground," he said, walking up to the metal gate and squinting.

"The darn fog is so thick, I can't see what's moving out there, but now, I can hear it, too."

"What do you hear?" asked Private Waters, reluctantly.

The overweight sex magnate turned around dumbfounded and said, "Eating sounds?"

"Hah! That's pretty funny there, Jerry. You have a wild imagination yourself," said Josh. "Eating? That's all you law enforcement guys think of, is eating and sex," he laughed.

"Shush! If you'd close that pie hole, you dummy, and listen, you'd hear it, too," said Waters.

"I've been driving this damn tank so long; I can't hear nothin'. What do you hear, Private?"

"Well, I'm not sure, but it sounds more, like a gnawing sound," he grimaced.

"Start the engine and turn the forward exhaust blowers on high. Let's try to blow that fog out of the way, so we can see what the hell is going on out there," said Waters.

"Good call there, soldier boy," shouted the State Trooper. The Abrams diesel cranked up, which shook the ground that the trooper was standing on, as the driver turned the machine a little to the left to give the blowers a better angle to feed the exhaust into the yard. They had to wait a minute for the engine's power generator to warm up, and then the driver flipped the switch to the forward blowers. Waters noticed, the tower guard shining his spotlight into the dark yard, too.

The light beams crisscrossed, each other's paths, as they flashed over the blanket of white mist covering the ground. The trooper was on his radio, as he walked forward to the chain-link fence, trying to get a better view. The driver then flipped on the headlights and then the blowers. The forced air gushed out along the ground, rolling back the fog to unveil the mysterious sounds that were emanating from the yard.

"RATS!" reported the Trooper, who was now back pedaling to the tank. Then he climbed up on it for protection. Private Waters stood up in disbelief, as the fog rolled away to reveal a moving sea of rodents. The furry swarm, scampered over the dead corpses in the prison yard, feeding on the lifeless carcasses. The tank driver closed the hatch and viewed the onslaught from the camera that was now recording the event and streaming the live feed to the command center, inside the prison.

"What in the blue blazes is that?" cried Warden Stephens, pointing to the monitors.

"Good, God! They are rats! Millions of them!" cried Chief Bunn, "Don't you ever exterminate those things, Stephens?" Bunn spurned.

The general got on the radio and asked who was sending the live feed, but, there was no answer. Captain Tatum, Warden Stephens, Chief Bunn, and the rest watched the rat feast, as they gleaned the dead, like a wave of locusts, decimate a field of grain. Flesh and bone alike, disappeared before their very unbelieving eyes.

171

The infestation was mind-numbing, as the rank and file stood motionless, witnessing the horrific event, before them.

"The rats are gnawing through the stiffs, like they're a big piece of cheese," commented Bunn.

"I don't know where they came from, but I'm sure that thing in the SHU, has something to do with all of this," reported Captain Ron to the others.

He'd just finished explaining, what had happened earlier in the Special Housing Unit, previous to the episode that was happening outside of his office walls. He walked over to the barred windows and watched the vermin feeding on the inmates and officers lying in the yard. He saw the tank sitting in the gateway, as the floodlights pierced the vapors covering the yard. It made him reflect back to his childhood, when he discovered a red, ant pile in an empty lot, near his home in Topeka. Tatum and his brother would catch spiders, in glass mason jars and then sacrifice them to the ravenous red ants that dismembered the spiders in a matter of seconds. Thousands of them swarmed over the arachnid aliens, who tried to crawl their way to safety, but were overpowered by the vast numbers of the red army. Ron remembered a pungent, sickening smell that came from the ant pile.

Finally, after many weeks of scrupulous entertainment, the two boys were tired of the sacrificial ceremonies and decided to destroy the ant pile to show their supremacy over the ants, dousing the three-foot high, pine-needle nest with gasoline and then lighting it on fire. Ron smiled, reflecting as he and his older brother danced, like natives in a war party, burning the ants at the stake. The flames shot up over fifteen feet high, as the cursed red army burned in a fiery epitaph.

"Burn 'em!" he barked, to the mesmerized bunch of officials who stood doing nothing, but watching the onslaught—just as Ron and his brother once did with the ants years ago.

"What?" cried Chief Bunn.

"You heard me. Fry the little bastards, before they come in here and eat us next."

"Good, God, man! Do you think they could?" cried Warden Stephens.

"Do you just want to stand around and find out?" said Captain Tatum, sardonically.

"General, does that tank have a flame thrower in it?" asked the prison captain.

"This is General Owens speaking. I want that tank at the south gate to torch the yard inside the prison, immediately," he ordered the commanding Colonel outside the front command post.

"Roger that, General!' responded Waters.

"Private Waters, did you receive that command, over?"

"Yes Sir, Colonel."

"Then light it up!" ordered, the Colonel.

The rank and file joined Captain Ron at the windows and watched as the Abrams M1 ignited the tip of the cannon and then spewed out, a seventy-foot flame. The bright light from the horizontal torch shimmered, across their faces as the yard burst, into a wall of fire.

"This is Captain Tatum. Open the south gate and let that tank in," he ordered.

The forty-foot-high gate rolled back, allowing the tank to get closer. The Abrams thundered forward, it's turret turning right, then left rotating the flamethrower, across the yard and scorched the yard full of vermin.. They scrambled everywhere, but were soon engulfed in the blazing inferno. Captain Ron smiled again, as he thought of his past days, as a young pyromaniac in Topeka.

The inferno roared and brought many inmates in B-Block to their windows, wondering what was going on in the yard. They watched the hose of flames incinerate their fellow inmates and whatever else, was crawling on the ground, that was too small, for them to see. They grew angrier, thinking that this was no way to treat their friends, or their enemies that is, to be turned into ash by their oppressors.

"Bubba! Look at this, quick," said LT, who saw everything outside their eight-inch window.

"Good gravy! What's goin' on out der?" cried Bubba.

"I don't know, Bubba. But I got's a real bad feelin' about dis. I sure do," said LT. Then they heard the other inmates screaming and shouting obscenities from their cells, as they objected to the carnage being performed outside their windows.

"You freaking Nazis!" shouted some, thinking of the Holocaust.

The hatred erupted all throughout the prison complex, as the guards tried to explain what was happening. The inmates went crazy again, thinking that they were being lied to, and they would be next in line to be cremated after, what happened in the yard earlier that day. Their paranoid feelings escalated, as fear and hatred drove many of the men to the brink of madness being locked helplessly, in their cells. Men began fighting, inside their units and then killing each other, as the massive, paranoid delusion spread faster than the fire in the prison yard. The guards used fire hoses to try and calm the riotous criminals down, but that only fueled their intense retribution. The alarms were sounded again, warning that the complex was under another siege. The command center inside Captain Ron's office lit up, as the barred gates rolled closed to seal off all the main exits in or out of the rotunda.

"This is insane," shouted Chief Eldon Bunn, covering his ears to protect them from the wretched electronic squelching of the alarm's security system.

"Somebody has to do something, before we all die in this place," shouted Warden Stephens.

Captain Tatum and his armored battalion of henchmen ran out of his office to the rotunda's main switchboard and control center at the hub of the prison. He knew how to handle things from there, because it was the nerve center of the complex. He tried to focus on the emergency procedures that he had trained for all these years, but he never imagined that it would ever, become a reality.

Chapter 17

"You ain't seen nothing, yet!"

Chaplin Barnett sprinted down the marble corridor of B-Block, witnessing the onslaught of the inmates. It was hard to breathe from all the smoke that drifted into the facility, from the burning carnage just outside the wall. She saw the flames shoot up into the sky through the glass block windows, which illuminated the interior arches of the block ceiling, sixty-feet high. Her flesh crawled with fear, as she heard the corpses crackle like kindling from the intense heat in the fiery prison yard. The pulsing, shrill sound of the alarms hurt her eardrums as she too, put her hands over her ears to try to protect them from the noise pollution. She backed up into a corner of the breezeway, screaming futilely, for the sirens to quit their vengeful singing when she noticed something very strange crawling along the ceiling, like a large spider. The chaplain thought she was hallucinating from hysteria and shook her head to try to focus her vision.

"My mind must be playing tricks on me because, I just saw an inmate crawling upside down on the ceiling," she said to herself. She again looked up into the shadows and knew that what she saw was for real. Her mouth dropped open, as she watched the orange-clad "spiderman" scamper along the beams, like nothing she'd ever seen before. Her hair stood up on the back of her neck when the thing stopped and rested in the rafters near the top gangway of the third tier of cells. It was a man with long dreadlocks, and he was making strange gestures over the cells.

"What is he doing up there?" she asked herself, looking around to see if anybody else, was a witness to her sighting. Her mind raced, and she no longer heard the blaring alarms now distracted by something far more sinister. His dark form moved around the rafters and then suddenly he stopped and turned around, sensing that someone was watching him—or it. Slowly, it crouched down as it realized that it was a woman, who was watching his every move.

Another burst of flame lit up the night from the five-ton dragon outside the wall. Finally, the Christian woman faced her enemy. Her eyes grew wide as the snake-headed shadow hissed violently, making obscene gestures at the frightened woman below.

Chaplain Barnett felt numb, as she hugged the wall to try to hide somehow from the advancing spider that was crawling down the glowing, block windows. She knew, she was in danger, but she couldn't move until a window burst from the intense heat outside.

The explosion rocked the corridor, as flame jetted inside B-Block, and a string of rodents that were on fire themselves jumped through the flames. The burning rats didn't get far into the corridor before Chaplain Barnett turned and ran for her life. She knew that the thing was after her. Her heart pounded, and she started to cry as she wondered, what in Heaven's name—no, scratch that—what in Hell's name that thing chasing her was. She made the corner and was headed down the main hall into the rotunda, when she met Captain Ron and his men. She was so relieved to see them, as they motioned for her to get down while they made a line formation and began to open fire on the creature behind her.

The demon slid across the marble floor on his rear end, like a baseball player would slide into second base at a ballgame. The lawmen's bullets riddled the marble floor behind him, barely missing him. He vanished behind a huge stone column as Captain Ron ordered his men to surround him. They thought they had him cornered, but how do you corner something that can crawl vertically up seventy feet and run on all fours, like a dog upside down on a vaulted ceiling?

Chaplain Barnett observed the twelve officers, as they continued the barrage of rifle fire, trying to hit the creature, like some video arcade game. Pieces of cement block and dust rained from the roof as they missed their moving target, and it disappeared along the thick rafters in C-Block.

"Lieutenant, take five men and kill that thing," Tatum ordered.

"Are you OK, Brittney?" he asked gruffly, holding out his thick hand to help the Chaplain up from the floor.

The sirens finally turned off, and everyone was shouting at each other still.

"Ah, yes, I think so. What was that thing, Ron?" she asked.

"An inmate named Watini—Mutumbo Watini, and he's a real freak, Chaplain Barnett. He has slain about twenty men, including Deputy Warden Dodd and Dr. Albert."

"What? Dodd and Albert? How? Where? I don't understand, Captain. What's going on in here?" she cried. Dr. Albert was her best friend even though he was an atheist. They used to make jokes to relieve each other's pent-up frustrations after working such long and difficult days at the penitentiary.

"We found them all filleted like fish, and they were hanging upside down in the SHU."

"Oh, my God! How horrible!" she wiped her tears with some tissue from her coat pocket.

"Yeah, it gets worse!" the Captain said, reluctantly.

"What on earth do you mean? How could it get worse?"

"Well, I'm sure their deaths were some kind of ritualistic killing. I ain't never seen nothing like it in all my career as a law enforcement officer.

"What makes you believe that they were a ritual killing?" she queried.

"You saw that thing!" he pointed down the corridor. "No human being can do that, and no human would treat others the way that thing did. It's been nothing but trouble since we brought him here," he barked and then straightened up as if he had just thought of something.

"Captain, describe what you saw in the SHU," she prodded, nervously.

"Candle burning in the interrogation room, a skinned rat was stuffed in the Doc's mouth, and they were all gutted, like in a deer hunt. What was really weird, were all the 'blood signs' painted on all the walls. Everywhere you looked, there are symbols painted in the inmates' and staff's blood in the entire Special Housing Unit."

"What?" she gasped.

"Yeah, you heard me right. It killed everyone in the SHU, including the inmates. The poor bastards were butchered in their own cells, just like Dodd and Albert. I can't prove it yet, but I think Watini is behind everything that's happened here during the past forty hours. Why do you—well, I don't know what the reason is, but I have never seen such a mess in during my whole career, either. I mean look at this place! It looks like a battlefield."

"Captain, take me to the SHU so I can see these signs that you are talking about. Maybe I can help determine what they mean. I studied anthropology in college, before I became minister. You know—primitive cultures and what not. Maybe there's a clue as to who this guy is," she said.

"I don't know, Chaplain. I don't think you could handle all the bloodshed and dead bodies in there—especially seeing Doc that way. God! It's just inhuman! But, then again, you might have a point. It seems this thing is from Hell and who better than you to fight it? Er,, uh, I mean to say …" he stumbled.

"No, you are probably right.

"The more I try to comprehend what I just saw and what's been happening in this prison, is not normal under any circumstances," she admitted, shaking some dust and fragments out of her red hair.

They were interrupted by more gunfire that echoed throughout C-Block as the radio squelched in mass confusion. "No, there! There, over there . . . AAAAAGGGGGHHHH!" cried the garbled voices.

The shooting stopped and both had the hair standing up on the back of their necks. They knew the answer before it was asked. The silence was the only answer they needed as, they all turned and ran back to the rotunda.

There were more National Guardsmen now, patrolling the corridors, and more outposts were set up inside the prison corridors. The main desk looked like a military command center as General Oswald barked orders to other officers, who then barked his commands to the waiting soldiers standing in formation. Over five hundred more soldiers, were inside the complex trying to restore law and order to the insane asylum. Captain Tatum didn't like losing control over the prison, but he had no choice. Things were totally out of his control, and he knew it. Chaplain Barnett could see it, as she watched his face grimace by the mere presence of the military and Chief Bunn's stern looks, as they passed by the control desk.

"You should be ashamed of yourself, Captain!" hollered Warden Stephens as he pointed his finger at him. He was blaming him for all the devastation surrounding them. Tatum turned toward Chaplain Barnett, grinding his teeth, and trying not to curse at them as he kept on walking down the hallway, past his office, and into the corridor to the Special Housing Unit.

"You know, Brittney, I'm not real religious or much of a churchgoer, but I have a funny feeling that we will all need your prayers, before this thing is over," he said somberly.

She reached up, tried to put her arm around the big lawman's back, and said, "Don't feel bad, Captain. There's always room in Heaven for one more hypocrite!"

They both chuckled, as he locked another clip of ammo into his M19 rifle. He ordered the remaining seven officers to stay tight and awake, and to look everywhere, including the ceilings. He unsnapped his dusty holster and handed the chaplain his 9mm pistol and winked at her.

"Here, take this. You still know how to shoot this thing, don't you?" he grinned, ribbing her about her past marksmanship. She defeated him in the Bureau of Prison's regional pistol championship the previous year.

They used to date one another, when she first arrived five years prior ,but after she got to know Captain Ron and his sinful ways, they soon broke up. He wasn't a God-fearing man, but he respected Chaplain Barnett's intelligence and her good looks. She was a prize worth catching, but her commitment to her faith in God and her abstention from having sex, until she was married, made her a target for jokes among the staff at Heavenworth.

The Chaplain cocked back the safety, loaded a bullet into the chamber, flipped the safety off, and held it by her side, like the professional she was. Smiling, she said, "You ought to know by now that I don't mess around, when it comes to men or guns. I figure I can handle them both just fine, thank you very much."
Some of the officers laughed at her cocky self-confidence, just like one of the guys, not knowing her talents.

The Captain gave her a big grin and said, "Yeah, don't I know it! The only thing is, we ain't shootin' at targets, if you know, what I mean?"
The Chaplain swallowed hard, knowing exactly, what he meant. It meant that when it came down to it, could she shoot to kill, if her life depended on it, or anybody else's, for that matter? O,r would she choose life and not death, of another human being according to her beliefs? She looked up at the vaulted ceiling, searching the shadows along the steel beams. She came to the conclusion, as she squeezed the rubber grip tightly that this was not a human being they were after.

185

Chapter 18

"Billy?"

P rivate Waters lit up a cigarette for the first time in his life. He needed something to remove the foul smoky, taste from his mouth, after torching the charred corpses, lying before him. His hands shook, as he took a deep inhale and then coughed. The driver's hatch sprung open, and Billy's head popped up from the hole. "Damn, it looks like hell, out here!" he said.

"You can say that, again, Billy!" said Colonel Waters, spitting out some tobacco, that was stuck on his tongue. "How can you stand to smoke these awful things?" he moaned, as the driver lit one up, too.

"I dunno. Just a bad habit I picked up in high school, I guess," Billy answered.

They surveyed the battlefield of debris, while hot embers glowed eerily in the darkness, reminding them of the remnants of a brush fire. Skulls popped apart, like hot kernels of popcorn cooking in a kettle. The black smoke rolled up into the air, leaving a haze trapped in the skyline turning the moon, into a blood red orb.

"Look at that moon, would ya? This place gives me the willies. I sure would hate to be inside this place, or even work here for that fact," said the driver.

"I don't know about that! Those guards make damn good money. Better pay, than what we're getting, sitting out here freezing our butts off in this dam fog," cried Waters again.

"Man, you sure do whine a lot. Why don't you quit the guard, if you hate it so much?"

"I dunno. I guess I like shootin' things. Where else, can I get paid to do that?"

"I dunno. Hey, where do ya suppose all those rats came from?"

"Jeeze, ya got me! I think every damn rat in the county was out there. I ain't never seen nothing that crazy in all my life, that's for sure," said Waters, flipping the cigarette into the air.

"Yeah, me neither! It was like out of some horror movie or sumthin, ya know?" said Billy.

"You can say that again. It smells real bad. All of them dead bodies burning up out there. Boy, we fried those rats up big time, didn't we, Billy?" cheered Waters.

"Yep! We had us a bona-fide barbeque. Yes, sirreee! We flamed their tails, right off their asses," laughed Billy.

"Yeah, all clear back here, General," reported Colonel Waters on his radio.

"Is the infestation over?" asked the four starred General.

Waters flipped on the floodlight and swept the field, revealing nothing, but ash and embers. "I'd say we got them pretty good, General."

"Good work, men. We're going to wait until morning to clear out whatever casualties, or what's left of their remains, that is. You won't be relieved until then, so stay at your posts until further notice," ordered the General.

Waters cursed, thinking they would get relieved, and he could make his hunting party later.

"Sum bitch!" he cursed again.

"Now what's wrong?" asked Billy.

"I was supposed to go deer huntin' with my brother and cousins. Dang this job, anyway," said Waters, as he took off his helmet and scratched his head. Billy didn't say anything. He fired up the tank and rolled it back a hundred feet next to the gate entrance and shut it off.

The guard in the east tower went back inside and fell asleep. It was all the action he could handle for the day. Waters bummed another smoke from Billy and lit it up like he'd been smoking for years. He climbed off the Abrams and walked over to water the bush again.

"Man, you pee a lot! You're worse than my old lady," sighed Billy.

"Oh, kiss my butt, Billy," said Waters, as he waved his wand over the bushes.

Again, Billy didn't say anything as Colonel Waters zipped up and walked back over to the tank, taking the cigarette out of his mouth. He said, "What's the matter, Billy? Cat got your tongue, or sumthin'?" He snickered and walked around to the front of the Abrams. Billy was gone.

"Billy? Billy, where are you?"

The fog returned, rolling along the ground, as the heat dissipated from the field of skeletal remains. Waters walked a circle around the tank looking for his partner. Just as, he came back in front of the tank, he heard a sound, like someone spitting loudly.

"Billy, is that you?" he asked.

Suddenly, an Army helmet dropped in front of him and bounced off the tank track, spinning in a circle, upside down. Colonel Waters jumped back a bit, shocked at the helmet that was wobbling, before him.

"Billy? OK, dammit this ain't funny," Waters said as, he bent over and picked up the helmet off the damp ground. He looked around, but didn't see any sign of Billy anywhere.

189

He set the helmet down on the tank by Billy's porthole, heclimbed back on the turret, and turned the spotlight, back on again.

"OK, pecker neck. I'll find you now," Waters chuckled, swinging the light around in the fog. "Nothing!" he said, shaking his head confused.

"BIILLLLYYYYY!" he shouted, into the silence of the night. "Now, where did he go? He knows better than to leave his post," thought Waters to himself.

Suddenly, he heard a loud belch come from the side of the tank. He looked around and saw nothing.

"Billy, is that you? BILLLLEEEEEEEEYYYYYYAAAAAHHHH!"

"PPPPPFFFFFFTTTTTTT!"A twenty foot long, sticky tongue struck outward, with the speed of a cobra, nailing Waters right in the face. His body jerked violently upward, into the night and then disappeared. The floodlight's, beam swirled along the top of the gun turret and finally, came to rest in front of the empty tank, as another helmet ejected into midair, banging off of it. The fog slowly parted along the roadway, as something very large was heading toward a snoring noise, coming from the east tower's silhouette, against the blood-red moon.

Chapter 19

"Whatever it is, it's really BIG!"

Two correctional officers, were standing just outside the wooden door of the prison chapel, as Chaplain Barnett researched the library, with her trustworthy assistants, Derek and Kyle Jackson, Terry Porebski, Lance Smith, Mongo, Bubba, and LT. She was looking for a book entitled, Demons, Witches and Warlocks. The library was extensive consisting of a couple of thousand books that were categorized by different religions. She probably could have found it herself, but she wanted the help of her prayer partners, knowing the inmates were born-again believers and were fearless in prayer. After spending time in the SHU with Captain Ron, she realized that they were dealing with some kind of demonic presence, especially after her little run in with inmate Watini in B-Block.

Captain Tatum went back to report to the command center to see if they, could find Watini crawling around the walls on the cameras. The only problem was, that the cameras were all facing downward toward the corridors, not up towards, the ceilings.

They had to get some kind of surveillance, temporarily set up to do that. Captain Ron didn't believe in ghosts, or goblins and figured Watini to be a homicidal maniac, running loose in his prison. He wanted to kill him, as soon as possible, before Watini killed any more inmates, or personnel. "It's got to be here, somewhere," she said, reaching up to a high shelf and exposing her bare stomach to Lance Smith, who was looking, on a shelf below her. He had just been introduced to her, because he was Porebski's cell mate. When she came to visit them earlier, Lance immediately fell in love. Her beautiful green eyes were so full of warmth, they glowed with Brittney's intelligent charm and demeanor. She shook his hand firmly when they first met, and Lance, liked her grip. She was not like other women he knew, and she was something for sore eyes, after being around all these brigands.

"It was no coincidence why everyone became a Christian," he thought, after meeting an angel like her. He just didn't get it and was still living in a carnal state of thinking. His libido was still in the past—when he could woo any woman he wanted. Brittney looked down and caught him gazing upon her flesh. She pulled out a book and dropped it on his head.

"Ouch," he moaned rubbing his noggin.

"Oh, I'm sorry, did that hurt?" she asked softly.

"Ah, well sort of," Lance said, feeling for a lump.

"You should pay more attention to the task at hand, rather than staring at my stomach," she jabbed.

"Sorry! No offense. It's just been so long since, I mean, I, er-uh." Lance stumbled, as she turned away, embarrassing him. They all laughed at Smith, which made him feel even worse, as he limped over to the drum set.

"Smooth move, hot dog. You really know how to score brownie points, don't you?" snickered Mongo, who was reading a newspaper in a chair.

"Found it!" shouted Derek, pulling the book off the top shelf of the bookcase. "It was lying flat and stuffed back in the corner. No wonder we couldn't find it. It looks like someone was hiding it, Chaplain," he said, blowing the dust off the cover and handing it to her.

"Good job, Brother Derek. She opened it immediately and thumbed through the pages, quickly scanning over the pictures.

"Just what is it, you're looking for, Chaplain?" asked LT as he looked over her shoulder.

"Sit down, you guys, and I'll be honest with you," she motioned to the red, folding chairs.

She sat down at her desk and browsed the book some more until they were all settled. Then she leaned over to see if the guards were listening outside of the door.

"Well, I'm not sure if, they want me to tell you this, but I'm telling you for your own protection," she whispered, as she leaned forward. "After I left B-Block during the riot, I was walking down the corridor when I could see the Army tank outside flaming the rat infestation out in the yard."

"Say what?" asked Bubba, who was now standing up and dwarfing everyone with his size. "Rats? What rats? The only rats are the ones doing time," he jested.

"Real funny, big man. Let's listen to what the Chaplain has to say, shall we?" asked Kyle, so Bubba sat back down in his chair. He was deathly afraid of those little dogs, as he called them.

"As, I was saying, I was walking, when I felt something weird, like someone was watching me and it wasn't the inmates in B-Block. My skin crawled and my senses tingled, so I stopped and looked around. I didn't see anyone except the guards hosing inmates down in their cells. Then all of a sudden, a burst of flame lit up the ceiling, and I saw it," she said, closing her eyes. The men swallowed hard listening to her story.

"What do you mean by seeing it?" asked Derek.

"I'm not sure, but I think it's a demon running loose in this place. His name is Mutumbo Watini. He transferred in late last night and since his arrival, all of these unexplained events have taken place in this facility."

"You mean the frogs and the riot in the yard today are <u>his</u> doings?" asked Bubba, wide-eyed.

"Maybe. I'm not sure what to think yet, but I saw him crawling along the ceiling, upside down like a giant spider, in an orange jumpsuit," she said quietly, looking again at the door.

"What? That's crazy! A spider?" barked Lance. "That's preposterous. You've been working here too, long, Chaplain," he said in disbelief.

"Hey, jerk wad! If she said she saw it, then she saw it," said Mongo, making a fist at Lance.

"Go ahead, Ms. Barnett and excuse my celley for interrupting you," said Porebski, politely.

"Very well. When it saw me, it began to chase me down the corridor into the main hallway, where I ran into Captain Tatum and his men. They froze when they saw me and told me to hit the ground, before they opened fire at it. I hit the ground, holding my ears from the noise, but somehow, they missed him with automatic weapons at close range. It crawled up a fifty-foot stone pillar and escaped, crawling among the rafters into C-Block.

Captain Ron told me they were hunting Watini down, because he had murdered all the inmates in the SHU as well, as all the guards. He took me down to see the evidence, and that's why I'm researching this book," she said nervously. The Christian inmates noticed her nervousness and were convinced that she had witnessed something frightful enough to be shaking so much, around all of them. She began to cry again, as she explained the ritualistic slaughter and the evil signs painted in the blood along the walls of the SHU. The strong men looked like schoolboys, sitting around a campfire and listening to horror stories told by their camp counselor. None of them ever imagined that they and their Christian beliefs would be faced with something as horrific, as this.

> "That's why you guys are all here with me now! I convinced Captain Tatum to let you men out to not only guard me, but to help me pray for wisdom and guidance during this awful siege. Captain Tatum, like the others, doesn't believe in God or Jesus Christ, but I know that you all do, and you believe in the Bible. We have to pray for God's help during this demonic crisis and try to help them all to combat this thing whatever it is," she implied convincingly.

Lance looked in disbelief, thinking they were all buying into her hysterical nonsense. He kind of was a believer in God, but not to the extent the rest of his miscreant friends did.

It was hard for him to just take for granted that the stories she was telling them were real. The door opened and one of the guards entered the room. He was dressed in black battle fatigues and wearing full-body armor. He posed a real threat as he held his M19 close to his Flak jacket.

"Is everything OK, Chaplain?" he inquired, noticing that she had been crying. She blew her nose with some tissue, not realizing that she had been sobbing so loudly.

"Yes, yes. I am OK, Officer. I'm just upset about what has happened today, that's all. There's nothing to worry about but thank you for checking on me. I trust these guys no matter what," she said confidently, breaking into a small smile at him.

The correctional officer tipped his helmet at her, like a gentleman, turned and went back out the chapel door. They could all see that he was on the radio, talking to Captain Tatum, who was just checking up on her.

"Man, we got's us a serious situation h'yer, yes we do," said LT as he walked over to the air-conditioner and turned on the fan.

"How we supposed to help ya, Chaplain Barnett? I don't know how ta fight some kind a demon," lamented Bubba, looking at the others faces and seeking solace.

"Listen, Brothers. We don't have to fear this thing, because our God is more powerful than all of the demons in Hell.

"We have to form a prayer circle and hold hands. I'll lead the prayer, but I need you guys to focus on the Holy Scriptures you have all learned in Bible Study Class. You know the ones, where Jesus cast out the demon 'Legion' into the herd of pigs in the field, and then they ran into the lake and drowned. Well, that's what we need to do," she advised.

"Well, we definitely have the pigs to cast the demon into," joked Mongo, referring to the guards. His joke broke the tension, as they all laughed at his quick wit.

"OK, OK, let's keep it together, you guys! This is serious business we're undertaking. What happens, if this thing brings more of his friends in here?" she asked them as she waved her arms in the air.

"You mean, like the frogs and the rats? Do you really think they came from him?" quipped Lance sternly. "Listen, I can't explain what's going on in here, but I don't believe in some demon conjuring up stuff and causing all this commotion. Come on now, really?" he added.

"Well, what do you think is going on, Mr. Smith? You think you have all the answers, but you haven't seen, what I have. Why would I lie to you or fabricate a story like this?" she asked.

"How do I know? Maybe to make us believe there really is a God," he mocked.

Then Chaplain Barnett became angry. She rose to her feet and stomped over to the doubter. She stared Lance right in the eyes, as if looking into his very soul. He became a little nervous as her green eyes pierced his mockery, searching for the truth.

"Maybe you should leave this chapel, Mr. Smith. We don't need your unbelief jeopardizing our prayers, do we Brothers?" she commanded, as the believers gave their unanimous decision.

"NO!" they all shouted. Lance was shocked and lost his confidence. He stepped back, although he did not take his eyes off their leader. He said, "Look, I don't mean anything by . . ." Chaplain Barnett cut him off. She put her hand over his mouth before he could say another word, pointed to the door, and shouted for the officer to escort Mr. Smith back to his cell.

He felt bad about having disrupted the group with his doubt and unbelief,f but thought it was probably best, before he caused any more trouble with the "Brotherhood." He stormed out of the chapel and was escorted by one of the officers down the hallway, leaving one officer still guarding the door. The attractive Chaplain turned and took her seat with the men. They respected her for her strong belief and example of leadership.

They all knew she was correct in what she was saying, as they all joined hands and began to pray. They started out with the Lord's Prayer:

"Our Father, who art in heaven, hallowed be thy Name.
Thy Kingdom come, thy will be done, on earth, as it is in Heaven."

Suddenly they were all frozen with terror when they heard a horrendous roar from outside of the chapel: "RRRRROOOOOOOAAAAAAAARRRRRRRRRRRWWWLLLLL!" They squeezed their hands tighter, knowing that what they heard could not have been good. The door flew open as Lance and the guards burst in, shaken by the horrendous roaring sounds that were echoing throughout the complex. A guard looked outside the door, as the lights began to flicker inside the chapel.

"What was that?" cried Bubba, wiggling his knees back and forth, like a little boy.

"It sounded like . . . like a big lion or something," reported Lance, shaking with fright.

"Keep on praying, you guys! It's all a distraction to throw us off guard," cried the Chaplain, holding onto their hands. They continued to pray louder almost shouting, as both guards joined the circle. Chaplain Barnett received knowledge from the Holy Spirit, and she led the prayer warriors through a series of worship.

The lights went out, and another ferocious roar emanated throughout the complex, followed by machinegun fire from the main annex.

The correctional officer's radios squawked, as they prayed.

"Do you see it?" shouted the Army soldier on the other end.

"No! I can't see a thing," another man shouted.

They heard more gunfire and then an explosion from a grenade went off, followed by more rifle fire. Chaplain Barnett didn't hear the others praying and opened her eyes. They were mesmerized by the drama unfolding over the microphones.

"Fall back, men," ordered General Owens, screaming over the battle sounds.

Lance peeked outside the door to see, if anything was down the dark hallway outside of the Chapel. It was silent. Then the lights went out, and the radios went dead, buzzing with interference. Then they heard men's screams of death echoing throughout the empty corridors. Porebski got up from his chair and joined Lance. They both held the door open, as they listened for any signs of life. That's when they saw four soldiers stop in the annex intersection, turn around, and start to fire their weapons. More inmates came to the door when they heard the rifle fire getting closer to them. "Pop, pop, pop, kapow, pop, pop, kapow," the rifles flashed as the soldiers emptied their clips and tried to reload their guns with new ammo.

Three of them were then lifted up in the air as if, snatched up by something. The remaining soldier dropped his rifle from sheer fright and slowly backed into the wall. They were about fifty yards from the Chapel.

"What in the Hell is that?" asked one of the guards, pointing at the hapless victims. The soldiers were screaming for their lives as they squirmed upside down, suspended 30 feet in midair. Then they were lifted a little higher up and vanished from sight. It was hard to see anything clearly because the emergency lighting had turned on from the prison generators. The prayer group had moved cautiously outside and now stood in the wide hallway. They had witnessed the horrifying event. They watched, as the other soldier dropped to his knees, surrendering to the invisible monstrosity. He was paralyzed with fear, as he pleaded for his life. Chaplain Barnett wanted to warn him to run, but none could say a word because, their throats had run dry as if stuffed with cotton. The soldier looked up, hoping the thing had granted him mercy, but a long, bloody tongue shot out from nowhere and snatched him up like a fly off of a flower.

"PPPhhhhhhhhhffffffftttttt!" went the thing's tongue, like an arrow flying through the air and just, as deadly. The tearful guardsman was gone. The Christians couldn't believe their eyes. Their minds were numb from trying to comprehend logic, as opposed to what they had just seen.

"Noooooo!" cried the Chaplain in tearful agony, pleading to the invisible force at the end of the hallway. Then without notice, the soldiers' bloody, metal helmets were spat out, like watermelon seeds and bounced like basketballs down the corridor toward the frightened bystanders. They all watched as the helmets slid to a stop just in front of them. Bubba shook, like the cowardly Lion, as one of the empty helmets spun like a coin and came to rest in front of him. Their mouths gaped wide, speechless at the relentless episode, until the invader noticed them and let out another gurgling roar of disapproval, "AAARRRRROOOAARRRWWWLLL."

"I think it's time to go, guys," said Derek Jackson to the others.

"Run for your lives!" shouted Mongo, tripping over Bubba.

"Come on, man, move it!"

The group broke out in a dead heat, sprinting down the concrete corridor, as fast as they could. They felt the earth tremble beneath their feet, as the huge monster thundered in pursuit. Its head knocked out the sodium vapor bulbs, as it gained ground chasing them. Kyle Jackson looked over his shoulder and could see flashes of the large hulking beast, as it destroyed the marble walls behind them.

"Hurry up, everyone! It's breathing down my neck," shouted LT, as he literally could smell the thing's hot, foul breath coming from behind them. They burst through the double doors to the prison's ancient gymnasium and ran for their lives across the shiny wood floor of the basketball court, to the far south end of the gym.

"Hold it here. I think we lost it," said Lance, his wound from the rifle, was bleeding, badly. He stopped the others, as they gasped and tried to catch their breath.

SSMMAAASSSSHHHH!

Suddenly, the entire wall structure where they had just entered, exploded into pieces, as the infuriated beast roared with discontent.

"RRRROOOOOAAAAAAARRRR"

They watched in horror, as the behemoth, bumped into the iron crossbeams that supported the arched ceiling above them. It bent up in half, breaking out the glass block windows, along the rooftop, as the demon struggled to get to its human meal. The thick iron beams, slowed it down long enough for the two correctional officers, who couldn't see anything, but opened fire anyway, trying to hit the invisible target that was towering before them.

"Bam, bam, bam, bam, bam, bam, bam, bam, bam, bam... ping, bam, bam." However, the bullets had no effect. They just disappeared into the thing's body mass, while the shell casings danced on the hardwood floor. The guards shot in a spread pattern, guessing its dimensions at fifty-feet high and a width of thirty feet. The rounds were a direct hit but still had no effect, on the invisible creature's advance.

"Chaplain, I've got an idea. Follow me downstairs, to the equipment lockers. Whatever that thing is, it's too big to go underground. Do you have your pass keys?" asked Derek Jackson.

"No, I don't. I left them in my desk in the chapel," she shouted over the gunfire.

"Here, take mine," shouted one of the guards, removing his off his key chain. Just as he tossed her the key, his body snapped up into the air and disappeared. The other guard continued to fire until, he was next. Mongo, Porebski, and LT all panicked and ran in the opposite direction from the others. "We'll try to divert it, Derek," shouted Porebski. He ran about twenty feet and then stumbled to the floor, narrowly escaping the arm swing of the creature. Three giant claws raked against the sheetrock, shredding it apart, like it was papier-mâché. Porebski got back on his feet and ran as fast as he could, to catch up to Mongo and LT.

"Boy, that was a close one," he smiled in relief running back out from where they had just come.

It was just enough time for the others to run under the overhead track, grab the downstairs railing, and hurry below, except for Lance and Bubba. A sign pointed down to the locker room where they were seeking shelter from the enraged beast. The thing's tongue zipped out, barely missing Lance, and hit the emergency fire hose closet that was mounted on the wall.

"I have an idea," said Lance to a wide-eyed Bubba.

"Quick! Turn on the water and help me hold the hose." The others ran downstairs, but Lance grabbed the brass nozzle of the hose and aimed it into the air in front of him.

"What are you doin' man? Is you crazy?" shouted Bubba, pulling down the red lever to "on." The hose straightened out rapidly, and a powerful spray of water blew out of the nozzle. Lance sprayed the creature, making it scream with rage. Bubba held onto the end of the hose with his partner, as Lance adjusted the spray nozzle into a jet stream. The torrential jet of water pelted the beast in the face, giving it visible form as the water doused over the angry monster.

"AAAAARRRROOOOOOOUUUUUUGGGGHHHH!" it shrieked in pain, from the hard blast of water.

"Hey man, its working! I don't think, he likes it!" shouted Lance, waving the hose. The two of them were soaked from the overspray, but they focused on battling the giant nemesis.

Lance aimed higher and blasted it in the eyes, turning the creature backward, as it struggled to see. It hit its head on a crossbeam and stumbled sideways, trying to gain its balance. Lance instinctively aimed the stream directly under, its hind leg. Its foot slipped out from underneath it, and the creature crashed to the floor with a thunderous BOOOOOMMM! It rocked the gymnasium, shaking the very foundations of Heavenworth.

"It kinda looks like a dinosaur," shouted Lance, to Bubba.

"Yeah, it kinda looks like a big ol' frog with nasty-ass claws," Bubba screamed back.

He looked over and saw Chaplain Barnett and the others shouting for them to come over. Lance winked at her and gave her a big smile, as if he had the situation under control, until her eyes grew wide, and she pointed at the creature. Lance quickly turned, but it was a second too late. The reptile's tail swung across the floor and batted the two heroes across the room. Bubba went through the wall, taking the brunt of the hit, while Lance skidded into a hydroplane over the hardwood floor. He bounced off the bleachers and into the corner of the gym. He was unconscious from the attack and appeared to be dead. The Chaplain screamed in horror and tried to rescue the two, but Kyle grabbed her tightly and carried her back downstairs.

"Let me go!" she shrieked, trying to break free from his firm hold. "Chaplain, there's nothing we can do for them right now, not until that thing leaves," he said.

"Kyle's right about that, Chaplain," said Derek, "There ain't nothing we can do except wait it out and hope for the best. Why don't you pray—that's what you're supposed to be doing, ain't it?" Derek locked onto her eyes, making a connection.

The truth hit her hard, and she went limp in Kyle's tattooed arms. He let her go, and she dropped down to the floor and started to weep for the gallant men whose lives, were lost while saving theirs.

Exhausted from fear, Derek and Kyle sat down on a bench against the wall and took a deep breath, praying that the creature would leave. They listened intently, hearing only the fire hose bang unattended on the wood floor. Water trickled down the stairwell, and the lights continued to flicker. Chaplain Barnett raised her head and brushed her thick hair back. She slowly regained her composure, while twisting a rubber band around a new ponytail.

"I don't hear anything! Do you think that toad left?" asked Kyle.

"I can't say. Why don't you run up there and find out?" jabbed his brother.

"Real funny, Lance. Where's the love of God in you, right now?" he bickered, back.

"OK, you two! Knock it off. Let's wait a few minutes before we go back up and check things out. I pray they are all right," she winced, holding her silver cross that was dangling around her soft neck. She took a deep breath and stood up when she saw Derek point to the stairwell, while holding his finger up to his lips, telling her to be quiet. Then he motioned for her to come over to them. She turned around and saw the thing's tongue extend down the railing like a probing sensor. She silently stepped over to the Jacksons and sat down in between them.

The dark, forked tongue shined in the dim light, quivering, like a rattlesnake trying to smell its prey. Chaplain Barnett closed her eyes and prayed that it would leave. Meanwhile, Kyle looked around for something to stab it with. The slithery muscle from the creature's mouth as it slowly came down the stairwell. The putrid, hot smell of death wafted from its gaping mouth at the top of the stairs. The tension continued to grow. They felt like ants on a log, about to be snared by an anteater, as the enormous tongue wiggled right in front of their faces. Kyle's eyes grew wide as saucers. He was thinking that this was going to be it when Chaplain Barnett had a revelation from the Holy Spirit. She popped the precious gift her father gave her—the silver cross from around her neck—and flipped it onto the creature's foul tongue. It retracted in the blink of an eye, and suddenly they heard the creature roar in a painful manner. It seemed to have choked on it or something as it backed away from the stairwell and began coughing violently. It screamed a howl, unlike anything anybody had ever heard before.

"AAARRRRRAAAAAGGGGGGHHHHH," it gagged again, clutching its throat.

Kyle ran up the stairs and watched the green, scaly behemoth gasp for air. It acted, as if it had swallowed hydrochloric acid, as smoke billowed out of its viper holes. The massive creature, finally hocked the deadly piece of jewelry to the floor in a wad of phlegm. The monster seemed totally caught off guard, by what had just transpired.

Kevin grew hopeful, as he studied the giant reptile's behavior. It blinked its blood-red eyes a couple of times and then turned away retreating back out of the flooded gymnasium.

"All right, Chaplain! That was quick thinking on your part," said Derek, smiling in relief. They heard the beast's heavy steps fade away into the distant corridor. "That was so cool! Chaplain, you are my hero," said Kyle hugging her tightly.

"I didn't do anything special. One minute I thought we were goners, and then I heard a voice tell me to throw my cross at the thing's tongue—and instantly, it went bonkers!" she beamed brightly. I know it was the Holy Spirit, because I was holding it when I was praying, and suddenly, I felt very calm and collected. I knew it would work the minute I thought it!"

"Wow! Now, that's cool. I really thought we were all dead men when its tongue, waggled within inches of our faces. I wanted to puke, I was so scared," Kyle laughed nervously. "You should see the size of that thing."

"We did! That water had some kind of effect on it because it became visible, but I wish I had never seen it," said Chaplain Barnett, shaking her head in disgust.

"Well, it reminded me of an overweight, dragon that needed to be on a diet," said Kyle.

"Really? I think it looked more like a big frog with teeth to me," said his brother. "Especially, with that sticky, tongue thing it has."

"It's definitely deadly! I think you are both right! I believe that thing, is a cross between a frog and a dragon. Maybe we should call it a "Frogon!" What do you think?" suggested the fair Chaplain.

"That sounds good to me, but let's just figure a way to kill it, before it kills us," said Derek.

Kyle went over to the phlegm pile and kicked it with his shoe. It reminded him of the green jello, they served in the cafeteria. He made a face, wincing from the smell.

"What is that Kyle?" asked Chaplain Barnett, who walked over to see it for herself.

"Praise the LORD!" she shrieked. "I see my cross in that stuff."

"Yeah, the Frogon coughed it up. It acted like it, was killing him o,r something," said Kyle.

"Yes, Chaplain, your cross saved our lives. I don't think the demon expected a 'Holy Snack' like that, if you know what I mean? It really affected it. Did you see the smoke come out of its nostrils?

"I wonder if, that was from the cross, or maybe because it's made from silver. You know, like silver bullets kill a werewolf," said Kyle.

"OK, Einstein, give it a rest, would you please," begged Derek. He watched Chaplain Barnett pull up her sleeve and reach bravely into the green goo to retrieve her cross.

"I got it," she said joyfully. "It was a graduation present from my father. He's a Pastor, too, and he gave it to me after I graduated from Seminary school. He said it would remind me of our commitment to our faith in Jesus Christ, and it would deliver us from evil," she reflected fondly, scrubbing it off in a puddle of water.

"Well, I guess he knew what he was talking about, didn't he?" said Kyle.

Derek shut the water off to the fire hose and ran over to see if Lance and Bubba were alive.

"Oh! My God! I completely forgot about the others," said the Chaplain, as she wiped the cross off on her coat. She pulled the chain over her head, flipped her hair back over the necklace, and then joined the Jacksons.

Derek found Lance stacked in a corner, resting against the bleachers. He felt his neck for a pulse. "He's alive!" he shouted to the others.

"Praise the Lord!" beamed Chaplain Barnett, running to him. Derek splashed some water on his face and patted it saying, "Lance? Wake up!"

Kyle crawled up on the bleachers, like he would a ladder and walked along the top row to the enormous hole in the wall that Bubba's body had flown through. He saw his good friend's mangled body, lying motionless at the bottom of the floor of the aerobics room next to the gymnasium. He looked back at the others and shook his head sadly. Chaplain Barnett cried, remembering Bubba's confession to her when they first met, and she felt so endeared to the "Big Fella," which was her pet name for him. She knew that if he was dead, then he was alive with Jesus, and she'd meet him in Heaven someday. But, as for Lance, she felt a terrible remorse, thinking that he wasn't saved and that he'd burn in Eternity, without accepting Jesus Christ, as his Lord and Savior. She couldn't help but wonder, if this was all some kind of divine plan from God. She reached for their hands and began praying for those lost souls who were murdered by the demons that were running amok in the prison. They all broke out praying in the "Spirit" against the forces of evil that even they didn't have the words to comprehend.

While they were praying, Lance regained consciousness. "Where am I?" he asked softly. "Man, you're here with us," said Derek, raising him up a bit. Lance coughed and winced in pain, holding onto his ribs.

213

"I think my ribs are broke," he gasped. "Try not to move, Lance. I'll go get some bandages from the locker room," said the Chaplain.

Lance reached for her arm and grasped it firmly saying, "Derek can go get them. I want to talk to you," he coughed again. "It's really important."

Derek rolled up a nearby gym towel, put it under Lance's head, and went back downstairs to get the bandages. He looked for Kyle, but noticed he had gone into the hole to check out Bubba.

The Chaplain scooted closer to Lance, wiping a tear from her eye. "Are those for me?" he grimaced, holding his side. "Some, but the rest are for Bubba. He's dead," she said remorsefully, now holding Lance's head in her lap. "What is it, you wanted to ask me?"

"Well, I think I met God!" he said, looking clearly intoher eyes. They grew wide.

"You saw God?"

"Yeah, at least, I think it was Him. The last thing I remembered was the beast's tail clobbering me. It knocked me out cold, immediately, but then I think I died."

"What are you saying? You are here, alive, and with me now," she smiled warmly.

"I know that, but I remember sliding across the floor, and the next thing that happened, I was floating in the air, looking down at myself, and seeing me lying against these bleachers. Then I saw the creature, and I remembered feeling really angry and wanted to fly over to kill the thing with my bare hands. you know, I felt invincible. Then all of a sudden, I was flying through this vortex of darkness, and I got really scared because I saw my past life experiences flash before me, and I was headed to the proverbial light at the end of the tunnel," he explained, not feeling any pain as he spoke.

"That's very interesting. Then what happened?" she asked, combing her fingers through his wavy black hair.

"Well, I'm not really sure, but as I was flying to the light, I heard voices, er,ah, you know, wait, they were more like screams, calling out my name, and all of a sudden my flight was jerky, like someone was grabbing my legs and trying to tackle me."

He took a deep breath, and then moaned as the pain returned. "I looked back at my feet, and that's when I saw them!" he said, in a bit of a panic.

"Saw them, who?" she quizzed. Lance started to sob uncontrollably, as he said, "The Minions of Hell! They were after me, Chaplain. They were horrible, and they wanted my soul," he cried and rolled his head into her lap, holding tightly to her legs. "I remembered freaking out and kicking them in the face and finally, escaping. Then a warm and peaceful feeling suddenly came over me. The next thing I knew, I was standing alone in a blazing white room. I could barely see the light, was so blinding," he whispered.

"Then I heard Him," Lance continued. "I knew, as sure as I'm here with you now, that it was Jesus, and He was sitting on a throne of white marble and gold. I knew it was the Judgment Seat. That's when I remembered Brother Porebski telling me about our sins being washed away when we accept Jesus Christ as our Lord and Savior," he coughed dryly.

Chaplain Barnett didn't say anything. She just listened to the believer in her lap. "So, you accepted Jesus Christ as your personal Lord and Savior?" she then asked him.

"Of course, I did. Right after the riot in the yard! When we were first on lockdown, Brother Porebski really chewed me out. He said the whole incident, was my fault in the beginning.

He said, I started it, and that I had no idea what I was getting myself into. I agreed with him and listened to him tell me why, I needed to become a Christian and do you know what?"Lance smiled.

"No, what?" said the chaplain.

"I did! I became a Christian and a member of God's Gang, not the other ganags in the prison. I really did feel horrible, after all the bloodshed I saw take place in the yard. My guilt was totally outrageous. That's when brother Porebski witnessed the story about Saul of Tarsus and what an arrogant snob he was, and how he murdered all of those Believers. I really felt a change in me when we prayed that Prayer of Redemption, and I made Jesus, My Lord and Savior," he avowed.

"Oh, that's wonderful! But why did you act the way you did back in the Chapel?"

"Because, I'm immature and wanted to get your attention," he smiled.

"So, you were at the Judgment Seat. Then what happened?" she looked sternly at him.

"Well, He said that I have a lot of work to do, and that I needed to protect you, and to relay a message back to you on how to vanquish the enemy," he winced again.

"JESUS, sent you back here to protect me?" she asked, looking puzzled. Then she dropped his head to the floor with a bang.

"You got some nerve, buster! If JESUS, sent you back to watch over me, then who is going to watch over you and your sore ribs?" she asked, kicking his ribs.

"Yoooowwwccchhh, Chaplain! I really did see JESUS! I wasn't lying about that, but . . . er . . . OK, so I was exaggerating about His orders to watch over you. That doesn't mean that what happened wasn't for real!" he shouted, rubbing his throbbing head. Derek came up from the stairwell and met the fiery Chaplain with the bandages.

"Here you go, Chaplain. I think I got what we need, . . . er, uh . . . where are you going?" he asked.

She didn't say a word, and he looked over at Lance, who was starting to get up off the floor by himself. Befuddled at first, he then understood the acting job that Smith had coordinated, so he could have some alone time with the Chaplain, but by the looks of things, he knew it had backfired on him, whatever his plan.

"What did you do, to get her so riled up?" Derek asked as he walked over to meet him.

"Oh, I just wanted to let her know I care about her and want to watch over her, that's all," Lance admitted

"Here, hold these, you phony, and fix yourself. I'm going to go get my brother. We'll meet in the Chapel, with the others. Try to be serious, about how we're going to survive all of this. Bubba is dead, and you're playing games. When will you ever learn that the world isn't about you, Lance? Grow up!" scolded Derek.

"I'm sorry, Brother Derek. I am truly sorry," he shouted back. He turned and watched the Chaplain storm out of the gymnasium, stomping through the puddles of water on the floor. Lance shrugged, looked up and said, "You see? I told YOU, they wouldn't believe me.

Chapter 20

"We got a plan!"

General Rocky Owens, drew the battle plan on a blackboard, explaining the details to his soldiers in the auditorium of the enormous prison. He was very concerned about the poor recon he had received from the officers, who were seated in the front row. Captain Tatum rubbed his aching head, popped some aspirin, and chased it down with some coffee. He liked his coffee strong with no cream but added some whiskey to it earlier, stirring it with his finger. One of the soldiers stared at the coffee, like a zombie, not listening to the general's ranting. Captain Ron offered him a drink with a gesture and handed it to the guardsman. The young recruit smiled a thank you and took a swallow. His eyes rolled back as he coughed hard from tasting more whiskey than coffee. He quickly handed it back to the Captain who whispered, "That will put some hair on your chest," he chuckled. The kid grinned in agreement and listened in to the Commander.

"OK, men. This Frogon creature, is no longer invisible and was last seen headed into C-Block, I assume to meet up with that demon inmate, Watini.

"The good news is, that we'll be able to trap them in a crossfire, when they come back out into the main annex. We have two machine-gun nests, here and here, blocking the outlets to A and B Blocks. I suggest we use a flame thrower immediately, when they are out into the hub, here," he pointed to the diagram on the board. We will have more than a hundred troops lined up along the sidewalls, divided into two groups of fifty men. Now, I want two bazookas, in those machine-gun nests ready to launch the minute you see them. We're gonna hit em' hard and fast. The minute the flame thrower is clear after the bazookas blast that Beast, I want you all to advance forward and spare no ammunition. We have to stop this thing from leaving the complex at all costs.

"If, we don't contain them here, then God only knows what kind of havoc it could wreak at the base. We got two Apache choppers circling overhead, and they have orders to dump their payload if we fail in our mission. You all know the ordinance those birds are carrying, so I'm warning you: If, the creatures breach the hub, get the hell out of there just as fast as you can, before those birds release Hell on earth.

"Do you copy that, soldiers?" he asked sternly, pushing his helmet back.

"Sir, yes, Sir!" they shouted in unison. "Good! Those new Harpoon missiles, on those birds can demolish this entire complex into a pile of rubble, so make haste and kill those things before they kill us! Synchronize your watches. I have exactly 11:15 p.m. Now, get going. We don't have a lot of time, and we must be ready when the enemy comes. Go ARMY!"

The men grabbed their gear and marched out of the auditorium into the main annex. No one said anything, as they were contemplating the arrival of something more hideous than they have ever imagined. It reminded many of them of a horror picture that they went to, when they were much younger and knew the good guys always won. But this was different. Many of them shot at the invisible creature, but their bullets had no effect on it. However, they were now told that it was visible, and it could be stopped.

The General encouraged them by saying, "You can't kill what you can't see," which made perfect sense to the military. But then again, how many times where they engaged with the supernatural? They marched passed Chaplain Barnett and her unarmed escort of inmates. They all gawked at her beauty and gave her a complimentary wolf whistle.

"Nothing cheers a soldier's heart up, like a pretty woman," said the handsome General, who was passing through the doorway.

"Why thank you so much, General Owens," she blushed, holding her hand out, to be kissed.

He smiled and kissed her hand, much to the ire of the inmates standing next to her.

"Where are you going?" she inquired.

"We're going down to the hub, to ambush that thing and kill it, once and for all."

"Do you think your guns will make a difference?' she barbed.

"Damn straight they will. We're going to hit him hard, with everything we got."

"I hope so, General. We ran into it in the gymnasium about an hour ago. Lance Smith sprayed it with a fire hose, and it suddenly appeared," she explained and introduced Lance.

"Well, I was worried about you, Chaplain. Where have you been?" asked Captain Tatum, sipping his Café Royale.

"She was explaining to me how inmate Smith here battled the creature with a fire hose, of all things," he stopped walking and asked some more questions. "So, when you sprayed this thing, it suddenly appeared?" he interrogated Smith.

"Yeah, I guess so. It turns out to be some kind of giant lizard, or dragon."

"It's a Frogon," said Kyle Jackson, butting in.

"A what?" asked Tatum, somewhat perplexed.

"You heard me, Captain. It's part frog and dragon, so I call it ‚a, Frogon," Kyle grinned.

"Is that, a fact? That would account for its tongue characteristics. Is there anything else, you can tell us about it?" asked the General.

"Well, it's kind of a mossy green color, scaly, has yellowish eyes, big claws, and it's about sixty feet tall and about thirty feet wide, General," reported Derek Jackson.

"It was invisible at first, when it chased us out of the chapel, and then it smashed through the gymnasium wall trying to get to us.

"It zapped two correctional officers, up in an instant with its tongue. It just appeared out of nowhere, and took them up in the air, devouring them whole. Then it came after me and another inmate. Its tongue broke open the fire hose catch, and so we turned the water on to try to buy some time for the Chaplain and the others by spraying water in a jet to hold it at bay," explained Lance.

"You guys are pretty brave," admired the General.

"It acted like it hated the water—until it became visible. Then I sprayed it in the eyes, blinding it temporarily, and it hit its head on a steel beam, which knocked it off balance.

That's when I aimed for his hind foot and soaked the floor behind it. It slipped and fell backward to the floor. Then in a split second, I was knocked out," said Lance. He rubbed the back of his head and stared at Chaplain Barnett, who just wrinkled her nose at him.

"Yeah, it has a tail like an alligator, only it's huge!" said Kyle,

"Well, that's a great report, men. Now, I have a better idea of what were up against," said the general, reaching for his microphone on his shoulder.

"Hey, wait a second. We're not done telling you what happened after that," barked Kyle.

"Not now, men! I have to go. Thanks," the general said as he tipped his helmet, smiled at the chaplain, and gallantly marched off to be with his troops, shouting commands over his microphone. "He didn't want to hear the most important part," whined Kyle, feeling rejected.

"I do, inmate!" growled Captain Ron indignantly, gulping the rest of his drink.

Chaplain Barnett could smell the whiskey on his breath, reflecting on some old memories. It was one of the reasons she no longer went out with the officer. He became rude and very mean when he drank alcohol. She rested against the wall, while Derek tried to explain what had happened with her cross.

The Chaplain thumbed through the thick book of demonology they had found, returning to the chapel. She had grabbed it and her keys, while locking the pistol in her desk. She'd glance up occasionally, from the colorful illustrations of demonic rituals and sacrifice, making sure the Captain and his guard were paying attention to what Derek had to say. She observed Tatum's demeanor and knew only too, well that he hated listening to any inmate about anything. His distain toward convicts was evident, no matter what the situation. His prejudice was deep-seated, and every once in a while, she gave the captain a scowl, correcting his attitude toward the Christian men who saved her life. He'd squeeze his baton, imagining how he'd like to bust their heads open, but he knew the Chaplain would have none of that. He hardly heard a word Derek said, before he interrupted him.

"Well, that's just like you Christians, thinking a cross could thwart a dinosaur. I'm sure it was terrified, as it ran out of the gym crying for its mommy," he mocked, laughing with the other correctional officers who were listening to their fearless leader.

"Well, actually, Captain, that's exactly what happened," said Chaplain Barnett. All of them immediately shut up, when she confronted them with the facts.

"That Frogon, or whatever it is, is a demon, and it was summoned by its Druid Master, inmate Watini.

Doesn't it all make some kind of sense to you that what's happened since Watini's arrival that things got really weird?" she pressed.

"Don't you think, that what's going on around here is a little surreal, or better yet, unbelievable? I mean, an invisible monster that can eat people whole, without stopping. What about the infestation of the frogs and the rats, that ate all those poor souls lying in the yard, earlier? Some of them were your friends. I think you'd better start believing, what we're telling you, because it's the only thing that makes any sense in this insane asylum. Here, look in this book," she turned and showed it to the officers.

"Do you see this picture? It's a story about demon worship and what was known as conjuring. Conjuring is a mystical form of magic, where Satanic High Priests summoned certain demons from the Netherworld," she explained fervently to the lawmen gathered around her. They ogled the picture, and then Captain Ron pointed to it and said, "You mean to tell us that this thing could be for real, and that you think that Watini is behind all of this?" he asked.

"Absolutely! It makes perfect sense, doesn't it? It shows here in this book that these ancient Druid Priests used to sacrifice humans, usually virgin women, to their earthly gods, who were creatures that represented different elements of nature. The entire ecosystem that they felt compelled to protect was comprised of living entities, such as trees, rocks, water, fire, the flora, and the fauna. "I studied them in college mythology, at seminary school. The Druids are one of the oldest, yet most organized secret societies, known to the world. They have been involved with more heresy of the Church throughout history, than any other form of religion. It is still believed to this day in certain circles of law enforcement and Christian scholars, that the Druids are responsible for more missing people than any other source. It's known to many of these secret, subversive organizations that the Druids are the most notorious of all the Satanic, cults. Their sacrificial, ritualistic murders are the abasement of mankind and are performed all over the world," she went on. "Did you know that children, especially females, are the main targets of the priests? They abduct them off the streets, and they're never heard from again. They are relentless, monsters that cloak themselves in high society.

"They are usually, very wealthy and powerful figures in government: scientists, lawyers, politicians, doctors, bankers, religious clergy, ,you name it, and they have their tentacles into everything. "I never heard of these guys before," marveled Captain Ron, dumbfounded.

"I know. That's how secretive they really are. They do not like, people to know about them. If you do, then it's usually covered up quickly and subjugated by an ulterior organization like the Illuminati, or the Dilderberg Group," she informed him.

"Hey, I've heard of those Dilderberger cats! They hate being associated with anything, but they are behind all kinds of conspiracy junk, especially manipulating world economies and such," said LT astutely.

"How does an inmate know anything?" snarled one of the officers, abruptly.

"Hey man, I read a lot. Unlike you fools, who only look at porno magazines," LT recanted.

"You know, boy, you got a big mouth," he said, angered by the remark. The officer took out his baton and swung hard, but was stopped immediately when a massive, tattooed arm caught his hand in mid-swing. It was Mongo. He held his hand, squeezing it until he dropped the stick to the floor.

"You better never do that again, if you want to live," said the giant inmate.

Chaplain Barnett jumped in between them, pushing Mongo back, before another fight broke out.

"Look here fellows, we all need to stick together if we are going to defeat this thing. It feeds off our hatred towards each other," she pleaded with them, touching a few of the others' hands, as they were going for their weapons.

Captain Ron stared at Mongo, ready to shoot him dead when Chaplain Barnett firmly grabbed his arm. "Don't do it Ron. You've been drinking, and we are all very tired and strung out emotionally, over what's happened here today. Please don't use violence. We must think about an alternative plan—just in case the Army fails."

"At ease, men. The Chaplain's right. We all know that what she is saying is the truth," said one of the officers.

"We're in denial about the whole damn situation and frustrated that we haven't been effective in bringing these things down," said the Captain. He felt defeated and looked away from Brittney's honest eyes.

"There. We can figure something out, but we don't have a lot of time," said the chaplain. "We have a plan, but I need your help, Captain, if we are to succeed. It might sound ridiculous to you at first, but I believe what Lance has to say could be the ticket to save us all," she implored the captain.

She pulled Lance up by the arm and introduced him to Captain Ron.

"This guy? He's the one that started the riot in the yard today. You want us to listen to him?" cried the Captain, reluctantly, glaring Lance in the eyes.

Lance stood up to the Captain, face to face, and said boldly, "I'm on a mission, from GOD!"

Chapter 21

"Now, what?"

The Frogon, popped the iron gates open, on the upper tiers, like doors in a snack machine, in the cafeteria. C-Block was under siege, and the inmates were trapped. They had no place to run. They could only shout in defiance, locked in their cells as they were, waiting for their turn with the inevitable. They heard their neighbors scream wildly and then succumb to a gruesome sound of bones, crunching in the creature's jaws. Its talons hooked the bars perfectly, as its bloody tongue darted in and out to retrieve its hapless victims. Most of the inmates died from heart failure, when the enormous amphibian spotted them in their cells with its glowing yellow eyes that acknowledged, their whereabouts. They tried in vain to hide somewhere in the tiny cell rooms. They tried to crawl under their bunks, or even to push a weaker cellmate out to offer to the giant eating machine, only to be zapped themselves by the Frogon's sticky, forked muscle. The braver inmates tried to fight, but it was futile to resist.

Hedeku admired the monster's malevolence, as it ravaged, its quarry with ease. He would raise his arms up and cheer ecstatically, with each human sacrifice. The demon's power was being fed too, as each inmate screamed in terror, hanging onto the barred doors and watching the others' demise, some even soiling themselves from fright. Hedeku danced in the rafters, relishing in the addiction of fear and the intense release of energy, as the beast reached up and ripped down a 100-foot gangway and sent it crashing to the floor below. The steel and iron structure crumpled, like tinfoil under the creature's scaly claws. The inmates on the first floor, could only listen and watch as their comrades died in vain. They tried to bend the bars with their puny arms, trying anything to escape the horrid epitaph that awaited them. Streaks of tears lined their unshaven faces, while they hoped and prayed that someone would, or could, save them.

Many of the inmates just went insane from the thought of being eaten alive. It was more than a mind could bear as the Frogon's intense roar blew out light bulbs and left many stunned with shattered eardrums.

There had been more than seven hundred inmates in C-Block, and now there were none. The great demon reached up to its master in the rafters overhead and started back for the main annex.

It was headed for B-Block. It held Hedeku in its talons, like someone holding a baby bird. It was truly, a powerful beast, knowing not to injure its master, only to protect him from any harm. The corridor down C-Block, was as dark as a train tunnel, making it difficult for the soldiers to see the monster, as it approached the hub. Hedeku stopped the beast, because he sensed the ambush ahead and so waited patiently, like a spider waiting for its prey to make a false move. The demon knew that the soldiers were unable to see them, lurking in the cloak of darkness, or they would have started their assault by now.

The Frogon breathed heavily, suffering from a bad case of indigestion. Hedeku rubbed the creature's stomach, like any good pet owner would do, trying to comfort the beast. The Frogon's stomach gurgled, and then it let out a bodacious belch: "BBUUURRPP," followed by a series of horrendous blows, of flatulence, relieving itself of putrid excrement. "BBRRAAAPPPHH!" A few of the soldiers, chuckled, at the sounds that echoed, throughout the annex. It was a mistake on the demon's behalf. It gave their location away, and the Army readied for the attack.

"Get ready, men," commanded the General, raising his arm up and making a fist in the air. He tried to see in the dark cave ahead and ordered a soldier to get closer to fire a flare into the tunnel.

The guardsman loaded a flare into his gun and proceeded slowly, toward the entrance to the corridor. He hesitated for a second, noticing a fluorescent green mist drifting out of the darkness and into the annex. The foul smell was absolutely, wretched. The soldier put his hand up to shield his face from the noxious vapors, that were wafting throughout the annex. He couldn't stand the odor and vomited in front of all his comrades.

> "What the hell is he doing? . . . Er, uh . . . what is that stuff?" asked General Owens, who was now lifting his shirt collar around his nose. "Oh, my God, that's worse than a stink bomb!" he gagged.

The commander watched the green haze drift out into the hub, making his men violently ill. It was an awful odor, that made him nauseous and his eyes burned, from the methane coming from the tunnel. Then he heard himself! "Methane? Soldier! Don't fire that flaaa . . ." It was too, late. The soldier fired at the moment the General thought it. In a split second, they watched a burst of light reveal the massive Frogon, who was perched in the entryway on its hind haunches. Hedeku dove back into the creature's clutch, and it covered him up with its massive claws. The flare ignited the methane gas, as it wafted over the heaving guardsman, setting the entire chamber ablaze.

> "Take cover!" ordered the General, who retreated with the rest of the fear-stricken soldiers.

His heart pounded, as he felt the advancing inferno. It was nature's own flamethrower, as it rolled over their heads, eating up the oxygen around them in the annex. EEEEIIIIIYYYYAAAHHH," screamed his men as they vaporized in agony. General Owens noticed, an open doorway to his right and leaped for his life, through the doorway just in the nick of time, as the Tsunami' of flames, roared past him. He could feel the heat burst passing the office, and his jacket smoldered with burned patches on his arms. He covered his head with both hands as another burst of gas, shot down the corridor. He started to weep, when he realized he had just lost two hundred soldiers. They were instantly vaporized by the inferno. His mind raced with emotion, wondering how on earth they could have defended themselves against such a hideous creature as the Frogon. He heard its fearsome roar over the flames, which shook the very ground on, which he was lying.

"God, help us!" he shouted, holding his hands over his eardrums. General Owens was a devout atheist, until now. He remembered an old Army quotation that he had read a long time ago: "There aren't any atheists in foxholes." He now understood, what the quote meant.

Meanwhile, standing outside of the prison complex near the South Command Center, U.S. Army Lieutenant Hutchinson, was reviewing prison blueprints with Warden Stephens and Deputy Chief Bunn, when the massive explosion blew a hole through the roof of the main annex. The earth shook violently, knocking the men to their knees, as they watched a fiery mushroom cloud billow over the prison.

"Good GOD, almighty!" said Chief Bunn, startled in disbelief. He looked at Stevens and could see the reflection of the mushroom cloud in his pupils. Then another explosion went off, and this one blew out all the remaining front windows of the administration building. Fifty-foot flames burst the glass shards into the air, forcing everyone to lie down for cover. The shards of shrapnel covered the entire front lawn, severely maiming, more military personnel and killing another forty-five soldiers. Warden Stevens peeked through his fingers and could see many soldiers dying from the blast. He began to shake like a leaf on a tree, thinking that he had to run away from this madness that was taking place at his prison. "We got to get out of here, Eldon, before we are both dead," Stevens whispered. "Eldon, did you hear me?" He turned his head and saw Chief Bunn's bloody face lying next to his. The Warden shook his arm to see if he was dead, but he knew better, as soon as he saw, that the District Chief's eyes were wide open. Blood trickled down his forehead, where a jagged shard of glass protruded.

Stevens got up and stumbled a bit, regained his balance and then ran like, a rabbit not even stopping to help other, wounded soldiers. The fear pulsed through his veins, like ice water. He only thought about his own, selfish right of survival.

"It's every man for himself," he murmured, as he ran across the barricades and headed for his car.

He didn't know why, but as, he was trying to open the door, he looked back at the prison and saw only mayhem, as some of his staff ran from the building on fire. The place looked like a war zone, with many casualties. He heard their screams for help, as two made it to the front stairs of the admin building and tumbled down the steps, but were dead, before they reached the bottom. Warden Stevens recognized one of the victims. It was Dr. Loomis, the house physician. He was wearing a dirty white jacket and his brown hiking shoes. Stevens remembered them because, the doctor wore them all the time, taking them off only when they went to play golf at the Country Club. Stevens opened the Rover's door and climbed in. He then reached over and opened the glove compartment to get a drink from the fifth of Scotch hidden there. He took a big chug from the bottle and wiped his mouth, as he watched the fire burn in the middle of the complex. He could visualize the exact location and began to tremble, when he heard the great Frogan's roar coming from the inside. He watched, as the Army medics scampered among the wounded, trying to save lives.

Warden Stevens took another long pull from the bottle, to try to wash away his guilty feelings, thinking about his dead secretary, who he had murdered on the way to the golf course. He remembered every detail, when she answered the door thinking he came back to apologize, until he clobbered her with his nine iron. He had repeatedly hit her, as he took out all his frustrations with each blow, until her pretty face wasn't. He knew the cops would find his DNA all over the place, but he was drunk and didn't even care anymore. He watched the flames burn his prison and sneered, because it reminded him, metaphorically, of his doomed career. All those years of sin, sex, bribery, collusion and now, murder. Stevens looked into the rear-view mirror and saw his darkened, red eyes. They were framed by deep lines of deceit and years of alcohol abuse. He stared longer, numb, knowing that the Devil owned his soul, and that this was the anticipation of evil's long sought-after retribution.

"I had it coming," he mumbled, finishing the bottle and dropping it to the floorboard. "You reap what you sow," he chuckled, fiendishly and started the car.

He turned on the headlights, pulled the stick shift into drive, and started to leave, when he saw the silhouette of dreadlocks sitting in the seat behind him, "NO! Not You?" he shrieked.

It was Hedeku, patiently, waiting for Stevens' thoughts to clear, while he was seated behind him all the time.

"How, how did you get in my …EEEEEYYAAAHHHHH!" The Rover rocked back and forth, for a few moments, and then it rolled slowly across the parking lot into, another parked car. The airbags deployed and the windows inside were covered in blood, as the demon warlock collected, another lost soul for Satan.

Chapter 22

"The Good Chaplain"

Chaplain Barnett, the Captain, his men, and the Christians were all out in the maintenance building looking for supplies, when the explosion took place. They all escaped injury other than their ears were ringing some, from the blast. Tatum and his men were escorting the Chaplain, because he had no other men available, or alive for that matter to help guard the convicts. There were twelve of them all together, and they thought their chances of living were better, if they all stuck together. Besides, Captain Ron wouldn't admit that he was scared out of his socks, and he knew that the Chaplain was knowledgeable, when it came to anything spiritual in nature. He remembered how many times, she would go on and on, about the supernatural findings of the Church, but he could care less. The only thing he wanted was to have sex with her, and he had acted nice until, their third date. They went out to dinner in a fancy restaurant in Kansas City, had a lot of wine, and they knew they shouldn't drive back to Heavenworth, where they both lived, so they got separate hotel rooms.

241

He rubbed his right cheek remembering the sharp sting, left by Brittney's hard slap to his face. He'd never been hit so hard by a woman, in his entire life, until that night. He told some of his single lieutenants the story about how she had slapped him sober. His face was red the next morning, when he woke from his sleep, and they drove back home. He said his plan was simple: A nice dinner, drink too much, and get a room. The only pitfall was that the Chaplain was not like other women, he had sacked in the past. It was usually a fool-proof plan, but not with her. He respected her enough to leave her alone, knowing they had to work with each other in the prison, and he didn't like the thought of her monitoring his charm, with the other female staff members in the administration.

The Chaplain was different in many ways, from other women. She was always polite, very generous, and she talked about Jesus every chance she had, which was a complete turn off for most of the men, who later gave up, trying to date her. She would go out to dinner with guys all the time, but she would always preach the Gospel and later would try to save them from eternal damnation. Some men did it, thinking they could get close to her by acting that way, but if she found out they were playing, then it was over, but she kept trying, no matter what.

Captain Ron Tatum, studied her as he guarded, the entrance doors and checked outside to see if, Watini was nearby. The Chaplain was reading her thick book of demonology, dragging her finger line by line, not missing a thing, as she read up on the Druid rituals. The Captain smiled, thinking what a great wife she'd make for somebody, just not him. He guessed she was in her thirties and wondered if, she had ever been laid. Then he felt guilty about his impure thoughts of her and raised his eyes up in the air to see if God was listening to his thoughts. He shook his head and reached in his back pocket and opened a can of chew. He dipped his fingers in, pulled out a big chaw, and loaded it in his lip. He put the lid back on tightly and looked over at the Chaplain, who was giving him a stern look of disgust. He smiled and raised the can offering her a dip, knowing, it would only further exacerbate her opinion of him. It did. He laughed out loud and checked out the inmates, who were busy filling up a couple of wheelbarrows. His men were armed, and they were making sure that the inmates didn't try anything funny, just in case they tried to escape. Then he thought how ridiculous a thought that was, because of the Frogon and Watini running around loose in the prison. He watched as inmate Lance Smith, walked over to Chaplain Barnett and heard him speak with her about his plan from GOD.

"Indeed," he said to himself silently, in disbelief, and then he spat a snoose stream, onto the concrete floor.

Captain Ron was jealous and self-centered, when it came to matters with "the Good Chaplain," as he would call her, facetiously. He squeezed his M19 tightly, thinking how he hated inmates. He thought they were all vermin, ever since the time he was attacked by Chino and his gang. It happened many years ago, when he had first started out his career in law enforcement. The cagey leader tricked him, into thinking he was a confident source of information, as Chino spoon fed him information about other rival gang members.

In the beginning, much of the info was true, and Officer Tatum quickly learned about the internal drug trade and the bribery that was going on inside of the Texas facility. Before long, Chino had finally trapped Tatum, exchanging favors for valued information. Internal Affairs got involved, and Tatum was under investigation for accepting money that was deposited in his bank account, by fraudulent wire transfers coming from California. He nearly lost his job, but was vindicated by an arrest made in Los Angeles, where one of Chino's hookers was filmed making a deposit into Tatum's bank account. She was busted by the FBI for other money-laundering schemes, and she admitted to setting Tatum up for the nefarious Sorreno Drug Cartel.

Tatum couldn't believe it at first, but he realized when talking with the ringleader, that he gave him little bits of personal information, which was all they needed to establish an outside identity and begin implicating him. It happens every day in the criminal justice system. Most officers never get caught taking the bribes and become Chingauhuas (slang meaning "slaves") for the gangs.

Captain Tatum was transferred to Oxford, Wisconsin, and Chino went to Pelican Bay in California. They never saw each other again—until two years ago when Chino was transferred to Heavenworth, where he met Captain Ron Tatum, and who gave him a real "welcome wagon" when he arrived.

Now, Chino gives Tatum, whatever he wants, whenever he wants it, including those "cash payments" left at a local tavern in Heavenworth for the greedy captain. But it was all a fog now, because of some giant frog destroying his dream that took him years to develop, and now he was watching the main annex burn to the ground.

Tatum went outside to take a look around in the flame-lit area next to the building to see if he could hear anything as to the whereabout,s of the Frogon.

"I wonder where he's going?" said Chaplain Barnett, noticing everything around her. "Who knows? He sure is a rough one," said Lance, sitting next to her.

"Yes, he's about as tough as they come, and he works at it," said the Chaplain. "What do you mean by that, Chaplain?" Lance asked her.

"Well, the Bible teaches us that there are two kinds of people in the world those, who believe that Jesus Christ is the Son of God and then there's all the others," she said, as she rested the book on her lap. "The only thing we have to do is confess with our mouth and our heart that Jesus is our sovereign Lord, and that he died for all our sins so that we can have eternal life. Pretty simple, right?" she said, as she looked intently into Lance's eyes.

"Well, I suppose so, but when I was little and went to church, I got tired of being told that I had to do this, or I had to do that. I saw so many people, who were hypocrites and didn't really take God as real. It was more of a 'rule book' of laws that everyone had to follow, or else," he said dismayed. "When I went to college at Michigan and got an athletic scholarship to play football, I really went off the deep end. I became a hero, during my second season as a starting quarterback, and everyone loved me. I partied and had sex with a different girl every other night. I felt invincible, like a god, and that I didn't need GOD, in my life.

"The professors taught me that GOD is nothing, but a myth, like all the other gods you know, like Zeus and Odin. Darwin's Theory of Origin is the bible of evolution and makes a great case that primates over millions of years, evolved into us. It seemed logical to only believe, what an expensive education was teaching me, and that they must be right, and that religion was nothing, but a big lie," Lance ranted.

"Wow! No wonder you are such a loser," she gaffed. "Listen, I've heard it all, well almost all, of what you are saying. Do you think we believers, just fell off a turnip truck, or something? But, I'm not here to judge you," she continued, "or anyone else, including the Captain. That's not for me to decide. It is up to people like me, though, to help people who are lost in the deceit of this world system. Nothing is new under the sun, but the academic world loves to proclaim itself as the scientific approach,' to the enlightenment of mankind. Everything they teach or have come up with in history, is a bunch of braggadocios findings that are totally unfounded and yet, they teach people that it is the absolute truth.

"It's true that medicine and science have come a long way after three thousand years of practicing procedures, but they are not even close to the Prophetic Word of GOD," the Chaplain concluded, standing and stretching her legs.

"So, what are you saying exactly?" asked Lance, rubbing his sore ribs.

The Chaplain smiled and looked at her watch, "Oh my! It's 12:30 a.m., and we don't really have time to discuss theology versus science. Let me put it to you, as simply, as I possibly can: How do you explain what is going on out there?" she asked, pointing to the prison. Lance realized she hit the nail on the head. How could he explain supernatural phenomena that had almost killed him? Instead, he was sent to GOD, who gave him a second chance to redeem himself, and it was GOD, who had given him the message on how to destroy the beast and to protect Chaplain Barnett from harm.

"How can I possibly deny what had happened to me only a few hours ago?" Lance said to himself. What she was trying to tell them all now made perfect sense. He jumped up to his feet and gave her a big hug, "You are right, Chaplain. I believe everything that you said to me is true, and I'm a fool for even thinking anything different," he said jubilant, to her amazement.

"I've been lied to all my life, and that's how I ended up in prison, because of my stupid, selfish ambitions, and here they almost cost me my life tonight. I don't believe this is all a coincidence, any longer. It's, a divine mission from God, to show the world that HE is good, and that its mankind's distain toward one another, that manifested itself through these creatures," Lance avowed, seriously.

"Exacto mundo, compadré," she beamed. "I think he's really got it," she shouted, loudly. The Jacksons and the others stopped for a minute to wipe the sweat from their brows. They had gathered most of the materials that Lance, and the Chaplain requested and joined her and Lance in opening some water bottles they found underneath a tarp. Derek handed one to both, of them and said, "Here, have a drink on me," he grinned.

"Thank you, Sir," sniled Chaplain Barnett.

"So, why are you so excited amidst all of this grief going on out there?' asked Mongo.

"Well, now, it has come to our friend's attention that there really is a GOD, because how can you explain, so much evil?" she asked, taking a big drink of water.

Everything she did, the men watched her every move, thinking she was so graceful, even drinking water.

"She's right, you guys, about everything. I just had an epiphany and worked it out with her," Lance said, opening his bottle and guzzled the whole thing in and then crumpling it.

"Duh! It's about time you figured out, there must be a GOD. I mean getting hit in the head by a fifty foot-tall demon, should knock sense into your big ego," chastised Kyle.

They all laughed and congratulated Lance on his revelation. LT was reading the Chaplain's book, where she had marked the page, and his eyes grew wide in disbelief. "Say, what?" he bellowed. "OK! We got all of the supplies, but where are we going to find a vestal virgin?" he asked, showing the sentence in the book to Mongo. They all huddled around LT to read the page and then looked at the picture.

"It says here that the Vestal Virgin, was sacrificed, on an altar to summon the Great Beast from Hell by the Druid High Priests. Once, this Satanic Ritual is completed, the Portal of the Netherworld would be opened, and the beginning of the end time would occur," Derek read out loud to the others.

"The Portal would allow all of the demons held in chains by GOD to be unleashed upon, all of mankind and would once again rule the world, as in the time of the pre- Adamic world, at the time of the Great Fall," he stopped and looked up bewildered. "You mean to tell me there are more of those things?"

"Do you think, that's why they are here? They are trying to establish Heavenworth, as the staging area for this portal thing?" wondered LT as he, rubbed his jaw. "Yeah, I think that is exactly, what's going. Where on earth, are they gonna find a virgin in this place?" Kyle asked, sarcastically. The Chaplain didn't say a word, as she wiped a tear from her rosy,

cheek, blushing.

"Chaplain Barnett, are you a virgin?" asked Mongo, poignantly. They all stared at her. She was standing under a dim overhanging light and looked them all in the eye and nodded her head, saying, "Yes, I am."

Captain Ron burst through the door, "Hey, you guys, come and look at this," he marveled. "Hey, what did I miss?" he asked, walking over to the Chaplain. "Why are you crying?"

"Oh, it's nothing really. What was it you wanted to show us?"

"You'll see. Follow me," said Captain Tatum.

"Don't you worry, Chaplain, we got your back," assured Derek, putting his arm around her.

They followed him outside, and they saw the Frogon, ravaging the remaining inmates in B-Block.

When they turned the corner of the building, they saw the Captain point up to the moon, "There! What is that supposed to mean?" The moon was blood red. It wasn't from the smoke of the fire because, it was drifting to the north and the moon had almost, reached its zenith.

"Chaplain, what does it mean?" asked Mongo.

"I don't know for sure, but the book talks about a blood moon, as the sign of the beginning of the end, as it does in the Book of Revelation in the Bible. I don't think we have much time left, until the portal is opened. Where would that happen in this place?" she asked, looking at the Captain.

"Anywhere, I guess," he shrugged.

"Where's the lowest elevation in this place?" asked a correctional officer.

"Gee, maybe the drain field in the south pasture, or it could be hey, wait a minute. We sent the maintenance guy down there earlier today, and we've never heard back from him, come to think of it," said the Captain.

"Sent him where, Ron?" asked Brittney tugging his arm. "The underground cistern," he answered.

"He went to poison the frogs. He said they were probably, coming through the storm drains and into the well water and were probably crawling up the sewer pipes in the prison," he reported.

"How big is the cistern?" asked Kyle.

"Oh, why, it's enormous. You could float a yacht in it," said the Captain.

"And, how deep, is this well inside of it?" asked Derek.

"Oh, gosh, it's deep. It's maybe a hundred, no, probably two hundred feet. Why? What's with all the questions? Do you guys know something that I don't?" he was getting upset.

"That's it, Chaplain. I know it is," said Lance confidently.

"Ron, how do we get there?" asked the Chaplain, nervously.

"We can go back inside and down the maintenance shaft. It crosses the yard, and the cistern is located underneath the pump house next to the power plant. Over there," he pointed.

"There's a tunnel underneath these grounds?" asked Kyle.

"Yep, there are six of them, and they go all over hell and back. Oh, pardon my English, Brittney," winked the Captain.

"Take us there right now, Ron. We don't have much time," said the Chaplain, walking back to the maintenance building.

"Wait a damn minute! I am not going anywhere, until somebody tells me what in blue blazes, is going on here," demanded the Captain.

"It's the Portal to Hell, Captain. Those creatures, are here on a mission to usher in a gateway from the Netherworld," said the young Chaplain Barnett.

"Right. A Nether, what?" said the Captain, confused.

"Here read this, Captain," said LT. He opened the book to the page where, it explained what they already knew. When the captain finished reading it, he looked up at the inmates and said, "Well, what are you waiting for? Let's get on it! What have we got to lose? I mean, I haven't been right for the past twenty four hours, so let's follow the Chaplain."

They marched back and saw the Chaplain, waiting at the door with her arms crossed. She didn't look happy, and they saw why, when Chino stepped out from behind her holding a 9mm pistol. He, Monk Samansky, and seven gang members were waiting for them to return to the maintenance building.

"Hey, Holmes, how's it goin'?" asked Chino candidly, as he shoved the pistol in Chaplain Barnett's ribs. "Me and my boys here, have been wondering, where you been. Then here you surprise us, with your return. C'mon in and meet the rest of mi amigos," he said slyly, holding the door open for them and motioning with the gun. "No funny stuff, Tatum, or else the Chaplain here, is gonna die," Chino threatened.

Captain Ron Tatum and his crew were caught with their proverbial pants down, and Chino knew it. Tatum had never surrendered in an inmate hostage crisis in his entire career, until now. He knew Chino was a cold-blooded killer, and he would have to do his bidding, for now. When they all entered the building, the other gangbangers disarmed them and then greeted them with a beat down. The Chaplain pleaded with Chino, asking him not to kill them, and then she picked up the book and showed him the pictures explaining to him what they had to do.

"We have to stick together, Chino. If, we don't, we can all say goodbye," she pleaded. Then she watched Samansky throw Lance across the room like a doll. He hit the floor hard and held his aching ribs. Then without warning, one of the gangbangers opened fire with his weapon and killed the kneeling correctional officers. Blood splatters covered the warehouse, as their bodies dropped to the floor.

"Nooooooo!" Chaplain Barnett screamed in defiance and then burst into tears. "You jerks! How can you be so ruthless?"

"I don't know, but it takes years of practice," joked Samansky. They all laughed.

"OK, you guys, pick the others up and get the Captain's keys. Looks like, we got a little adventure here, with the Chaplain," said Chino. He grabbed a handful of the Chaplain's thick hair, pulled her toward a stack of crates, and then made her sit down. She complied, while rubbing her scalp. Then she watched Chino walk casually, over to the kneeling Captain and thought,

"This was it for him." Chino hit the Captain across the face with the pistol, knocking him to the floor. Tatum knew, there was no love lost between him and his arch enemy, but it didn't matter now, because he was unconscious before he hit the concrete. The brutality of the other inmates was a stark contrast of reality, between them and the Christians. Chaplain Barnett turned her head away, as they kept punching the Christian inmates, and spouting words of hate and disdain toward them.

Suddenly, amid the hateful beat-down, her hair stood up on the back of her neck. She could sense the demon's presence, almost, as if he were wearing a tracking device. Just when Samansky, walked over to kick Lance in the ribs again, Watini attacked him and slit his throat, where he stood.

The big man grabbed his throat to try to stop the bleeding, but it was too late. The Monk turned to Chino with a helpless look and dropped to his knees and fell face first into the ground. Watini moved swiftly, stabbing and slashing the other, gang members. The Chaplain winced, as the greater evil destroyed, the lesser. The Sorrenos started blasting away, spraying bullets wildly, and trying to hit the daunting demon, who literally leaped about like a circus acrobat. He leaped, twisted, and somersaulted through the air, making it difficult to shoot him. Suddenly, the Chaplain was pulled to her feet by Derek Jackson, and they ducked behind the crates to escape the wildfire of the M19s. Derek looked up to the skylights and dreaded what he saw coming near the east windows, it was the Frogon.

"Come on, Chaplain. We got to get out of here right now," he said, as he helped her to her feet. They bolted for the tunnel exit, followed by Kyle, LT, Porebski, and Mongo, who was carrying Lance, like a newlywed bride. Chino was infuriated, but he was trapped behind a maintenance truck, as he watched them try to escape. Then, as if a hurricane hit the front of the building, it was torn off by the Frogon, as it shrieked in defiance: "RRROOOOAAAAARRRR!"

Chino trembled in fear and crawled under the truck to protect himself from the falling debris, while many of his men were being snatched up into the air by the Frogon's lethal tongue. "Zot! Zot, Zot!" Sounded its tongue

He knew he was trapped, until he saw a lone soldier helping the Captain toward the tunnel exit.

"Oh, no you don't," yelled Chino. He dashed out from underneath the truck, like a rabbit, out from its hole. Just then, he looked over his shoulder and saw Watini's hideous face, as he hissed his orders to the rampaging monster.

Chino instinctively realized the Frogon, was after him. He turned and fired his 9mm, at the maintenance truck's fuel tank. He emptied the clip and the vehicle finally, erupted into a ball of flame, repelling the scaly, beast backward. The explosion knocked Watini off of the creature's shoulder and into a pile of fallen debris. Chino shaded his eyes from the fire and could see that the witchdoctor, was impaled on a long sprinkler pipe that was juxtaposed, out of the rubble.

"Yes," Chino shouted, making a fist pump. He hid behind a support column and watched, as the Frogon plucked its skewered master into the air and removed the pipe, just as someone would remove a skewer from a shish kabob. The Frogon seemed lost, as it carried its master gently between its claws, like a child would a wounded sparrow. The hulking beast covered Watini and then charged through the south wall, to escape from the ensuing flames.

Chino was relieved and took a deep breath, while he rested against the column. He stared at the dark tunnel entrance and reloaded a fresh clip of ammo into his pistol. He cocked the mechanism and ran into the tunnel entrance, chasing after the others. He wanted to finish what he had started, to kill the Captain, once and for all.

Chapter 23

"and let there be, Light"

The Christians had suffered tremendously, as did the Captain, but they were happy to still be alive, unlike so many who died, that night at Heavenworth. They rested near a storm drain leading from the south side of the prison complex. The inmates nursed each other, while the Chaplain, cared for Captain Ron. General Owens, tried to raise his troops by radio, but the signal couldn't penetrate through the deep ground swell of earth. The lighting was faint, but adequate enough to see each other's face and mend their wounds. The General marveled, at the engineering that went into building the great, brick labyrinth winding before him. His flashlight pierced the darkness, revealing intricate spiraled patterns of brick and mortar lining the long tunnel walls that, were covered with a bright green moss. The moss was iridescent, when illuminated by the flashlight, and it clung in large clumps, dangling off the leaking walls.

The heavy smell of mold, filled the air, as he walked downward to investigate the tunnel's features, that led to the great cistern they reviewed from prison's blueprints, earlier that evening.

The four main tunnels, were fed by a complex system, consisting of hundreds of smaller storm drains that spouted downward from twenty-four-inch pipes. It was a microcosm of life and heavy with moisture. The light reflected tiny, rainbows, as they crossed over the large entryway. Each tunnel eventually, led into the cistern. The cascading waters grew louder, as General Rocky Owens slipped on some mildew and fell backwards, but he caught the railing, just in time to regain his balance.

"Whoa! That was close," he sighed, walking further into the tunnel. He turned and looked back, where he had come from and could see a dimly lit opening where the others were, but he wanted to explore what his options were as he went further down the walkway. He finally passed under a large brick arch, and knew he was getting close to the cistern.

The General noticed something unusual, as he got closer the level of noise had dissipated. The sounds of the rushing water were now nothing but a babbling brook instead of the raging waterfalls, he was anticipating. He stopped and knew something was wrong. He aimed his flashlight straight ahead of him, but the light seemed to be engulfed in darkness. He tapped the flashlight on the rusted, pipe railing a couple of times, thinking his batteries were low, but they weren't. Then he pointed the beam upward, but it barely lit up the ceiling.

"Huh, that's funny," he said to himself, needing the vote of confidence that was quickly leaving him. He looked back again and could barely see the archway at the opening. "Man, this thing is really huge," he said nervously. He finally came to the realization that he was in the middle of the cistern—directly over, what would be a water pool. He leaned cautiously over the railing and pointed the flashlight into the huge gaping hole before him.

The brave General swallowed hard, as the beam vanished into the vast darkness of space beneath him. It frightened him to know the stark realization of what a real bottomless pit looked like. Suddenly, he felt something fly near him, and he quickly flashed the light in the air over his helmet and saw nothing. He knew it was something.

"What the heck was that?" his voice echoed. Startled and hearing the echo of his own voice, the General removed a star from his lapel and tossed it over the railing. He listened for a ping noise, but heard nothing.

"How deep is this thing?" he wondered. He removed his 45mm sidearm and ejected the shell out of its chamber over the edge and listened, again nothing. "This is crazy," he thought, scratching his head.

"Whooooosh," came the sound again, whizzing by his head. The General cocked his pistol and held the flashlight in front of him, as he slowly retreated off the gangway.

He finally, made it back to the archway, when he heard more sounds of air rushing over his head. His skin began to crawl, as his imagination started to get the better of him. He turned and ran just as, fast as his boots would move. He didn't even bother looking back, to see if those things were following him. He ran all the way back up the tunnel and was relieved, when he saw the Chaplain and the other human beings. He was out of breath and leaned against the wall to try to catch it back, when LT asked, "Hey, General, what's up? You look like you saw a ghost, or something," he kidded. The General finally got his breath back and said, "I did!"

"You did what?" LT asked, not smiling now.

"I don't know, what I saw? I didn't see anything, but I sure as heck felt something, that I couldn't see," he gasped.

"Oh, no! Uh, uhhhh! I ain't going down there Chaplain, if there's spooks down there. No, sireeee. I'd rather go back out there and fight that overgrown toad, than mess with them spooks," whined LT loudly.

"Settle down, LT. What happened, General?" asked Chaplain Barnett.

"I'm not quite sure. I don't believe in ghosts or demons, but after dealing with that thing out there, I don't know what to think anymore. I'm jumpy and feel real out of place. Do you know what I mean, Chaplain?" he paused.

"Well, considering the events of the day, I think we all feel that way, Sir," said Derek.

"Yeah, and now, were looking for some kind of Portal to Hell," whined Mongo, as he wiggled, a loose tooth in his mouth.

"A Portal to Hell? Well, that's what it is. I saw it. The cistern is completely devoid of water, and there's a gigantic black hole that's bottomless. I threw one of my star pins over the railing, and I never heard it ping, or anything. It's real creepy down there. I agree with him and suggest we go back and take our chances with the Frogon," said the three-star General.

The rest of the Christians moaned in disbelief, knowing the report was not good, and things were definitely looking worse, instead of better.

"Listen, men. We have simply got to keep praying and keep our faith up, or else we will lose. You all know that if you do die, you are headed for a better place than here, that's for sure," assured the Chaplain. "Did you think Satan was going to make things easy for you? I mean really!

"You call yourselves, men? Why, I've never seen so many chickens out of the henhouse, since I left the farm," she dissed them. The Chaplain stood to her feet, walked up to the General and stood upright. "General, are you a Christian?' she asked fervently.

"No, Ma'am. I'm military born and bred. My whole family is Army, at least the ones, who are still alive. My father didn't believe in GOD, but my mother sure did. He wouldn't let her take us to church, or have anything to do with GOD," he admitted openly.

"Well, I think it's time to change your mind, don't you?" she asked.

"Considering what I've seen today and just saw a few moments ago, I've been asking myself a lot of questions about God, but I don't have time right now, to go to Bible school, Chaplain."

"You don't have to go to school to accept Jesus Christ, as your personal Lord and Savior, soldier," groaned Captain Tatum, shocking everyone, as he regained consciousness sitting against the wall.

"Oh, Ron, thank GOD you are coming around," said Chaplain Barnett.

"Yeah, I'm coming around. Don't you think it's about time I did?" he grimaced, painfully.

"Yes, but I'm stunned, to think you ever listened to me," she said, dabbing blood, off the Captain's cut lip.

"General, you and I both know, that after tonight, if there's evil, like, this stuff we've battled, then surely there must be some good, somewhere. If, his name is JESUS, then I suggest we accept him and get on with living, because there is nothing we can do that's going to stop those things out there," said Tatum, sitting up. His right eye was swollen completely shut, and his face was badly bruised from Chino's pistol whipping. The Christian men felt bad for Captain Tatum. Porebski tried to help him get up to his feet, and Captain Tatum indignantly chastised him.

"I can get up myself, you dumb Polack," he barked.

"Ron! You'll never become a Christian, until you forgive these men, what you've said and done to them," Chaplain Barnett, said boldly.

"What? Forgive these scumbags? Why, I'd rather eat scat!"

"Ron! What did I just say to you?" she goaded the Captain, squeezing his sore arm.

"Well," he mumbled, "Alright, but it doesn't mean they can walk all over me, if I become a Christian, right?" he asked the Chaplain. "That's right. Isn't it, men?" she sought their approval.

The Christian men all looked at each, other and then Porebski said, "Well, if he can love a Polack, then I can love a jarhead, too," he smiled holding out his hand to be shaken by the Captain. "Oh, I suppose so," said the Captain, and he shook Porebski's hand.

"OK, then, repeat after me, Captain and General. Uh, take your helmet off, General, please," she smiled, as the Christian men snickered. They were excited about the new men coming to JESUS CHRIST, when they heard another voice enter from the shadows. It was Chino.

"What about me, Chaplain? Can GOD forgive a murderer, like me?" he asked pointing the gun at them.

"You rotten son of a dog." winced the Captain, but the Chaplain put her hand over his sore mouth, before he could say another word.

"Yes, Chino! GOD, will forgive you, too, if you are honest in your heart, ask for His forgiveness, and accept JESUS CHRIST, as your Lord and Savior.

The General slowly withdrew his pistol from his holster, when a vice-like grip, grabbed his hand and squeezed it so tightly, he had to let go of the weapon. He turned to see who almost crushed his hand, and Mongo just smiled, standing behind him.

He nodded and said, "Pay attention, Sir!" pointing to the Chaplain. The General obeyed.

"You know what, Chaplain? I heard everything you people have been talking about, and I stood back here, in the dark crying like a little baby. I believe there's a GOD, but why did HE do this to me?" he sobbed, honestly, shaking the 9mm at them.

"Chino! Look, GOD didn't do this to you. You did this to yourself. You have to accept responsibility, for your own sins or else, He will not, forgive you. The grace and mercy of GOD, are so big, bigger than we will ever know. Until, the time we see HIM, on Judgment Day, is when, we will understand what HE did for us by giving up HIS only SON, to save us and not to condemn us," preached the Chaplain. Captain Ron couldn't believe his eyes when Chino handed the brave woman of GOD the gun and fell down on his knees, crying at her feet.

"If GOD loves us, then who can be against us?" she quoted the scripture, as her faith began to perk. The rest of the male audience stood awestruck. They couldn't believe their tired eyes, seeing the Chaplain for the first time, as the compassionate Disciple of CHRIST, they knew, she was.

The love of GOD radiated from her face, glowing with goodness, as she demonstrated to them, all the power of forgiveness.

It was miraculous! She knew, no fear and illustrated the courage and compassion to willingly forgive and love the man, who had wanted to kill her, earlier. They all took a knee, as she led them through the Sinner's Prayer of Redemption. The power of the HOLY SPIRIT, was present in that tunnel, as the Chaplain prayed for them all to be forgiven and cleansed from all their sins, from this moment forward, by the Blood of JESUS CHRIST that was shed for them at Calvary.

"And do you all repent of your sins and ask for the forgiveness of your sins to JESUS CHRIST, OUR LORD AND SAVIOUR, whose blood takes away all of our sins and washes away all of our iniquities?"

"Yes, I do!" each responded.

"And do you vow to make JESUS CHRIST, who is the Lamb of GOD, your personal Lord and Savior and believe that HE died, was buried, and rose again on the Third Day and into HEAVEN, and is seated at the right Hand of the FATHER?"

"Yes, I do!" each said, loudly.

"Then ask JESUS into your heart right now and thank HIM for HIS sacrifice, for each your lives. You may also ask, for the Gift of the HOLY SPIRIT, to descend upon you now, and show you the Way, the Truth, and the Light, in JESUS' precious name. Amen," proclaimed the Chaplain.

When she opened her eyes and to her amazement, every man was lying face down on the walkway. She started praising the Lord, singing over the re-born Christians, who were lying before her. The Peace of GOD, filled each one of their hearts, as they got up and began to greet each other, as new creatures in CHRIST JESUS. The Captain didn't want to be hugged, but Chino did and so did, the General, who no longer felt, fearful of the dark.

"Are you sure people can change, with a few simple prayers, Chaplain?" asked Captain Ron, glaring at Chino, who was apparently jubilant, talking with the other Christians.

"Prayer's help, but it's, JESUS, who changes people, Ron. Plus, it helps, if a person wants to be changed. God gave us all free will and doesn't force anything on us, that we don't want. You must have faith and believe in HIM to make a commitment of faith. In Hebrews, Chapter 11, verse one, it says, 'Faith, is the substance of things hoped for, but is the evidence of things, not yet, seen.'"

"There you go, saying all that crazy, scripture lingo. You know, I have a hard time trying to understand that stuff," Ron pouted, buttoning his shirt collar.

"You have to try to think about what's being said. It will come to you eventually, now that you have finally agreed to serve HIM and not the enemy," she said, helping him put on his jacket.

"Who is the enemy, Chaplain? I've been trained my whole life knowing that those crooks, thugs, and murderers were my enemy, and now we're supposed to be buddies. Come on get real," argued, Captain Ron.

The Chaplain grabbed the Captain's vest and pulled him close to her saying, "Ron, you have got to let go of the hatred that's inside of you, or it will destroy you. Surely, you felt the presence of GOD a few minutes ago, didn't you?" she asked, staring into his eyes.

"Well, I think I did, but my distrust is starting to come back, making it feel like, it's all a big joke," he glanced over at Chino.

"Ron, listen to me very carefully. The Devil comes to steal, kill, and destroy. I can see that Satan, is already trying to take what you just received and fill you with unbelief. Just listen to your inner thoughts. They are probably racing around inside of you and robbing the Peace of CHRIST, even while we speak with each other, aren't they?" He didn't say a word, but he gave her a nod and took the gun Chino gave her and pushed her aside. He quickly cocked it and pointed it at Chino.

"OK! Happy hour is over! I'm making the rules now, and we're going to cross the tunnel and head up to the pump house, as planned.

I figure we'll be safe for the time being, from those demons up there," he pointed the gun to the ceiling, then back at the inmates. "General Owens and I are going to guard you JESUS freaks, and if any of you makes one false move, I'll shoot you like the dogs that you are. Capish?" said the snarling Captain.

The men heard the bullet load into the chamber of the 9mm and were dumbfounded by the twist of fate, making them doubt once again. The Chaplain didn't say a word. She picked up her book and walked in front of Chino and looked him in the face.

"It's OK! Don't worry about him. What happened to you is real, and no one can take that from you now, not even Captain Tatum," she assured him. Do you trust me?" she asked.

Chino smiled and grabbed her arms gently, moving her to the side of him, and stared back at Captain Ron saying,

"Don't worry about me, Chaplain, I'm cool. I know JESUS forgave me of my sins, and I don't have to feel guilty, about who I am, anymore. What's a relief from a burden that weighed heavily on me. But, what about him," Chino asked, pointing to the Captain.

"You gonna shoot us in the back, like you did the others, back in Texas?" he challenged the Captain.

"Don't give me any ideas, grease-ball, if you know what's good for you," the Captain growled back.

"Come on you guys. Let's get going, if we're going to help anyone else," said the Chaplain, putting her arm around Chino and turning him away from the Captain. She knew the captain would shoot him if they stayed any longer.

"What's he up to, Chaplain?" asked Derek, turning on his flashlight, while taking the lead. They marched down to the cistern and could hear the General talking things over with the obstinate Captain, but he marched along with them.

"Watch your step, it's pretty slippery up ahead," warned the General.

"Man, this place is huge," said Mongo, watching a rat crawl along a brick ledge in the tunnel. "You can say that, again," marveled LT, looking over the railing into the darkness.

They finally arrived at the archway of the cistern, where they stopped before entering. "Hey, why are you stopping, Jackson? Get a move on," barked the captain, licking his sore lip. "Wait a second, Captain, I thought I heard something," said Derek, as he leaned out, trying to hear the sound again.

"What did you hear, Derek?" asked the Chaplain.

"I don't rightly know, Chaplain, but it sounded like something flying," he said.

"I heard the same sounds, when I came here, too," said General Owens, walking up to the Chaplain. "There were sounds of flight, and I could feel them pass over my head, as I got closer to the center of the hole up ahead," he informed them.

"What do you think it is, Chaplain Barnett?" asked Lance holding his ribs tightly. "I don't know, but let's keep going, until we get to the middle of the gangway. We'll stop there" she said.

"Man, it's dark in here," said Porebski. "The lights must be out above. I can hardly see a thing."

They walked into the middle, and they all heard the whooshing noises flying over their heads. They were looking over the edge of the railing, into the giant black hole, when Captain Tatum shined his light into the tunnel, he asked, "Where's the water?" They all looked back at him like he was crazy.

"This is supposed to be filled with water, all the way up to the walkway," Tatum said.

"Well, guys, I think we've found the Portal, don't you?" asked Chaplain Barnett, candidly.

"Yep! It looks like, the Portal to Hell to me, all right," commented Kyle Jackson, as he then hocked up a phlegm and spit it into the hole. "Man, there you go again. You just got to antagonize someone, even if it's the Devil, himself," said Derek, shaking his head.

"Shhhhh!" said the Chaplain, holding up her hand to silence the squabbling, brothers. She leaned over the railing and tried to listen better. Then she removed her cross from around her neck, kissed it, and tossed the shining silver necklace into the cavern.

"Chaplain, what are you doing?" asked Lance, but then he saw everyone staring in disbelief. The necklace was suspended in the air only a few feet in front of her. They were stunned by the unbelievable event, as the holy artifact turned, slowly in mid-air. "What the heck is going on, Chaplain?" asked Mongo backing up a few steps. "I ain't never seen something like that, in my life," mumbled a wide-eyed LT. The necklace floated and hovered slowly, until the Chaplain held out her hand, and it returned back into the open palm of her left hand, and then she said, "Thank you!" Much to the others' amazement, there was no one there, only the darkness.

She closed her hand and smiled. This scared all of them, and they backed away from her, needing an explanation.

"Well, gentleman that proves everything the book was saying is true," she spoke adamantly. "What on earth are you talking about, Brittney?" marveled the unbelieving Captain. "The book explains everything, but I will tell you that we are standing directly above the Gates to Hell. What you just witnessed was an act of Holiness, which means nothing that is sacred, or holy, can enter Hell, itself. I know my cross is sacred, because it has been blessed, and it represents Our Master, JESUS CHRIST, the Lord over us all. Good and Evil.

"So," she continued, "even the spirits of the Netherworld must respect and obey the spiritual laws that have been in effect for thousands of years." Then she put the necklace chain over her thick auburn hair.

"You mean to tell me that those sounds we have been hearing are . . ." queried the General.

"Yes, General! They are spirits entering the Netherworld of Sheol," said the Chaplain, flipping her hair back. "They are the lost souls of the dead, and they are waiting for Judgment Day."

"Are you telling me those things are for real, and they're flying around us, now?" asked the General. "That's exactly, correct, General Owens.

Now, aren't you glad you accepted JESUS CHRIST, as Your Lord and Savior," she beamed.

"Roger that," he saluted her.

They stood in awe as the Chaplain, explained what Sheol was and why it was so important to accept salvation, so they would not be a lost soul waiting to be judged. They acted like little children, as they listened to her vast knowledge of the Bible. They felt the confidence it gave them, at this time of fear. Captain Tatum, finally started to believe what she was saying was true and not a bunch, of poppycock. He looked up toward the dark ceiling thinking, "What if I'm wrong?" he worried. "I've been lost my whole life, and no one ever cared about me, like the Chaplain did. She never gave up on me, even when I've been such a creep to her," he lowered his head in shame.

"Are you, OK, Captain," asked General Oswald.

"Yeah, I'm OK. I suggest, we get a move on, if we're going to stop that thing up there. If the Chaplain, is right, and I believe she is, then we only have a few more hours until daybreak, and I'm not interested in finding out what else, can crawl out of that hell-hole," said the Captain.

They all agreed with him, but the Chaplain insisted, they stick to their original game plan. The plan that brought them to the warehouse in the first place.

She explained Lance's vision to General Owens, Chino, and Captain Ron Tatum, bringing them up to speed, until she came to the virgin bait issue, and why she thought, the demons chose Heavenworth prison and not, someplace else.

"You mean to tell me those things are here for you, because you are a virgin?" cried Chino.

"She's not only a virgin, but she's a 'sanctified virgin' who serves GOD, you idiot," said Derek.

"Well, I'll be!" said the General. "If, that don't beat all. This whole thing, just keeps getting crazier by the minute," he said, shaking the cobwebs out of his mind.

"Where do you suppose, we set this trap for this thing?" asked Captain Tatum.

"In the gym," said Mongo, rubbing his arms to get warm. There was a stiff draft coming up from the bottom of the dark pit. He looked over the railing and saw a strange light, begin to flicker in the distance. "Say, Chaplain, what's that light way down there," he asked, pointing. They all leaned over and saw the flickering light. "I don't know what that is," she admitted, squinting her eyes to see it better.

"I know, what it is. I've seen it many times, before when scouting enemy positions. It's a campfire," the Captain said, looking at the Chaplain.

They all came to the same revelation that she did, except Chino. He didn't get it. "Who would have a campfire in the bottom of this hole! You don't think that's El Diablo, do you?" he asked fearfully, backing away from the railing. "No, the demons are roasting marshmallows down there, what do you think it is?" said Kyle sarcastically. Then they could faintly, hear the echoes of people crying in pain and agony. They all turned and started to run back up the gangway toward the maintenance building. But Chino slipped on some slime and skidded off the gangway, hollering for help.

Captain Tatum was the nearest to hear his cry for help as Chino was dangling by his arms and hanging off the bridge way. At first, Tatum turned and ignored him, as he began to follow the others, who couldn't hear Chino. The Captain licked his cut lip, reflecting about the pistol whipping he had received earlier, and he kept on walking. Chino screamed, as loud as he could, but the vastness of the cavern swallowed his plea for help. His arms burned and were feeling weaker, as he tried to swing his foot up to the walkway, but he couldn't quite get his shoe to catch the mossy edge. He could hear the moans rising from the depths, as he hung on helplessly. He looked down and could see Hell's fire. He began to sob, "Noooo, El Diablo, please! No," he begged, but his grip was slipping. He squeezed for dear life trying to hold on.

While Chino, was hanging there in the darkness, he prayed, "GOD, I don't want to die, please forgive me," he cried tearfully. He could feel his hands starting to let go, and he tried to scream. But his throat was as dry as dirt, and nothing would come out. The gang lord knew, it was over, and he thought to himself, "Why would GOD listen to a killer, like me," and he let go.

"Gotcha!" said Captain Tatum. He had knelt down, stretched out over the bottom rail, and caught the limp Chino, by his right arm. Chino looked up and couldn't believe his eyes, as the Captain strained mightily, to pull him back up to safety. "Thanks, Holmes! I thought I was a goner for sure," said the relieved Christian. "You're welcome. Just don't let it go to your head," growled, the winded Captain.

"Why did you do it? Now I owe you big time, Homey," said Chino as he sat up against the railing. "I ain't your damn Homey, so quit calling me that before, I throw you over again," he said.

Chino smiled and closed his eyes, trying to rejuvenate. He knew only too well, that if the circumstances had been different, he would be roasting more than marshmallows in Hell, with El Diablo.

Chapter 24

"Let's eat! Maybe just a bite, or two?."

"Of all the bad luck," moaned Mongo, holding his hands up in disgust. "Now, what are we going to do?" The wreckage had buried the exit back through the maintenance building. They all sat down to take a break and get some rest.

"Where have you guys been?" asked the General, taking off his helmet.

"Oh, we got hung up a little back there," Chino smiled. The Chaplain eyed the Captain, thinking something, must have happened but, didn't question them.

"Well, what can we do now that Plan A is gone?" she questioned the group.

No one said anything for a while, as they tried to regain their senses. They were tired, hungry, and badly bruised from their epic journey. The Chaplain could tell they were all running on fumes, and the best thing they probably could do was to get some nourishment.

"I think we need to eat something and quickly, before we die from starvation," she opined.

280

They all nodded their heads in agreement with her. "Where can we get some food?" yawned the General, rubbing his sore neck.

"Well, we can go through the west storm drains, which should lead us up to the chow hall, so long as the drain is not damaged. It comes up through the kitchen galley and into the main food storage shelter," advised the captain.

"How do you know about all of these underground tunnels and what not?" asked LT.

"I know everything there is about this place. We practiced many drills underneath this place preparing for every kind of emergency you could think of, except something like this," he said.

"Well, I'm glad you did, because I could eat a horse right about now," said Mongo, rubbing his stomach.

"Yes, I think that goes for all of us. Ron, how do we get there from here?" the Chaplain asked, kindly.

"Follow me," Captain Ron said, waving his hand for them to come.

They moaned and complained, as they got up off the cold floor, but they were happy just thinking about eating some hot food. Just imaging eating a mouth-watering steak, or fixing up a giant cheeseburger could push a person a long distance.

The Army used the thought process, as part of their survival training, the General mused, to himself. He imagined that he was eating some hot French fries, smothered in ketchup.

The Christians marched again, following the Captain's quick pace. They came to a metal door that none of them had noticed, when they passed by it earlier. The Captain jingled his keys and found the skeleton key that fit the ancient lock that was bolted in the door. None of the inmates ever got used to that dreadful sound, of the jailer's keys rattling their cell door locks. It was always a constant reminder of their incarceration.

"I didn't see this door earlier," said Chaplain Barnett, pushing some cobwebs away. "That's because you weren't looking for it. You never notice anything, unless you're looking for it," said Porebski, with a heavy accent.

"That makes sense to me," said Kyle, rolling his eyes up in his head, as he passed the Chaplain.

"These drains haven't been walked in for years. GOD only knows, what will find up ahead," said Captain Tatum. "When it rains, there are all kinds of things floating down these tunnels. We've found stuff, like diamond rings, money, needles used by addicts, all kinds of treasures, but mostly mud and such," he informed them all. "Just watch your step, as best you can," he cautioned.

"Watch your step he says. I'm blind, as a bat and feeling my way along these slimy walls," whined Kyle, as he shook something off his fingers.

"Would you be quiet, you big baby. Waa, waa, waa, just like a little baby," mocked his brother, who was right behind him.

"Eeekkkk!" squealed the rat, the General stepped on.

"Damnable rodent!" jeered the General. "I can't stand those things after serving a tour in the Philippines. They are all over the place down there. Good thing they eat them, or they would be really out of control," he said, distastefully.

"They eat rats, really?" asked Mongo, wiping a web from his mouth. "Oh, yeah! The Asian cultures, pretty much eat everything. It doesn't matter what it is. If it can crawl, fly, or swim, they eat it. They just chop it up and wok it with some peanut sauce, and you don't know what it is, unless you are brave enough to ask them," informed General Owens.

"OK! You can stop now! I'm losing my appetite," grimaced the Chaplain.

"What's the matter, Chaplain? Don't like eating black beetles and a side of snake?" he snickered.

"Hardy har, har!" they all guffawed. The Chaplain held her tongue. She was getting queasy just from the idea of it all.

Captain Ron flashed the light back in her face and could see that she was getting green. He knew, she was a meat and potatoes type of girl and didn't care much for spicy or Thai foods. Even, though she was from the deep South, Cajun wasn't ragin' with her.

"You know, what I likes to eat?" asked LT. "I like's my Uncle Joe's smoked brisket of beef, cooked medium well, or maybe even a platter of his world-famous barbequed ribs. Hmmnnn, hmmnn! Just move your hands out of da way, or else, you gonna git bit," he smiled big.

"Now, you're talking, Brother LT. That's my kind of food, too," giggled the Chaplain.

"Ya'll know, dat's American food, right der, yes sir," LT continued. "Ya'll 'memba Bubba? Dat boy spent over two hundred dollars in one sittin', eatin' dose ribs. I ain't never saw a man put food away, like he could, no sir! No one," he started to choke up from the memory, of his recently lost cell mate. "He was a good ol' boy, dat Bubba was, yowser." It grew cold and silent as they traipsed through the muck, and the grim thought of reality had struck them again.

"Hey, Captain. I can see some light at the end of the tunnel," said Kyle happily. "Hope it's not a train," punned Mongo.

"It's probably an air shaft. They line up all along these tunnels, as we get closer to the surface. It shouldn't be too much farther," he said brusquely.

They welcomed the fresh air. It cleared the stench away, from the decaying rot in the tunnel. Each member filled their lungs with the cool air, as it revitalized their senses.

"Oy! I needed that," said Porebski, inhaling deeply.

As they marched further along, the Earth began to shake, knocking matter off the tunnel and into their hair.

"What's that? It can't be an earthquake, could it?" shouted the Chaplain shaking something, out her hair.

"No. It's not an earthquake. It sounds, like a tank, or a heavy . . .," the General didn't finish his sentence, as their hearts began to pound. They knew exactly, what it was. It was the Frogon. "Shhhhh, quiet, don't say a word," whispered the Captain, who was squatting down on his heels looking up, hoping it didn't hear them. They all stared skyward, as the thunderous pounding of the dreaded beast's claws stomped above their heads. Dirt filtered through the cracks from the intense pounding. It was nerve-wracking, and they tried to be as, quiet as a church mouse, hiding. The dust grew heavy, as the Frogon stomped around the grounds seeking the Christians' whereabouts. It began to lean forward, listening to the ground.

The creature snorted loudly, as it started to rake the surface with its powerful hind claws, like a chicken scratching up, some feed. It pecked its way along the ground and then stopped suddenly, directly over them. The great Beast had caught the scent of their fear beneath it. The Frogon reared up on its hind haunches and began to howl, at the blood red moon, as any instinctive hunter would, summoning to another that it had found its quarry.

"What's it doin' up there?" Chino, whispered.

"Shhhh!" shushed the Chaplain, but it was too late.

The earth began to tremble, as the Frogon clawed up the earth in huge clods, shredding the surface of the yard. It was coming after the Chaplain, like a bird on a worm. The dust made them begin to cough as more terra firm, fell on top of them. They stumbled in the quaking tunnel, trying to keep their balance, when the brick ceiling caved in behind them.

"Run for your lives!" screamed Mongo, as he helped the Chaplain to her feet.

Once again, the creature's tongue jutted into the tunnel, narrowly missing the Chaplain and Mongo. It rose and listened to their steps as they plodded in the muddy tunnel below. The Frogon stomped over to a nearby air vent and tore off the galvanized cover. It peeked with one eye down into the tunnel. Then it waited patiently, as the Christians made their way to an intersection of an adjoining tunnel. The ventilation shaft was directly above it.

The Frogon drooled heavily, as it waited impatiently, for the unsuspecting victims.

"Down here," shouted Derek, taking the lead along with Captain Tatum.

"Wait a minute. What's that moving in front of us?" asked Tatum, trying to twist the focus of his fading flashlight. "I don't know," said Jackson.

The Captain tapped the flashlight, against the wall to bring the ailing batteries back to full beam to illuminate, the tunnel ahead.

"RATS!" he shouted to everyone.

"Back everybody! Turn back! There's a herd of rats, heading our way," Kyle Jackson, said frantically.

"Oh, that's just great," cried Mongo, bumping into Chino and knocking him down. "Hey, Holmes! Watch where, you're going, man," he warned the big man.

A thousand of the remaining rats, had escaped the Army's earlier attack and now, escaped down the shafts seeking shelter there, until the thunderous Frogon, agitated them, again. They bounded down in the dark, just as the waiting Frogon, shot its sticky tongue into the air shaft. The Frogon felt the vibration of the rats, thinking it was the Christians. The massive muscle flicked around in the tunnel, swiping the interior chamber, of the shaft and swiping many of the angry, vermin.

The rodents bit and gnawed, at the startled Frogon's tongue, as it retracted it back up the air shaft from the tunnel. The Frogon roared agonizing in pain and went beserk! It danced around, helplessly jutting its long sticky tongue, in and out of its gaping maw. It tried to scrape the rats off with its claws, spat them to the ground, and then stomped on them, like the stinging insects, they were.

The Captain heard the roar and stopped, shining the light back down the tunnel. He saw that it was nearly empty of the ravenous, rodents.

"Hey you guys, stop! They're gone," he shouted.

"What did he say?" Kyle asked LT. "I think he said they're gone," answered LT.

They all stopped. They could hear the Frogon's pounding dance, just above them.

"What do you think happened to it?" asked Porebski.

"I think that thing was waiting for us, and it got a little surprise instead, from our furry little friends," said the General.

"Now, that's what I call, 'divine intervention,' chuckled, the Chaplain.

"It looks clear back there. I say we make a run for it," advised the Captain.

"Well, let's get going before that thing digs us out of here," said the General, wisely.

"I agree. I think it sucked up most of the rats down there. There might be a few left, but not enough for us to worry about," Captain Tatum, said.

"Where does that other tunnel lead to, Captain," asked the observant General.

"I think it leads to the SHU, but don't quote me on that," said Tatum.

"Let's stick to the game plan and get something to eat," said the Chaplain.

"I agree. We can't fight on an empty stomach," said General Owens.

"OK, then, let's move out," commanded the Captain, once again taking the lead.

"Chaplain, get behind me. If, there are any more of those rodents up ahead, I'll squash them for you," said Mongo, going ahead of her and leaving her at the rear of the pack. "You're my, hero, Mongo," she said proudly, patting him on his muscular back.

"What about me, Chaplain? Ain't I your hero, too?" wondered Kyle Jackson.

"You are all my heroes," she beamed brightly.

"Shhhhhhh, we're almost to the shaft. Be quiet," warned the Captain. He shined the flashlight's beam up into the shaft and leaned over as he looked upward to make sure the coast was clear. "Come on, quickly. It's clear," he said quietly, and they all tiptoed passed the ventilation shaft.

They could hear the Frogon whimpering, like a wounded animal, destroying the remaining rodents.

The group crossed over another storm drain in the floor, where water trickled down in the dark, hitting another grate in the subterranean chambers, below. The moon's eerie red glow lit the air shaft and then the tunnel faintly. They used their hands to balance themselves and blindly felt their way through the tunnel. They traveled another two hundred yards, before the Captain told them they were almost to the exit. They were relieved for the most part, thinking that the Chaplain was correct in stating that it must have been a "divine intervention" as the rats had attacked the creature, rather than them. They could hear the Captain's keys rattling in the door lock, and then it opened with a rusted creaking sound, just like in the horror movies. The door was blocked by something—it only opened narrowly.

"Hey, Mongo, I need some muscle to open this door please" asked the Captain, politely.

This shocked the other inmates, thinking it was the first time they'd ever heard him be polite, about anything.

"Man, did you hear, what I just heard?" whispered LT to Derek. "Yes. Now, that's something," the older Jackson whispered back to him.

They heard the two strong men groan, as they shoved the rusty door forward. It knocked over some boxes of food that were blocking it.

The two kept shoving the door, until it was three quarters open, and then to everyone's amazement, the Captain shook Mongo's hand.

"Good job, Big Fella," obliged, the grateful Captain. "Er, uh . . . you're welcome, Captain," said Mongo, smiling proudly, acknowledging the rare moment.

They all wandered around the huge stockroom, looking into the boxes to see what they could eat, immediately. They knocked over crate loads of canned goods from the shelves as they searched for something that they could eat. Finally, Chino opened a box full of bananas.

"Hey, homies, look what I found," he said as he proudly held up a banana. "Let's eat," said Kyle, reaching up and grabbing it out of his hands.

Then he handed out the bananas, like they were going out fast. The hungry men peeled them and scarfed them down quickly, moaning with pleasure. Chino dispensed the entire box, until he noticed something odd. "Hey, homey, where's Chaplain Barnett?" he asked, bewildered. They all stopped eating for a second and began to walk around the stockroom looking for her.

"Chaplain where are you?" they shouted, puzzled by her sudden disappearance.

"She was right behind me, when the Captain called me forward," said Mongo, clearly upset.

"Where is she?" asked Porebski, lifting his arms up in the air, dumbfounded. The stark realization hit them instantly, and they all looked back at the dark entry leading to the tunnel. They didn't know, where she had gone, but they had an overwhelming fear come over them, knowing that she was, indeed, in serious danger.

Chapter 24

"The Beginning of the End"

The Army Apache Warbird, launched a Harpoon Missile, into the back of the giant Frogon, as it crossed the compound into the smoldering main annex. It was a direct hit, blasting the monster forward, face first into the charred rubble. The plume of smoke rolled into the air, causing poor visibility for the chopper pilots, as they aimed the spotlight over the debris, searching for the carcass of the Beast. They made another pass over the annex, wondering where it had disappeared. One of the pilots turned the Apache's main rotor over the smoldering debris to fan the black smoke away in order to get a better viewpoint.

All of a sudden, the Frogon leaped into the air and snatched the unwary pilot from his stagnant position. It wrapped its powerful talons around the hovering Apache and brought it to the ground. The chopper exploded into a fiery ball, killing the two-man crew aboard her.

The Frogon crashed back into the charred embers, creating a huge cloud of ash. The cloud of glowing embers rose quickly, like a giant bonfire and blocked another horrified pilot's, view plane. The pilot jerked the joystick hard right and banked the chopper to avoid the blinding smoke and fire that billowed a hundred feet, into black sky.

The Frogon hopped out of the ashes of the wreckage, crawled up the north wall of the massive prison rotunda, and disappeared on the opposite side of the domed roof. The pilot banked left and circled around the dome, while gaining elevation. He armed his 80mm Gatlin guns and strafed across the dome. The shells fell, like golden rain from the blazing side gun, which belched its own brand of fire back at the hiding beast. The bullets ripped along the rooftop in parallel lines, tearing chunks of solid concrete up, like it was made from Styrofoam.

The Frogon shrieked, as it momentarily lost its grip, and the gunner could see, that it was bleeding a bright, fluorescent green from its wounded left, hind leg. The creature scampered around the giant dome, seeking shelter from the pesky chopper's stinging barrage of bullets.

"It's hit! I think that's blood dripping down the dome," said the co-pilot. The chopper was a good fifty feet above the dome, not taking any chances, as the others had. He kept firing bursts into the dome, keeping the Frogon off guard. He was hoping it would grow weak and fall from its lofty perch.

The pilots radioed for more ground support, and two Abrams M-1A, Battle Cats responded. They were stationed in front of the administration building, in the parking area to the south. They sped over the front courtyard, smashing through the shrubbery, while firing multiple rounds into the dome. The Frogon was getting pummeled for the first time, as the Army regiment poured it on.

The wounded monster roared in defiance and swung its dragon-like tail. It was like an angered alley cat, as it smashed the columns off the side of the rotunda. Then it clawed its way to the top of the dome and smashed the cell towers off the dome, like they were branch twigs. It curled up in frustration, cried in pain, and then peed all over the dome. The urine looked like streams of green molten lava, as it ran off the dome and dripped down to the ground.

"Will you look at that," pointed the Apache pilot.

"Yeah, man! It's really pissed off. Let's nail that thing," said the Co-pilot.

The Apache made another pass and banked a left turn. Then suddenly, the molten splatter pelted the Apache chopper and burned a hole in the rear rotor blade. "We're hit!" said the pilot, jostling for control. The Frogon flung more of the molten matter, into the air, by whipping its massive tail, like a catapult.

The highly corrosive material smacked into the spinning chopper's windshield, burning holes through it, which then dripped onto their bodies.

"AAAAARRRRRGGGGGGHHHHHH!" they screamed.

The Frogon then circled to the opposite side of the dome, away from the artillery fire, using it as a shield against them. It watched the smoking chopper plummet from the sky, as it crashed into the prison fuel depot building, with an ensuing explosion, of smoke and fire.

"BAAAARRROOOOOOOMM!" it shook the compound.

The tank commander witnessed the whole event. He was standing in the gun turret, atop his Abrams. He shielded his eyes from the blinding flash of the explosion that was adjacent to their position. The gunner reported that the monster was moving, again and was now crawling like a tree frog, head-first down from the dome and down the front of the administration building.

> "Sir, we got to get out of here! That thing is coming right for us," he panicked. "Beat feet, now!" he ordered, without a second thought. "Load another round and kill that thing," he commanded to the gunner.

The tank was in full reverse and traveling at top speed. It knocked down some small trees that outlined the parking lot and then ran over some parked cars. He watched the other Abrams tank try to make a stand by firing one round, after another, but missing the rampaging Frogon.

The remaining troops surrounding the south flank, opened fire with everything they had, but nothing seemed to slow the massive beast down. It flicked its long tongue out and snatched the other tank commander right out of his turret, like a fly off a lily pad.

Spotlights surrounded the perimeter, featuring the towering Behemoth, as it stopped and yanked the tank turret off the ground, by its cannon, then effortlessly, hurled it into space. The gunfire ceased, as the soldiers stood in awe of the monster's tremendous strength and watched the turret soar, through the air into the Army's munitions trailer that, was parked near the prison's main entrance.

When the tank hit, it had ruptured the trailer and ignited it like a fireworks display on the Fourth of July:

"VAROOOOM! POP! BANG! BOOM! KABLAMMO!"

It was uncanny, how every move the Frogon made was strategically placed by creating the greatest force of damage that it could possibly have made. The soldiers ran for their lives, retreating through the pastures of the stampeding buffalos and into the surrounding foothills.

They wondered what it would take to suppress such a supernatural juggernaut, as it roared mightily at their defeat. The lone remaining tank, which rammed the old prison bus, was stuck and could go no farther. Its commander blazed gallantly away, firing his 55mm machine gun at the oncoming menace that had hunted, them down.

The driver flipped the forward hatch lid open and crawled out of the tank, followed by the not so, unlucky gunner.

"ZOT," darted the Frogon's tongue, dragging the flailing soldier into its, munching machine. The machine gun ran out of ammo, so the commander reached for his side arm and began to fire it. The sixty-foot-tall demon stood over him and roared, popping the commander's eardrums. It then reached down and plucked the 38-year-old U.S. Army Captain up by his helmet and hoisted him into the blood-red, moon lit sky. The other soldiers hid in the shrubbery and watched with horrified anticipation the demise of their comrade in arms. The Frogon snorted arrogantly, as it studied the insignificance of humanity, while the deaf soldier squirmed, between its talons. It was making a mockery of all the spectators, driving fear deep into their numbed psyche, as it hoisted him up a little higher into the air and dropped him whole into its gaping jaws, like a piece of candy.

The Frogon further, terrorized the grounds, as it sought out any of the remaining human pestilence from behind thick clusters of shrubbery. The soldiers acted, like frightened cottontails, as they tried to hide, in the landscape with their camouflaged fatigues. They could run, but not hide from the amphibious, Apex predator. The Frogon sniffed them out, one by one, zapping them up with its tongue, or snaking them out of drainpipes. There was no place to hide. The lucky soldiers who had survived the night, were the ones, who kept running and never looked back.

The Frogon was merciless, as it sought to destroy all forms of life, man or beast. It even devoured a couple of buffalo, that were pasturing, in front of the prison. The fires blazed in the battlefield, void of life, as the Frogon crawled back up to the top, of the decimated dome and stood on its rear haunches, roaring victoriously to the blood-red moon. .

Meanwhile, back in the subterranean tunnels, the Christians searched for the missing Chaplain. When they arrived at the intersection where the ventilation shaft was, they had found her silver necklace lying in the muddy floor that led to the Special Housing Unit.

"Look," said General Owens, picking up the crucifix, "the chain has been broken."

"Well, at least we know, where she went. Now, we can follow the trail. Look here at the two sets of footprints leading down the tunnel," said Captain Tatum, flashing the beam of light down the mossy, brick tunnel.

"God, I pray she's OK," said Mongo with remorse, hanging his bald head low.

"Well, she won't be for long, if we don't hustle and find her. I'm sure Watini will prepare her for his little sacrificial ritual, like she told us he would," said Kyle vigilantly, shaking his fist.

"Who's Watini?" asked Chino. "He's the demon, that killed Samansky back in the warehouse," said Lance, holding his ribs. "You mean the dude with the dreads?" Chino quizzed.

"Yeah Bro, that's him, alright," said LT, nodding his head. "Look here, Holmes, I saw that dude get shishka-bobbed back at the shack. When that Frogon thing was after me, I blew up a truck, and the blast knocked that dude off the rafters," bragged Chino.

"He landed on a long piece of pipe that went right through him. I saw it with my own two eyes, Homey. It was the last thing I saw, before I chased you guys into the tunnel," said Chino.

"Well, if he's dead, then who abducted Chaplain Barnett?" asked the confused General. Nobody answered.

"Well, someone or something had to take her. It snatched her right out from under our noses, and we have to find her right now. So, let's get going," ordered Captain Tatum, frantically. He envisioned her face, as he took the lead down the long tunnel.

No one said a word. Their thoughts and prayers were with the good Chaplain. They were angry with themselves that they had lost her to the enemy, and each man felt a horrible sense of guilt, knowing she was such a great person, and they would feel horrible losing her.

The Chaplain loved them all, in a very special way, and they all knew it. She had ministered to each one of them on different occasions at their time of need and helped them however, she could.

Mongo remembered the time his mother had passed away, and it was Chaplain Barnett who broke the news to him. He cried like a baby in her arms, as she comforted him, even though it was against regulations to touch an inmate in any manner. He knew that she was the bravest person on the staff when she would meet with inmates, one on one in her office, although a CO was usually waiting out in the hallway.

In nine years, of her Chaplaincy, she had never been harmed. She would let the inmates use her phone to call home on occasion, knowing, they didn't have much money, earning only twelve cents an hour. The pay phones were the biggest rip-off the Bureau operated, charging them twenty-five cents a minute for a call. They were even charged, if they left a message, since they could not take incoming calls. Most of the inmates respected her, even if they weren't saved.

Chaplain Barnett could brighten a roomful of the meanest inmates and turn them into lambs, by the time she left. She was truly a rare and genuine individual. You knew you could trust her with anything. The men were ashamed that they had thought sexually, about her, especially knowing now that she was a virgin and in her late thirties.

She was saving her virginity, for the man she would marry someday, and apparently, that hadn't happened yet. She would be a treasure worth keeping, and, knowing that it made all of them run down the tunnel instead of going at a slow trot. They loved her, like they loved JESUS, at least the Christians did that, knew Him. She was the best example for them to know, the love of CHRIST, because she walked in righteousness and loved each one of them. Chaplain Barnett did not judge them, and that's what made her so special.

Derek and Kyle remembered her for her generosity. She would give them supplies that she had purchased with her own money, many times, when the Bureau would not cough up for needed equipment repair for the band's instruments in the Chapel. Or there were the hundreds of times, when new arrivals came into the prison and needed shower shoes and hygienic supplies. The Chaplain organized a tithing system for the Christian Brothers in the prison to purchase supplies from their personal commissary lists and then donate to the chapel locker. When a new inmate arrived, they could come to the chapel to get a shaving kit from them. It was a real blessing to many of the inmates, and they always thanked them, for it.

They reached the SHU and could see the door was opened wide leading into the front offices. General Owens and Captain Tatum removed their side arms and proceeded slowly into the office, sweeping their weapons, as they looked for Chaplain Barnett.

The others remained in the tunnel, until the coast was clear. "Clear!" shouted the Captain, putting his gun back in its holster. He checked the monitors on the watch desk, but they were all out of commission. It was dark in the room, because all the power was out from the damage incurred to the facility. The flashlights were growing dim, too, and they needed to replace them.

"Jacksons, check the back room and get the high beam LED lights. They're on the shelves to your left, third door down. There should be four, or five of them in there. They should help us to see, better because, those babies really crank out some candlepower," he boasted, as he searched the desk drawers for ammunition. He found half a bottle of whiskey and removed it from the file drawer. He twisted the cap off and then looked around him to see if, anyone was watching, he tilted it up in the air and began to take a swig. But noticed the bloody reminders left on the walls by the demonic Druid that had the only woman, he had ever really respected.

Captain Tatum stopped immediately, remorseful over the loss of his staff, put the cap back on the bottle, and put it back, where he had found it, and closed the drawer. He felt the overwhelming burden of responsibility, remembering that he had shot his own man, earlier while trying to shoot Watini. He closed his eyes tightly as the haunting images flashed through his mind.

He relived the moment seeing that thing crawling around the ceiling. He jumped up from his desk, pulled out his pistol, and aimed it at the ceiling, thinking it was watching him again.

"Are you OK, Captain?" asked the startled General who was walking past him.

"What? Ah, yeah, I mean no. I mean, I don't know, Rocky. I'm so spooked about all of this, that it has me on edge. I keep visualizing Watini crawling around on the ceiling. I'm hallucinating with reality," admitted the Captain, wiping the sweat from his brow. "I mean, look at me. I'm shaking like a leaf," he held his quaking hands out in front of him.

"Don't feel bad. I went through the same thing. It's called Post Traumatic Stress Disorder. Soldiers who have been in heavy combat get it all the time. Your brain wrestles with the reality of what it was taught to believe, as opposed to the horrors of the unbelievable, explained General Rocky.

"It's a big cover-up in the military, and the psyche wards are full of veterans who are drugged out on all kinds of pharmaceuticals, trying to neutralize the frames of horror trapped inside their minds," added the General, patting the Captain on the back. "We've been through an awful lot today, and we're not done yet. I need you, Ron, so don't wig out on me now, Brother," he assured him.

"I won't," said the tired Captain. "I need a vacation, that's all," he smiled. "That makes two of us! Listen, how do you feel about letting the guys, handle a weapon?" asked the General.

"Scary," declared the Captain, "but considering the circumstances we're in, who cares?"

"I believe the more guns, the better off we are in hunting that thing. Who knows? One of them might get lucky and kill it," offered the general, picking up a 9mm from the floor.

"Well, hopefully it and not us," joked the Captain, dropping his clip out and reloading it.

"This 9mm hasn't even been fired. Who should I give it to?" asked the General, watching the bright spotlights come down the corridor. Captain Tatum took it from him and handed it to Chino.

"Here. It's for your own protection," said the Captain.

Chino pulled the hammer back and loaded a shell in the chamber.

"Thanks, Holmes," he grinned, showing the weapon to the others

Where's ours?" asked Porebski.

"You can find plenty of them lying around the dead soldiers. Arm yourselves, but don't take anything that you can't handle. I don't want to get shot by any of you. If you need a brief training on a rifle, or how to use a grenade, ask me," ordered the General. They all concurred.

"Man, these LED spotlights are the ticket, they shine forever," said Mongo, flashing the bright beam around the room and noticing the bloody drawings on the walls. "What are those?" "Those are Druid worship, symbols to Satan. They were painted with the blood from my men and the dead inmates who were killed earlier this evening," said the Captain. "The Army bagged the bodies and took them out of here," he continued. He pulled a cup from the dispenser and lifted the water cooler back upright. "Drinks are on me," he smiled, pressing the button to the gurgling jug.

After, they hydrated, they made their way to the Chapel and armed themselves to the teeth with rifles, handguns, and grenades. Mongo found an 55mm machine gun and wrapped the extra belts around his neck. "Look at me, guys! I look like Jesse Ventura, in the Predator," he said, waving the gun in front of him. General Owens gave him a two-minute drill on its operation. They tested it, by firing a burst into the wall ahead of them: " BBBBBRRRAAAAAAPPPPPPPP! It works fine," grinned Mongo.

"Now, that's what I call firepower," giggled the giddy inmate. "We'll follow you, Mongo," said Kyle warily, walking behind the man-child.

They heard strange sounds of pipes clanging and glass breaking from the devastation that surrounded them. Piles of rubble and debris were strewn everywhere, as they pushed forward.

They hiked through the gutted annex, hardly recognizing it, as they used to pass by it daily to go to the chow hall. The entire auditorium had collapsed, and they could see the eerie red moon on the horizon. They knew time was running out, but they had to get to the Chapel and fulfill the mission Lance was given by GOD. Dead inmates and soldiers comingled, in the charred carnage; no signs of life were left anywhere. It was all a grim reminder that they were blessed to be alive and were hoping to find the Chaplain soon, in the same condition.

"Where do you think she is?" asked Kyle of his older brother. "I don't have a clue, Kyle, but I'm praying for her protection, nonetheless," he whispered. They walked over a huge wall that collapsed where they could see the legs of the unfortunate soldiers extending from under it. The General turned his head in disgust and wiped the tears from his face.

"Such a waste," he wept. They made it to the Chapel and immediately, went to work. Mongo, Porebski, and Kyle climbed up on the altar and pried off the huge wooden cross that was mounted on the wall.

The bolts snapped, and it crashed to the red-carpeted floor, below them. They got down and lifted it up on the altar, using it as a workbench. They had machetes to hack the bottom, vertical end of the cross into a point.

The General and the Captain, kept watch in the hallway, while the men worked, chopping the wooden cross into a giant stake. It was eighteen feet in length and eight feet at the horizontal cross section. They lifted it up and took it to the door, but they couldn't get it out. The cross section was too long—it would not fit through the doorway.

Mongo then shot out the wall, with his new toy making it just wide enough, so they could get the cross out. They packed it down to the gymnasium, laid it on the floor, and LT shimmied up an exercise rope to the side of the gym. He carried a sixty foot rope that he drape,d over his shoulder. They had retrieved the rope from the Construction Shop that was near the SHU.

"Be careful up there," warned Derek.

LT was serving ten years for burglary, he was a professional cat burglar, and they realized that he was the man for the job. They watched the way he balanced himself, as he walked across the ceiling support beams. Then LT sat down on a steel beam in the center of the ceiling and tied one end of the rope around a cross beam and dropped the rope. They tied another rope to it, and he pulled it back up to himself. Then LT fed the longer, second rope over the center beam to the floor.

The inmates fastened a harness of a smaller rope, around the cross, and then eight of them hoisted the cross halfway up into the air, so that it was suspended horizontally about twenty feet from the center beam, like a pendulum in the middle of the gymnasium. "I hope this works," said the Captain.

LT wrapped the end of the rope, around another support beam and tossed the excess rope to the team waiting below him. "OK, pull it back," he called down to them. They struggled with their footing on the damp floor, but finally raised it back, like a hammer swing. LT quickly fastened another rope, and the trap was set. But he had almost forgotten to put on the finishing touch. LT walked back across the beam like a tightrope act, holding his arms out for balance. He knelt down and removed his crucifix from around his neck, remembering that the Chaplain had given it to him, when he first arrived at Heavenworth. He said a quick prayer and then laid flat on his belly on the steel beam. LT stretched out his left arm, barely reaching the front tip of the cross, and draped the neck chain around the end of it. The cross caught the spotlights below, and it flashed, like a star in the sky. He got up and slid back down the exercise rope to the floor. "There. That should do the trick," he said as he brushed his hands off, smiling.

"You think this thing is going to work?" doubted, the four-star General.

"Hey, General," said Lance, "if GOD, told me to do it, then I'm going to follow HIS plan. Besides, nothing the Army has done has stopped that creature. Derek saw how it reacted, when the Chaplain flicked her cross on the Frogon's tongue, and it went nuts," Lance continued, pointing up to the suspended cross on the ceiling.

"Well, I hope you're right, even though it seems pretty medieval. One thing though, how do we pull the trigger?" asked the weapons expert.

"We shoot the rope that's holding it back," Lance explained. "Who's going to shoot that rope in the dark?" asked the puzzled General. Lance scratched his head, then, thinking that maybe the General had a good point.

"I know! Let's fasten a flare cartridge to the rope and then tie some string on the pin and hang the string down to the floor. That way, anyone can pull the trigger," advised LT.

"Man, you are slick! Nice touch adding your cross to the tip, by the way" praised Derek, giving him a high five.

"That should work, but you have to go back up there again," said the General. "That's perfect, all we need now, is the bait," said Lance. "Who's going to be the bait?" asked General Owens, looking for volunteers.

"I'll be the bait," said Chino "That thing didn't catch me the last time I saw it, and it won't this time, either" he said confidently. "Besides, I'm the fastest guy in here, next to LT."

"OK, then, let's go find the Chaplain. I think our best shot is splitting up though," advised Captain Ron.

"Me, too," said General Owens. "I'll take Lance, Mongo, Porebski, and Chino. That will leave you, with LT and the Jackson brothers."

"That sounds good to me. Let's synchronize our watches. I have four thirteen, a.m. Let's sync now. You guys go down to A-Block and then swing over to the powerhouse. We'll double back to the tunnels and down to the Pit. We only have two hours until sunup, so we got to make haste. Every minute counts," said the worried captain.

"Whoever encounters the Frogon leads him back here and kills it. The others, hopefully, will find Chaplain Barnett. I have a sneaking hunch Watini, has her held hostage at the Portal. If, he's going to have a virgin sacrifice, I think he'd do it over the Gates of Hell, don't you guys?" asked the General.

"Before you all go, I have something for you," said Derek. He opened a canvas satchel and distributed cross necklaces to those, who didn't have one. He gave one to Captain Tatum, one to General Owens, Chino, LT and Lance.

"I found these in the Chaplain's desk, when we broke into it back at the Chapel," he explained. He then removed a bottle of Holy Water and opened it. Hold them out and let me bless them with this Holy Water. The same goes for your ammunition, too. You can never be over prepared, when fighting against the supernatural," he assured them all.

"Come on, Jackson, we ain't fighting vampires for GOD's sake," moaned the Captain.

"I know, said Derek, "but the bullets that were fired from the Army and your men never harmed them, so if, we don't try something different, especially, knowing what we've seen well, let's not be foolish and take any chances. Besides, the Chaplain would want to do the same thing, if she were here" he said, defensively. So, they held out the guns, the ammo, and the crosses, as Derek said a prayer and then sprinkled the Holy Water, saying: "JESUS, Bless these men with, Your anointing from on high.

"Protect us from evil and guide our actions with, Your, mercy and grace. Lord, GOD, sanctify our lives, protect Chaplain Barnett from the enemy, and lead us to rescue her from Satan's demonic forces. Give us victory over the enemy. This I pray in JESUS' name. Amen."

"Man! Did you feel that?" asked the General.

"Yeah! It felt really good! It felt like a wave of warmth washing through my entire body, from my head down to my toes," smiled the Captain.

"That's the HOLY SPIRIT! The anointing of GOD, is upon us," Mongo said, joyfully. "That's correct, Brother. That's why we should pray, about everything we do," said Kyle.

"Hey, David killed Goliath, with GODs anointing, and JESUS stole the keys from Hell, overcoming sin and death. So, we too, are more than conquerors, in CHRIST JESUS," quoted Porebski, in a heavy accent.

"I'm ready to go kick some, Frogon tail," cheered Chino, tucking his gun into his belt.

"Thanks, you guys," said General Owens. "I would have never thought GOD was real, until tonight and to think that I got saved in a prison, by a bunch of Christian inmates. I'm starting to understand the big picture," he added, as he spread the chain over his head. He looked at the cross and smiled, as they left the gymnasium to go find the chaplain.

Chapter 25

"Chaos"

The men walked out of the gymnasium, talking about the Frogon, when they encountered Hedeku, just as he was leaving the Chapel. Time seemed to stand still, as they were in shock to have run into one another, so unexpectedly. The Chaplain wasn't with him, which really set the fuse off with the crusaders. Hedeku's dark figure was ominous, to say the least, as his onyx eyes and snaking tongue glistened in the reflection from the spotlight. Mongo had the lead and swung the mini gun up, and opened fire. ":BRRRRRRAAAAAAAAAAAAAATTTTTTTT!

Fire belched out, from the rotating chambers of the 55mm, as Mongo strafed the corridor, trying to hit the bounding demon. The others watched in awe, as Watini's image flashed, before their eyes, like a stuttering film clip of images following, one after another. The bizarre movements defiled gravity and all human logic.

"Get him!" ordered the Captain, firing his M16 rifle. The Christians opened-up with gunfire, blazing away at the freakish orange target, as they moved their arms up, down, sideways, but always missing the dodging demon.

No matter where they aimed, it was a Nano-second, too late. They were shooting behind him instead. The bullets sparked, as they ricocheted off the walls of the long, concrete corridor. Then the daunting devil, made a flying lunge, behind a pile of rubble and ran down the opposite corridor.

"Blast it all to Hell! How could we all miss that thing? It doesn't make any sense," cried the General, dropping a clip from his M16 and reloading another, into his weapon.

"It's gotten faster, than when we first saw him, in the maintenance building," said Chino, in disbelief.

"Man, I saw that thing get skewered. I swear I did," he said, rubbing his tired eyes.

"How are we supposed to kill that thing? We all shot at it, and it didn't even faze him," cried Mongo, throwing the empty mini-gun to the ground in disgust.

"What was in that sack, he was holding? It looked like we caught him red-handed stealing, something out of the Chapel, didn't it?" asked Kyle, observantly. "I can't remember. I was too busy shooting at it," said Porebski.

"Yea, I saw the bag, too, Kyle. Let's go in the chapel and find out what it could have been," offered LT, as they all, moved down the corridor and went into the chapel to look around.

"Man, oh man, will you look at this place? It looks like, a tornado hit here," said LT, surprised by the mess they had found. "We didn't leave this place looking like this, did we?" asked Derek, picking up a Bible from the floor and putting it back on the altar.

"What on earth do you suppose it was looking for in here?" asked the Captain.

"I have no idea, but I think the Chaplain must be OK for the time being, or else, why would the demon be snooping around in the Chapel?" Derek pondered. The bright spotlights searched throughout the Chape,l until Kyle noticed something unusual.

"Hey, big Brother, do you notice something is missing from here?" he asked, pointing to the empty candelabras lying on the floor.

"Candles? He came for the candles," said Derek, "but, why?" he asked them.

"Maybe you can't have a virgin sacrifice, without them," offered Mongo, candidly.

"That's just crazy. Why take some candles?" asked General Owens

"Who knows? But, if Chaplain Barnett's still alive, we have got to find her, and I mean right now," said the Captain, frantically. "Let's get out of here before it's too late."

As, if on cue, the Frogon announced its arrival:

"RRRROOOOOOAAAARRRR!"

It was thundering its way down the annex, toward the Chapel wing.

"Well, that saves us the trouble of finding it," joked Porebski, as he ran to the exit. They all ran out of the Chapel and into the hallway. The Frogon spotted them and charged down the corridor. Pieces of the ceiling shook loose, as its massive weight shook the ground, vehemently. The crusaders ran for their lives, back down to the gym to lure the monster, into their trap. Chino helped the Captain back to his feet, after he had tripped over a spent gun belt that was lying on the dark floor. They turned and saw the Frogon's enormous, hulking outline fill the massive corridor. Its warty head occasionally hit the vaulted ceilings, knocking debris to the floor below.

Chino removed his 9mm and stood defiantly in front of the gymnasium entrance, firing his pistol:

"POP, POP, POP, POP, POP, POP, POP, POP, POP"

He emptied the clip and looked in disbelief, at the weapon, because it had no effect whatsoever, so Chino threw the gun at the advancing Frogon. He turned and ran for his life into the gym.

"Get ready! Here it comes," he shouted, crawling over some wreckage and getting into position. They turned out the spotlights and waited for the beast's momentary entrance, into the gym. They could see the opening of the gaping hole that was once, a wall barrier leading into the gymnasium. Dark shadows, of twisted beams and insulation dangled loosely from the ceiling of the demolished entrance, as the Frogon entered the gym. Its gigantic outline was terrifying, and the Christians struggled desperately, not to faint while, holding their strategic positions.

The Frogon sensed something was amiss, as its long, snaking tongue, tasted the humans' fear in the air. It hunched down a bit, trying to let its eyes adjust to the dark void, of the gymnasium, uttering a low rumbling growl, "GGGGRRRRRRRRRR"

The men could feel the rumbling vibrato that gurgled forth from its deep throat, like that of a sixty-foot-tall alligator. It slowly made its way into the gym and then lashed its tongue out, against the forward bleachers, where Kyle was hiding. Its tongue rattled the wooden bleachers, narrowly missing him, only because he was lying down between two rows of seats.

Kyle sobbed, silently in the dark and closed his eyes tightly, praying for his life, as the deadly force missed him, again.

"Over here!" shouted Derek, turning on his light and aiming it up to its slanted, yellow eyes, exposing his whereabouts, to the demon dragon. It stood upright, startled by the Christian's boldness, but then it grew wary of him, as he stood at the other end of the gym. It growled loudly and looked about in the darkness, but it didn't see anybody else, as it tried blocking the blinding, high beam., with his claw.

"Bok, bok, bok, you big chicken," Derek stammered, scratching the floor, like a chicken flapping his arms. The others watched his bravery, and knew that in any second, one wrong move could be their last.

"AAAAAARRRAGGGGGGGAAAARRRRRHHHGGG!" snarled the Frogon, snapping its sharp teeth into the air. It reached out blindly in front of it, taking a cautious step. Then another light clicked on, to Derek's immediate left, as he then shut his own light off.

"Hey, there, Big Ugly! You ain't that bad! Just look at you, acting all big and bad," jaded Porebski, wiggling his behind, as he taunted the bewildered beast. That was the straw that broke the Frogon's scaly back. It lunged into the middle of the basketball court, roaring its anger: "RRRRRROOOOOOOAAAAAARRRRRR!"

"BANG!" The flare flashed brightly, blinding the Frogon momentarily, while exposing its menacing presence. The rope popped and the giant cross released and swung down through the air, directly at the startled, behemoth. The air whooshed aside, as the wooden missile made its way towards the Frogon's wide yellow, throat. The Frogon, gasped in unbelief, as its reptilian eyes grew wider, recognizing the glimmering silver cross that streaked towards it. It reared backward on its hind legs to defend itself, but the sharpened cross struck home, piercing through the beast's lower jaw, then up and impaling it in the brain. The Frogon stumbled, while raising its claws to its throat and the ropes snapped, from the steel rafters.

The Christians, heard the cross strike its target and turned on their spotlights, to watch the beast fall backwards, crashing, dead on arrival, in the rubble, beneath it: "BADA-BOOOMMM-CCCRRASSHH!" They couldn't believe their tired eyes, as the Frogon's enormous tail rattled, a final death throw to defeat. It was totally silent, no one said a word. They just listened to the sweet sound of air gurgling, out from the Frogon's bloody, lungs.

"Praise the Lord!" shouted LT, giving Kyle Jackson a bone-crushing hug.

"It's really, dead?" stammered, the General, walking cautiously toward the beast's talons.

"Glory be to GOD! We killed it! It's dead! HALLEJUAH!" shouted Derek, jubilantly running, across the gym.

Captain Tatum giggled, with joy, not uttering a word, as he kicked the beast's scaly belly with his boot. He didn't know what to say, or how to say it, but tears began to streak down his dirty cheeks, in unbelief. Mongo hugged everyone, with a big squeeze, shaking each one of them, as if, they were a saltshaker and singing,

"Ding, dong, the Beast is dead, the wicked Beast is dead," he merrily danced.

Lance was congratulated, by the vivacious Porebski, who slapped him on the back saying, "I knew it vould vork," he laughed, heartily.

They shined the lights, on the Frogon's head, and they could see the bloody tip of the cross jutting out from the top of the creature's skull, just above its scaly brow.

"Aha, what a shot!" cheered Lance, pointing to it. "Right between the eyes," he cheered.

"Congratulations men, we did it," grinned, the Army General, proudly.

"Uhhh, just a minute there, General," said Derek.

"What is it, Jackson? Can't you be happy and take credit, when credit's due?" "Well, yes I can," Derek said, "but, it was GOD, who should get the credit, not us," said Derek, looking and pointing both his index fingers, upward.

They grew silent, realizing, it was indeed GOD's plan and infinite wisdom that destroyed the living nightmare, which had ravaged and killed thousands of lives that night.

"He's right, General. If, it weren't for GOD, we would all be dead," said Lance, soberly.

"Amen to that, Brother!" said LT, who dropped down to his knees and folded his hands together to pray.

They all dropped, one by one, to their knees and thanked GOD for HIS grace and mercy in their lives. They praised him out loud, while raising their arms up into the air and prayed for HIS, continued blessings and their deliverance from evil.

Then they realized that they had to press on, to find the Chaplain. They rose to their feet and formed a prayer circle, holding each other's hands while standing in front of the slain demon, as they said The Lord's Prayer. They finally, understood the revelation of Scripture, in Romans 8:31, "That all things are possible, with GOD, because if, GOD is for us, then who, can be against us?"

Chapter 26

"Can you hear me, now?"

Chaplain Barnett struggled vigorously, trying to loosen the bonds of rope that entangled her, but it was, to no avail. The gag that was stuffed into her mouth was dry and suffocating. She was empty of tears and couldn't cry anymore, as she sat alone, in the dark cell, tied to the ancient electric chair, in a secret level of security, below the SHU.

"No wonder they called this the Special Housing Unit. It's more like, the chamber of horror," she thought to herself, faintly seeing other ghastly devices of torture lying about the dim lit room. It had become a dark closet, where the guards' discarded things for more than hundred years. Some items were not that dust-covered, such as the wooden box that looked like, a miniature wine press, leaning against the wall. The prison supposedly had disbanded electrocution, back in the sixties and switched to hanging by a rope instead, as a form of "death sentence" in the State of Kansas.

Now, they used lethal injection, as a more hypocritical way to execute someone, who murdered someone else. It was Old Testament. No doubt about it, seeking an "eye for an eye, or a tooth for a tooth." The Chaplain was bitten continuously, about her bare ankles by the bold prison rats that chased each other, about the room. She couldn't see them, but she could hear their shrill squeals to one another, after regaining consciousness, over an hour ago. The last thing she remembered was Mongo passing her in the tunnel, when she saw something move in the dark tunnel that adjoined theirs. A blood-caked hand went around her mouth, as someone very strong jerked her away and dragged her down in a different direction. She knew it was inmate Watini, as he dragged her against her will, to the SHU, and that's when he rendered her unconscious.

Chaplain Barnett could hear the faint sounds of gunfire and explosions, that came from all directions, around the prison. She wondered each time, if it was the good guys, finally beating the bad guys, but after so many disturbances it didn't matter, anymore.
She closed her tired, burning eyes. It felt so good to close them from time to time, because it soothed them. It was the only form of relief she had, other than meditating on the Word of GOD.

"Why was GOD testing me," she prayed, thinking it was something she had done.

"Oh, that's ridiculous, that's just Satan, always there to make you feel guilty about something, even though you didn't do anything wrong at all. "SATAN, YOU ARE THE GREAT LIAR," she shouted to herself, shaking her head back and forth, as she tried to clear her mind of his tormenting thoughts. "Think good thoughts, Brittney," as, she pushed back in the uncomfortable chair. She could smell the putrid musk of moldy urine in the room.

"Lazarus! Hello, my kitty cat. Mommy misses you, sweetie pie. Do you miss your Mommy?" she tried to delude herself, thinking about her fat cat, at home. Her chapped lips stung, smiling about the happy vision, of her loving pet. "Don't you worry, Lazzy. Mommy's coming home soon," she hoped.

Suddenly, the metal door opened slowly and in walked Hedeku carrying the duffel bag of items, he had retrieved from the Chapel. Chaplain Barnett recognized it, immediately. It was her gym bag that she had left in the Chapel, so she realized that's where, he had gone. Then she heard a voice, at least, she thought it was a voice. The accent was British, eloquent, educated, perhaps from Oxford, she thought, to her amazement. She perked up in the chair, as she watched the dreadlocked demon untie her. Her wrists were rubbed raw with severe rope burns, and her neck was chafed, by the filthy hemp.

Hedeku worked quickly. He placed a noose over her head and around her neck. He tugged the slack out of the rope, and the knot slipped securely against, the back of her neck, choking her. He pulled her head back against the wooden chair and hissed his snaky, black tongue in her face. His eyes were completely blacked out, and the Chaplain could literally, see her reflection in his glazed eyes. She was terrified by what she saw.

Her captor's face, was narrow, dark brown, and bony. It was highlighted with two deep scars that disfigured what could have been at one time a handsome man, she thought, observing him. His dreadlocks were black and grey, with highlights of light brown strands streaking through his scalp. He had a bad case of dandruff, and he stank to high heaven as his face moved about hers, his tongue twitching like a rattlesnake's. The chaplain couldn't stand the sight of him. She closed her eyes while turning her head sideways, but she was brought forward by his vice-like grip attached to her chin. Hedeku groped her, and she almost jumped out of the chair. She felt so violated by his inhuman touch to her body. She squirmed, but he jerked the rope around her throat and slammed her head against, the chair, painfully. She stayed conscious, but she wanted to die.

"Sssssssoooooo, Chaplain, let me introdusssssseee mysssssellffff," hissed, the voice inside her head. She opened her eyes, and Hedeku's snakey, tongue flicked at the tip of her nose., but she didn't see his lips move at all, which created more fear in her heart than she could possibly imagine.

"Who are you?" she stammered, to herself.

"I am Hedeku, aaaatt your, ssssssserviccssssssee." He hissed, Chaplain Barnett couldn't believe her racing mind, or trust her befuddled thoughts, as she tried to comprehend the demon's uncanny, supernatural abilities, to read and speak in her mind.

"How is this possible? You are communicating with my mind without moving, or using your voice box," she asked nervously, searching for any signs of humanity, in her captor's expressions.

"Yess, its truly amazzsssiing, issssn't ittt," said the demon, voraciously, fondling her again. "Please don't do that," begged the Chaplain.

Hedeku hissed loudly, baring his fangs and then licked her face, denying her requests. "I caann tassste yourrr virginn feeaarrr. And Iiii, like ittt."

"You're nothing, but a sordid heap of rubbish from Hell," she shrieked defiantly.

"At least you underssstaaanndd mmeeeee, now, ha,hah,hah,haaa!" it laughed, standing upright and holding the rope, like a leash, on a dog.

"Why, are you here?" she asked angrily, relieved he was leaving her alone for the moment.

"'I have come so, those mortals who have life, will lose it and ssserrve the one truueee Masssster, fforrevveerr. We will onccce again, rule the world," Hedeku said, tugging her to her feet.

"Where are we going?" she asked, struggling unsuccessfully.

"Iitssss time for you to die and free our people." Hedeku lifted the bag off the floor and pulled her back down the dark tunnel. The Chaplain realized the demon could see in the dark, because he never once stumbled, while leading her down the dark corridor. She trudged behind him helplessly, slipping and sliding in the mucky tunnel. She could tell they were headed back to the Portal in the cistern. The Chaplain tried to remember what it was, that she had read earlier, about Druid priests and demonic possession, but it was all a blur as Hedeku snapped the rope tighter around her neck. She could barely swallow, as the knot choked her soft throat..

Suddenly, Hedeku fell to his knees, dropped the bag to the ground, and screamed in agony, as he reached for his throat. He hissed loudly, while rolling on the tunnel floor, letting go of the rope. Chaplain Barnett fell back on her bottom, landing in the mud, as the tension was gone from the leash. It scared her and yet, for the first time she felt relieved watching the hideous man roll in pain, but from what, she had no idea. She instinctively knew that something happened, but she couldn't imagine what it was.

She didn't care, though, as she got back up to her feet and ran back to the SHU, as fast as, she could. The hissing noises faded, as she distanced herself from the Druidic demon. Running blindly, she loosened the noose and removed it from, her chafed throat.

"Chaaaaaaplainnn, itsss usseelessss tooo ruuunn," it telepathed, angrily, but Chaplain Barnett kept running for the SHU. She saw the dimly lit doorway, just ahead of her. Her heart raced as she felt that she was, almost there. If she could just get to it in time, she could close and lock it, from the other side.

Suddenly, Hedeku appeared in the doorway. She could tell by the outline of the dreadlocked figure that was now, blocking her way to freedom.

"NO! How could you be there, when . . .?" she stopped in midstride, looking in absolute shock, and wondering how, he got ahead of her. Terrified, Chaplain Barnett started to back pedal slowly, not trusting her perception of reality, as Hedeku stood motionless in the doorway.

"Why isn't he chasing me?" she wondered, walking back toward the Portal. She turned about face to start running again and felt his vice-like, hands grab her arms.

"NO . . . Nooo, no" she cried in disbelief. Her legs went limp as, she tried to reason how he could be in two places at the same time.

"Iiittss qquuuiittee eassyyy, Chaplainnn. Iiii control your thoughttsss and cann projectt myy imaggesss too your punyy brainsss. Thhaaaatt wasss noottt meeee up thherre," he hissed in her ear. She looked back to the doorway and saw that it was empty. She began to sob, as Hedeku put the rope over her head and dragged her back again, to the Portal. "Youuu sseee, iitssss uselesss," he hissed mockingly.

The Chaplain's spirit was down, but not out. Her eternal optimism kept the demon quite amused, as they made their way down the ramp to the archway. She could hear other voices coming from the cistern, giving her hope, once again.

"Help me! I'm over here," she screamed at the top of her lungs. "Maybe it's them," she prayed, looking for her heroes.

"Hah hahhhha hah aaaaaa," the Hedeku laughed, loudly, throwing his head back. She heard the voices getting louder, as they started towards, the gangway.

Then, to the Chaplain's horror, she saw what he was laughing about. The voices were not voices she knew.

They were the moans, of the "lost souls" hovering inside filling the Pit, miles deep, before her. Her throat was dry and locked up, as her muscles tensed in terror. "NOOOO!" she cried, hopelessly, struggling with Hedeku as, he presented her front and center.

"Noooow, noooow, Chaplainnn. They've been waaittingg forrr youuu."

Chaplain Barnett, was sick to her stomach, seeing the wretched demons swarming around in the Pit of Hell. They were deformed, hideous images that were half human and half beast. Some had antlers and some had horns. Some had feminine qualities, and some were men. Some had eyes and some had none. Their noses were snouts, like cows, goats, pigs, and wolves with sharp canine teeth or jagged squares of yellow and red. Worms and bugs fell from their unkempt manes of scraggy hair, but their cries were merciless, agonized pleadings of torment. She thought she was going insane, after witnessing, such a calamity of pain.

Swirling black shadows, of forlorn spirits, whizzed over their heads, flying to and fro, along the vaulted ceiling. They seemed to disappear right into the brick and reappear again, elsewhere in the tunnel. Chaplain Barnett struggled with her senses, witnessing things she couldn't have possibly never seen in her wildest nightmares, but were in abundance before her very eyes.

Hedeku, the Demon Druid High Priest, worked quickly, removing the Chapel candles from the bag. He lit a torch he had made of rags dipped in gasoline. He melted the bottoms of four, large, white candles and attached them to the top bar of the railing.

As, the demon built the makeshift altar, Chaplain Barnett wept, while lying on the slimy, gangway praying to GOD, and thinking about JESUS' last moments, at Calvary before HE was crucified. She remembered her father and all the good things he had taught her, when she was a young girl growing up and helped her in her rights of virginity, when she would come home in tears, accosted after prom dates and dances. She remembered, how he consoled her, telling her that peer pressure was nothing that could harm a person unless, they allowed it too.

Her Dad had prepared her for the worst in life, and now she was feeling the strength of the HOLY SPIRIT, filling her body with the love and support of JESUS CHRIST, as she remembered, Psalms 23: "Even though I walk through the valley of the shadow of death, I will fear no evil, for YOU are with me; your rod and your staff, they comfort me. You prepare a table before me, in the presence of mine enemies. You anoint my head with oil. My cup overflows. Surely, goodness and love will follow me, all the days of my life, and I will dwell in the House of the LORD, forever."

Chaplain Brittney Beth Barnett, ordained Christian Minister, rose to her feet, no longer fearing, what was transpiring around, her. The demons seemed to recognize, her renewed strength and shrieked even louder, trying to haress her and break her connection with the HOLY SPIRIT. She walked up to Hedeku, who was putting a red satin, robe over his head, in preparation for her sacrifice. Startled he looked into her green eyes and saw the Face of GOD.

"Aiiiiiyyyeeeeee! It'sss you, the Nazarene!," cried the Druidic Demon. Hedeku put his hands up in front of her face to hide from her gaze, into his dark soul. Hedeku was terrified, for the first time in his life as he stared down to the Pit seeking support. Chaplain Barnett compassionately walked over to the now, shrieking Hedeku and touched his cheek with the back of her soft hand. He fell down on his back. "Doooon't touccchhhhh meeeee," he hissed vehemently, as if she were inflicting pain. He crawled back and pulled himself up onto the railing. Then he pulled out his bloody knife and lashed out at the Chaplain, cutting her left shoulder.

She stumbled backwards, against the railing and fell in between the lighted candles. The wound burned, as blood began to stain her jacket. Hedeku crouched toward her for another attack, while she was down.

He held the knife high, ready to lunge upon the virgin, when she looked up again and said, "I forgive you!"

She might as well, have hit the advancing demon with a double-barreled shotgun blast. Hedeku froze, perplexed by what she just said, to him. Somehow, the remaining human consciousness of Dr. Mutumbo Watini, Cambridge Professor of Anthropology, recognized the offertory remark, she delivered to his soul. The sharp dagger, dropped out of his hand, and he fell to his knees in front of the Chaplain. The Pit reaction sent a violent quake in outrage, at the High Priest's actions. The vaulted ceiling cracked, above the Pit, and fire filled the three-foot wide split, which came, from the Gates of Hell.

"JESUS loves you and HE died for your sins, too. It's not that late, you can repent and be saved," shouted, the Chaplain boldly, while holding her bloody, shoulder and struggling to get on her knees. As, she watched the dreadlocked man kneeling in front of her grimace in pain, she recognized that inmate Watini was battling the demonic possession, of his soul. He growled, spit up, and rolled violently on the gangway, wrestling with the Druid demon, Hedeku. The Chaplain began to pray, as she laid her hands on Watini and rebuked the evil spirit that possessed him: "I REBUKE YOU IN THE NAME OF JESUS CHRIST! DEMON, COME OUT!"

Watini laid on his back and shook, like he was being electrocuted, and when she removed her hands off him, it came out of him with a hideous roar: "RROOOOOAAARRAAWWW." A looming black mist, gushed from Watini's mouth and flew into the air, swirling as would a screaming wind. Chaplain Barnett attended to the spent husk of humanity that transformed itself, before her very eyes after the exorcism. Watini's eyes were bloodshot, but white with blue irises. His tongue returned to normal. He was weak, and tears filled his eyes.

"Thank you, Madame, whoever you may be?" said Watini, with a Colonial English accent. "I do say, I've been a bit out of sorts, as you may have noticed."

"Er, ah, yes, just a little bit," she smiled kindly, holding his head in her lap. "You're English, aren't you?" she asked him.

"Yes, I'm from Windsor. My name is Dr. Mutumbo Watini. I'm the Director of Anthropological Studies at Cambridge University in London," he grinned slightly, as he shook her hand. Then he saw the gruesome images hovering over their heads. "Good Lord! What in the devil is that?" he asked, pointing in the air.

"You don't remember, do you?" queried, the Chaplain.

"No, I don't remember anything except, that I was having these dreadful, nightmares," he replied, rubbing his head and then felt noticed his dreadlocks.

"What on earth is wrong with my hair?" he cried, pulling a dread in front of his eyes. "Where am I, and what am I doing in this cavern?" he ranted, as he sat up. Dr. Watini couldn't believe his eyes. He looked about the enormous cavern that was filled with shrieking demons. "It....it....it's real, all of this? It's real?" he asked, as mesmerized by the startling discovery of horrors, swirling around him. He reached out for the Chaplain, "You're hurt?" he asked. "I'll be OK. It's you I'm worried about," she said standing up. "Am I in Hades then?" he asked her, intently. "No, not yet, but you're pretty close," she said, looking over the railing down below. "That thing above you is a demon that possessed you, and you were about to sacrifice me to his boss, who lives, down there," she pointed below.

"Good Lord. I'm so sorry! I don't remember a thing, really, I don't. How can I make it up to you?" he implored the Chaplain. "You don't believe in God, do you?" she probed. "Well, not really, but seeing all of this, I'm sure there is some logical explanation," he replied.

"Well, there is" she said. "You, my dear Doctor, have been murdering people all over, this place. You were possessed by that shrieking demon that's flying around our heads, and you can't imagine all the damage and horror you have brought to Kansas," the Chaplain informed him.

"Kansas? You mean to say I'm in Kansas? In the United States?" he ogled her, in disbelief. They both dodged the angry Hedeku, as it swooped down in between them.

"That thing right there, is a demon that has possessed you for a long time, judging by the length of your hair. You were transferred here, forty-eight hours ago, as a violent prisoner and this place where we are standing, happens to be underneath, Heavenworth Federal Penitentiary. I am one of the Chaplains, who works here," she said checking her wound.

"Please, I don't know what to say! I feel awful, and I'm so confused," he said. Then he looked over the railing and saw the demon hordes fighting each other for space. His eyes grew wide, and his heart pounded, when he saw the fire down below. "Is that what I think it is?" he pointed.

"Yes! That's Hell down there, and we've got to do something to stop those minions from Hell" she offered. "But, let me ask you something, Doctor.

337

"Seeing all of this, do you believe in GOD, now?" she inquired. He paused and looked at her and said, "I don't know. I've been schooled my whole life and committed to evolution, so committed that I have given my heart and soul to a career of educational values that totally disprove the existence of GOD. I'm an anthropologist, cave men and such. I don't know, if I could refute all of what I have learned and taught others, that the Bible is a bunch of poppycock," responded, Professor Watini.

Chaplain Barnett could not believe her ears, or her eyes, as the Doctor denied GOD, even while, standing amid a demonic conundrum. She thought she had seen it all, until now. "It's no wonder you've been, demonically possessed. You're a veritable hotbed for demon seed."

"I mean, good Lord, I just exorcised you and now, even in the midst of all that I've told you and all that you see, you still deny GOD's sovereignty? Unbelievable!" she exclaimed, as she slapped her forehead. "I'm sorry to disappoint you, but it is what it is," said Dr. Watini, shrugging his shoulders.

Chaplain Barnett started to cry, "I'm sorry, too. Because you could be hit seven times, worse than what you were before," she said, looking around at the gathering storm above their heads.

"What is happening to me?" he asked, as he jerked a couple of times.

"It is what it is," said Chaplain Barnett backing up, slowly along the railing, watching the demons getting ready to attack the Doctor of Evolutionary Anthropology. She couldn't bear the thought of him going through it all over again, as she ran over to protect him. But just then, she was yanked back off her feet by a huge, tattooed arm.

"No, you don't, Chaplain," said Mongo wrapping another arm around her waist, as she kicked and struggled. The rest of the crusaders took aim at Watini, as he was jerked about the gangway, like a rag doll. He began to levitate into the air screaming in agony being repossessed , by Hedeku and a demon horde.

"Fire!" ordered Captain Ron.

"Blammo, blammo, bam bam bam, rat-a-tat-tat, bang, bang, pop-pop-pop!" blasted the firing squad.

The Christian men overheard the whole conversation, between the Chaplain and Watini. They gave him his chance at salvation, but he chose denial instead. They grimaced, watching the bullets penetrate the human host, just as, the demons entered him at the same time.

"Noooooo," shouted Chaplain Barnett, as she was being carried away, up the gangway and back toward the powerhouse where, they had just come from. The others, kept blasting away. The gunfire echoed in the cavern, chasing the other demons back down into the Pit. Watini's body levitated into the air, and the demons shrieked, because of the holy bullets that penetrated the human.

General Owens pulled a pin from a grenade and lobbed over it to the half-dead, Dr. Watini, who caught it midair, and he seemed to give a faint smile, while they hit the deck.

"Give this to your boss," the General, shouted as Watini went over the railing and tumbled down the Portal.

"KAABBOOOMMM!!"

The crusaders, jumped back up to their feet and leaned over the railing, firing bullets, dropping hand grenades and tossing cross necklaces and Holy Water, down into the Pit. They were angry and wanted revenge for the injustice that was brought, against them this night. They kept firing, until they were out of ammunition, and then they threw their weapons down into the hole. They pulled the pins of more hand grenades tossing, them down, as well. They laughed for the first time in a long time, feeling victorious in their conquest of evil. It was a good feeling, as they heard the grenades echo and flash, in the darkness below.

"All right, men, we hit them with everything we've got," said the Captain smiling happily. "Not quite, Captain," said Chino, as he removed his cross, from around his neck and held it dangling over the railing. The others looked at him, as if he were crazy, but then they thought, Chino was right. They all removed their neck chains and held them steady over the Pit of Hell.

"Now, of all the weapons of warfare, we know this is the strongest of them all. It's the power of JESUS CHRIST, who died on a cross, to save a wretch, like me," cried Chino. "Amen!" said the other ten. They launched the flashing silver crucifixes down into the hole and watched them disappear into the darkness. About a minute later, the cavern began to rumble with a tremendous force.

"Oh, oh," warned LT, as they all turned and started to run back up to the tunnel. "Hurry," shouted Mongo, waving them on with a spotlight.

"It's caving in!" hollered, General Owens, as a brick banged off his helmet.

Bricks rained from the ceiling behind them, while the ground shook beneath their feet. They could hardly keep their balance, as each one of them helped the other to make their way through the tunnel of the powerhouse and out of the doors to the rear gate, of the prison.

The entire prison complex quaked with the magnitude of a seven-plus, on the Richter scale. The hundred-year-old brick buildings collapsed from the thunderous vibrations, rattling beneath them.

> "Look there," screamed Chaplain Barnett, pointing to the yard as it began to sink into the giant portal. They watched the turf get sucked into the cavernous hole, as did the "Big Red" wall. There seemed to be no end, as it continued to engulf the entire facility, swallowing anything near its opening. They saw the hole begin to swirl, like a maelstrom at sea, as the guards' tower tumbled into the vortex, followed by A-Block, the powerhouse and, eventually, the charred carnage of the main annex.

The Christian survivors kept running for their lives, while the sinkhole screamed with a life of its own, grinding the evil prison in its voracious jaws. They came to rest on a hilly pasture, just east of the complex and sat down, exhausted from their escape, and pondered the devastation.. The slow, crunching noises emanated from the grinding of concrete and twisting steel beams together, like some horrible recipe of disaster. Massive wooden crossbeams snapped, like dry bones popping from afar. A gray cloud of dust hung over the gaping hole, while a news helicopter circled the mayhem below, trying to film the nightmarish event, in the early hours of morning.

The sun was breaking over the horizon now, illuminating the drifting clouds with bright colors of orange and lavender. They could see that the moon was back to normal, settling in the northwestern sky.

The Chaplain rose to her feet, feeling the warmth of the sun on her face. She thanked GOD, closing her eyes and feeling HIS presence among them. She looked over her flock, like a shepherd taking pride in each and every member of her fold as, they laid themselves to rest in the green pasture overlooking the Missouri River. No one spoke about anything, while they witnessed, the entire prison complex being devoured, by the supernatural phenomena.

They were reflecting and thinking about their friends and cellmates who died, such horrible deaths that night and, yet they were the blessed ones, who lived. It was a humbling feeling, and it left them numb for the most part as, they thought about what had happened and what if they, like Watini, hadn't converted to a belief in JESUS CHRIST. They thought, about how they might have been tormented in Hell for an eternity.

The Chaplain lamented over the lost souls, especially Dr. Watini's, as she prayed for them, all. She watched the administration building crumple up, like soda crackers and fall into the gaping hole from Hell. The grinding rotation began to slow, as though its appetite was finally becoming appeased, as the north warehouse building disappeared, last.

"Look, its slowing down," said Mongo, standing up and pointing to the mile wide crater.

"I think it accomplished, what it wanted to do in the first place," said Captain Tatum, now standing next to the Chaplain.

"Oh, and what is that?" she asked sordidly.

"It came to teach us, how precious life really is and how corruption can destroy everything, you ever loved," he said, looking into her eyes.

"Oh brother, it looks like, we got us a love affair going on here," grinned LT.

Chaplain Barnett blushed and held out her arms to all of them. "I just want you to know, that I love you all! I, want to thank you for what you did in there. It took a lot of courage to defeat those demons and still prove you had enough faith in GOD, to not let evil stand in your way. Many others perished, and they will all be judged at the Throne of GOD. Today, you are more than conquerors in CHRIST JESUS, who loves you. Remember, wherever you are in life, that GOD, is always with you, through thick and thin," she spoke confidently, giving each man a big, hug and a soft kiss on the cheek.

"Here, Chaplain, I almost forgot," said Derek, removing her necklace out of his pocket.

"You were right about never leaving you. Thanks, for loving all of us and never giving up on us. I think we all, learned a lot from you and what a treasure you are," he said earnestly, as he fastened the cross necklace, around her neck.

She cried and kissed the crucifix, having thought, it was gone forever. She remembered Hedeku, ripping it off her neck in the tunnel, earlier.

Then, as if on cue, they heard the grinding sound come to a halt. The edge of the mile-wide hole, had completely consumed everything that once stood, on the property. The edge of the pile of rubble, had come to rest, just in front of the only remaining structure on the property.

The dust settled to reveal the arched, stone entrance gate to the prison, with an old, rusted iron, sign that read, "HEAVENWORTH." Just below it, there was an engraved plate of scripture, it read:

"Repent: for the KINGDOM of HEAVEN is at hand!" Mk 4:17.

"AMEN."

Jeffrey James Rickman
Author / Artist / Publisher

Rickman is a creative, Christian author, artist and self- publisher, "living the dream" in Bend, Oregon. He has written five novels, (four are fiction and one non-fiction), a novella and a children's book series, entitled "The Amazing Adventures of Fuzzy Bug", (all are pending publication). Rickman's talent has materialized into a platform of inspirational leadership, encouraging others to not give up on their dreams. His motivational themes are provocative and highly entertaining. Further information can be found at:

www.ingramcontent.com/pod-product-compliance
Lightning Source LLC
Chambersburg PA
CBHW030919260626
47169CB00002B/320